FROM THE WRITER OF FIN...
THE ROOKIE, A...

a novel

SKAVENGER'S Hunt

MIKE RICH

29

34   24   21   N T C H Z 36

Published by Inkshares, Inc., San Francisco, California
www.inkshares.com

Edited by: Staton Rabin & Matt Harry
Cover design by: Will Staehle
Interior Design by: Kevin G. Summers

ISBN: 9781942645801
e-ISBN: 9781942645818
LCCN: 2017938051

First edition

Printed in the United States of America

For Gigi

I'll be home for Christmas
If only in my dreams

—Recorded by Bing Crosby, 1943

PROLOGUE

Under the Elephant's Watchful Eye

IT WAS LATE afternoon on Christmas Eve, and twelve-year-old Henry Babbitt was alone.

Alone in New York City, no less—where it was snowing hard on the eight million residents. And frantic weather forecasters were saying the worst was yet to come.

Technically, Henry wasn't completely alone, but that's how he felt inside; the type of feeling he'd felt a lot over the last couple of years. As if something very important was missing.

It was that kind of alone.

His best friend had left a half hour ago, so right now it was just Henry—all five feet two inches of him, in his dress-formal Nikes—and the towering and startled African elephant standing ten feet away. Fortunately, the animal was both motionless and indoors where it was still nice and warm.

The room. Not the elephant.

New York City's American Museum of Natural History was on Henry's shortest of short lists of favorite places to spend time. Especially now, when the place was nearly empty, and he was completely by himself.

Merry Christmas, big guys, he thought to himself as he looked up at the eight well-preserved elephants, the tallest of which loomed eleven feet over him. *See ya again in the new year, I guess.*

Just today, he'd heard more than a few museum visitors calling his eight buddies "stuffed" elephants, but Henry's father had always insisted he never use that word.

"They're not 'stuffed,' son. They're 'preserved.' Doesn't that sound like a much better term for such a dignified beast?"

So "preserved" is what these eight majestic elephants would always be—at least to Henry Babbitt.

He took a quick glance at his iPhone.

4:10 p.m.

No new text from his mom yet, although there were plenty of messages in ALL CAPS on his phone screen saying she was:

ALMOST THERE! BUT I THINK I'VE MOVED AN INCH IN THE LAST HALF HOUR. THIS SNOW IS GETTING DOWNRIGHT NASTY OUT HERE!

Y'know, I think that's the only time I ever hear the word "downright," Henry thought to himself as he tucked his phone away. *When it's snowing and it's not just "nasty" anymore. Don't worry, Mom, I'm doin' fine here. Everything's good.*

He sighed and scratched the back of his neck, wondering what he should do next. His blue eyes scoured the cavernous room with the slightly amused twinkle his mother said was always there, even when he was frustrated or irritated. Henry wasn't either of those things right now, despite a somewhat furrowed brow that was usually there as well. Right now, his brow was more furrowed than usual because of the red, white, and blue New York Giants winter hat covering most of his forehead, the ear dangles bearing the NFL shield providing a solid finishing touch.

His mom had been out taking care of some last-minute Christmas shopping, an annual tradition because of her annual habit of waiting to the very last minute to buy presents. Henry didn't mind; it meant he had a bit more time to tour the surrounding exhibits of Akeley Hall: the black rhino, the gorilla of the savanna, the watering hole that was always being visited by the giraffes, zebras, and gazelles.

None of the mammals in the exhibit were quite on the same level of majesty as the elephants, at least not in Henry's book, but still, the entire exhibit was pretty awesome just the same.

The museum had been scheduled to close at 5:00 p.m., but that was before the snow had started falling sooner than expected. Once that happened, there'd been an announcement that the museum would be shutting down early.

Fortunately, they'd been able to squeeze in Dr. Riggins's Annual Christmas Edition of "Meet the Scientist." Riggins dropped by each month with a presentation that usually mixed science with history. The topics included stuff like Einstein, Edison, and Eiffel—"The Three E's," he always made a point of calling them. Henry loved it when he said that.

Today's lecture had been especially good. Riggins had explained how Einstein's theory of relativity could actually make Santa's delivery in a single night scientifically possible. Jeremy Nack—one of Henry's few friends from Regis Middle School— had gotten so excited that when his parents picked him up, he'd almost made Riggins repeat the whole thing over again.

But that was an hour ago. Now it was just Henry and the— *BZZZZZZZZT.*

His phone rumbled in his pocket and he took it out for a quick glance. Onscreen were the dozen or so previous texts from his mom, including the one she'd just sent:

I'M OUT FRONT!

Henry fired off a quick On my way and tucked the phone into his bulky winter coat, hiking the bag of books he'd checked out from the school library for holiday break a bit higher over his shoulder. The strap landed right on the massive red scarf he'd yet to fully wrap around his neck. Once he did that, about the only thing anyone would be able to see of him would be his rosy, thin cheeks.

"Whoa, Henry, you're still here?"

Henry turned just as Dr. Riggins walked up, apparently heading out into Snowpocalypse himself. With his red beard and enormous sky-blue North Face coat, he looked as if he were getting set to climb Mount Everest.

"Oh, yeah," Henry answered him. "I was just waitin' for my mom to get here. She just showed up."

"Ah, good to hear," Riggins seemed relieved, pulling off his doctory-looking glasses to make sure they were clean. "The snow's getting downright nasty out there. Four inches already, another six inches expected overnight."

A second "downright," thought Henry. It really must be gettin' bad out there!

"Yeah, well, my grandparents' place is pretty close by," Henry opted to say. "We should be okay."

The champion of The Three E's gave him a nod. "You want me to walk you out?" he asked. "I just gotta pick up a couple things in the Discovery Room."

"Nah, I'll be fine," Henry assured him. "Thanks anyway, Dr. Riggins. And thanks for today. It was really great."

"You're more than welcome, Henry," Riggins said with an almost protective smile. "Hope the break's a good one for you. I know the next couple of days have gotta be, well . . ."

He stopped before finishing the thought. Henry offered a faint smile and nodded, knowing Doc R was just trying to help.

"See you next month then?" Riggins asked as he hiked up his own bag of books. "Might have a new thing or two about Eiffel for you. Really interesting stuff."

"Yup, sure will. I'll be here."

Riggins gave one more nod and a wave over his shoulder as he walked out.

"Merry Christmas, Henry."

"Merry Christmas, Dr. Riggins," Henry called back as his phone buzzed with what he guessed was a follow-up text from his mom out front. A quick look confirmed as much:

HERE! Oops, I mean, I'm here. No shouting in my text messages, right?

Henry smiled. His mom's arrival came precisely at the right moment, being as Akeley Hall was now completely empty. Not a creature was stirring, not even a security guard—and it was fairly common knowledge among movie-watchers what kind of things could happen if you ended up spending a night in this museum.

With one last glance of respect toward the towering elephants in front of him, Henry wrapped his scarf around his neck and zipped up his winter coat. He headed for the exit . . .

. . . ready to begin his very favorite and most difficult night of the year.

ONE

Christmas Eve

EVER SINCE IT had happened, Henry usually found himself on the boring side of the window. In other words, the "inside" side, precautions being precautions and all.

He was on the boring side right now, sitting in the passenger seat of his mom's car as he looked out on the downright nasty snow coming down. Twelve-year-old boys closing in on thirteen shouldn't be on this side of the window, Henry knew.

They should be outside.

Not always, of course, but certainly a lot more than Henry had been allowed to be over the last couple of years. Playing sports, hiking, the occasional camping trip or two—those kind of activities were now simply out of the question. He didn't need to remind himself that this was his mom's doing.

Not that he'd be doing any of that right now anyway. Thanks to the snow pelting down on the windshield of his mother's old Ford Expedition.

"Well, I sure am glad Dr. Riggins was able to get his lecture in. I know how much you like him," Eloise Babbitt said as the gridlocked holiday traffic on Central Park West finally decided to move. A few feet later, though, it stopped again.

"Yep, it was really great," Henry replied, eyes locked on the bright screen of his phone. "There were like thirty kids there."

"Ah, that's nice," Eloise replied while tucking her shoulder-length sandy-blond hair—the section of hair up front that was blocking her view at least—back under her finest purple dress beanie. She stole a glance in the rearview mirror, her one dimple deepening with growing concern.

A good part of her attention, of course, was on the unrelenting snowfall outside. The Expedition had four-wheel drive, but it wouldn't help if they remained stuck bumper-to-bumper in the street-turned-parking-lot surrounding Central Park.

"You would not have believed the number of people still shopping only an hour ago," Eloise remarked. "Yes . . . me too, I know," she added with a smile. "Everybody's busy, busy, busy."

"The museum was pretty much empty," Henry informed her. "'Cept for the elephants."

"Mmm," she replied, her eyes locked on the worsening weather.

A text from Jeremy popped up on Henry's phone:

8p tonight. Sci-Fi. The Tick Loves Santa!

'Scuse me? **Henry responded.**

It's great. Just listen: After a bank robber disguised as Santa falls into a neon sign he gains the improbable power to duplicate himself. Multiple Santa is born! The Tick must get over his Santa-worship in order to fight the legions of Nicks. Best line in the whole thing? When he's about to be swept away by an avalanche of Santas, the Tick screams, "It's a yuletide!"

Cool. I'll check it out, **Henry typed.**

Henry hit "Send."

WOOOOOOSH.

"Henry?" Eloise asked. "What's the latest on this weather? I mean, look at all this!" She glanced at her son. His eyes were locked tightly on the screen of his phone. "Y'know, I could be wrong"—Eloise sent him a quick smile that he caught—"but I don't think your video game's gonna have the forecast."

With the glow from his phone illuminating his face, Henry knew he at least needed to fake a quick internet search.

"Same as before," he said with a firm look at the latest NBA standings. "Six inches of snow tonight. Clearing tomorrow."

"Keep me posted on that," she nodded with a worried look. "Oh, and can you check your hair, please? We're almost there. Want you lookin' sharp as ever for your grandparents. *Tu es un beau garçon, oui?*"

"Yes, *oui.*" Henry nodded and pulled off his hat, hoping his usually messy copper-colored hair was still in passable holiday shape—or as his mother had just insisted in her favorite language, that he was a "handsome kid." She'd been fluent in French most of her life, and Henry was getting to the point where he wasn't half-bad himself.

"Okay, and one more thing to remember," his mother continued, craning her neck for a long-shot parking spot as she had been for a few blocks now. "Once we get out? I want you inside, and I want that jacket to stay on at all times. Understood?"

"Yes, Mom," Henry answered with a quiet sigh, unable to resist a quick look up from his phone.

They were getting close now. Even though he'd been there countless times, Henry never got tired of seeing the front of his grandparents' place. It was as if a sculptor had taken these already-perfect steps, columns, and outcroppings, and then etched them with royal shields and patterns that turned the whole staircase into this amazing frame for the walnut front door. Tonight, with all the snow, it would look spectacular.

"Six inches tonight, wow!" Eloise shook her head as she switched the wipers to a notch just below their most frenetic speed.

He stole a glance at her as she tightened her grip on the steering wheel.

Mmmboy, here we go. She's headin' straight to Worry Land. No stops. I am gonna look soooo good wearing my winter coat at dinner tonight.

Henry knew that never in a million years would he say anything like that out loud to her. First of all, he wouldn't want to hurt her feelings, but more important: there was a part of him that understood why she worried. He didn't like the overprotective part, but he did get it.

Henry's father, Nathan, had been one of New York's very finest attorneys—a loud and strong voice for those who needed that kind of voice most. In other words . . . a lot of people.

And when Nathan Babbitt—tall, yet wide-shouldered, like his son was on a path to be—wasn't helping those in need, he was finding adventure; the thought of that, especially this time of year, was heartbreaking for his only child.

"Henry," his father had always promised him with a sparkle in his eye, "when you get a little older, we're gonna sail somewhere. We'll climb the highest mountain we can find. And when we're done with that adventure? We'll find the next one. Okay?"

"Okay," Henry whispered to himself in the here and now, quietly enough that his mother couldn't hear.

The last time he'd heard those words was two years ago, the year a car had run a red light at West 96th and Riverside, hitting Nathan as he walked across the street and taking his life. Thanks to that, there wouldn't be any adventures at all for Henry with his dad. Not then. Not now.

Not ever.

There were still moments when Henry allowed himself to dream about the journeys they would have taken together, but those moments weren't as frequent anymore.

The one person Henry's heart really broke for, though, was the one who was right now looking for a place to park. The loss of his father had ripped a hole in Henry that hadn't even come close to healing yet, but it was a different kind of wound for his mother. Her pain was a crushing and permanent one.

To say that Nathan and Eloise had been in love, Henry's grandmother had told him only a few months ago, was to undersell the very meaning of the word.

They lived to be with each other.

Home. Away from home. Anywhere.

And when his mother's Volvo started having problems this past summer—even though she had loved, loved, loved the car—she decided to keep Nathan's midnight-blue Expedition because he had loved it.

It had enough miles on it—more than a hundred-thousand—that every once in a while, the transmission would slip out of drive and into neutral. And when it did that, it would make this ever-so-slight clicking sound. The service tech had said Eloise should get it fixed, but she'd told him she wanted to hold off, and Henry knew why.

The times when it did slip out of gear? Making that soft click?

It was almost as if Nathan was still there, shifting his SUV. The same SUV that was supposed to take Henry on so many of those adventures.

Henry sighed, knowing his mom probably still had a few more rules to cover, Christmas Eve–related or otherwise.

"Okay . . . so . . . I need you to stay inside once we get there," she continued, immediately confirming his hunch. Just then, though, she discovered a Christmas miracle in the form of a suddenly vacated parking spot.

"Whoa, whoa, whoa—look at *this*!"

She hit the accelerator to block the dark red Mercedes trying to cut over from the middle lane—an impressively aggressive move even in Henry's eyes.

"Annnnnnnnd, *yes*!" Eloise put the finishing touches on the parking job, even though it required a quick nudge backward and another one forward to get it juuuuust ri—

CLICK.

Her hand stopped an inch above the gearshift.

The acceleration had prompted the transmission to slip out of drive and into neutral, even though the glance she shared with her son suggested otherwise.

Eloise looked at the gearshift for a long moment before gently pushing the Expedition into park.

"Gotta get that fixed someday," she said with a tiny swallow. "Not tonight, though, right?"

"Tonight? Are you kidding?" Henry answered her. "Last thing we're gonna do is give up *this* spot on Central Park West . . . on Christmas Eve."

Their shared loss had made Eloise's smile come less frequently, but when she did flash her smile—as she was right now—it was stunning.

"Love ya, kiddo." Henry's mom leaned over and gave him a quick kiss on the top of his head.

"You too," Henry replied back.

"Okay, so . . ." She was getting back to the rules, which sounded firm, but were tucked inside a friendly voice. It was this kind of stuff that really gnawed at him.

"Stay inside."

"Yes, Mom."

"Careful on the concrete steps. They'll be really slippery."

"Got it, Mom."

"And try not to bother your grandfather too much. I don't want him filling your head with any of those crazy stories of his."

"What? Why? I like his stories," Henry frowned as he dumped his phone into his pocket.

"I know you do." Eloise nodded. "Same as your dad." Then she added with a sad smile, "I just worry his stories are maybe getting, I don't know, a little bit crazier ever since . . ."

She sighed, followed by her son doing the same a half second later.

"Great, perfect," Henry muttered with both disappointment and frustration. Before the last word was even out, he regretted the tone he'd just used.

"I know, I know," his mother replied, "I just . . . he misses your father a lot too." She finally got around to turning off the Expedition. "This time of year's rough on all of us."

TWO

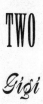

Gigi

"HENRY NATHAN BABBITT, just look at you!"

Henry's grandmother—who'd been "Gigi" to him since he first started talking—wrapped him in an embrace so tight it sent his gloves and book bag to the floor.

He'd already taken off the gloves as a precaution on the front step—which really *had* looked terrific covered in snow—but only because he knew his mother had looked away for a second, no doubt checking for icicles that might fall on him.

"Hey, Gigi," he managed to say into the arm of her burgundy dress.

"Hey, Gigi? Hey, Gigi?" she said with a smile wider than the front door wreath. "Don't you have something else to add to that? This isn't just *any* day of the year, you know."

"Oh, sorry," he corrected himself. "Merry Christmas, even though Christmas Day really isn't until tomorr—"

"Merry Christmas to *you*! Much, much better." She embraced him again, constricting him enough that the smell of pumpkin pie coming from the distant kitchen completely vanished for a moment.

Wow, Geege, you're in midseason form. Two hugs in two seconds.

"Hello, Margaret," Eloise said with a kind smile, before instantly correcting herself. "I mean, Merry Christmas." She pulled off her hat and her hair fell perfectly into place, which served as a reminder to Henry that he'd forgotten to check his own.

"You too, dear girl." Gigi hugged her daughter-in-law tightly and gave her a kiss on the cheek, winking at Henry. "See? At least one of you knows what to say on Christmas Eve. Come, come, hand over those coats now."

Henry shot a glance toward his mother.

Okay?

Eloise shrugged, her eyes suggesting that ditching his coat was probably all right—for now.

"Henry?" Gigi asked. "I've heard rumors your latest grades took a nice step forward from last year. Is that so?"

"Well, I thought it was pretty okay," Henry answered. "I did get an A in history, which kinda made up for the C in math. We can skip talking about chemistry if that's okay."

"Well, you've had a lot on your mind," she said, hanging their coats in the front hall closet. From there she led them through the dining room and straight into the kitchen. Henry knew the holiday path from experience.

The inside of his grandparents' home was every bit as stunning as the snowy front entrance. It featured hickory hardwood floors and high ceilings along with tons of artwork that blended paintings from both a hundred years ago and one year ago. Henry knew squat about all that stuff, but even he could tell his grandmother had a knack for it. All you had to do was ask her.

The elegant elderly woman was dressed head-to-toe in her annual Christmas wardrobe: a red floor-length dress with decades-old sparkly stuff around her neck and a flour-coated green apron that right now featured a splattering of turkey grease.

It would have looked nice on anyone, but there was a reason the word "elegant" always jumped to mind with Gigi. At five foot nine—she avoided saying five ten for some reason, even though she was—and with somewhat short silver hair that any Ice Princess would have rocked, she always looked great. At least ten years younger than her real age of seventy-eight.

"All right, coats are up," Gigi said, finishing the first piece of business and quickly moving on to the next. "Henry, if you could help me choose the perfect Christmas music, ideally cheerful now and then quietly cheerful at dinner." She then sped back into the dining room, immediately adjusting the placement of all four water glasses before giving them a youthful thumbs-up.

Eloise sent Henry a smile that he knew carried a heavy dose of heartache.

Gigi had always made a strong effort when it came to Christmas, but she'd really gone overboard the last two years. Henry figured that if she ever stopped for even a single second, especially on *this* night, it wouldn't be good.

Ding! Ding! Ding!

The oven timer chirped from the kitchen—and even though Gigi was in her midseventies, she actually scurried into the adjoining room for a look-see.

"Half hour more and this turkey should be all ready to go." Gigi waved for the two of them to follow. "Henry, can you grab me the Christmas oven mitts, please?"

"Sure. Top drawer over here, right?"

"Right you are—OW!" she confirmed while nearly burning her hand just opening the oven. "Maybe only twenty-five minutes more," she said, waggling her hand. "I think that's what the mathematician in me would recommend."

"Here ya go, Geege." Henry returned and looked up at her as he held out a pair of mitts that once looked like snowmen, but were now long-charred by the oven.

Annnnnnnnd, yup, there it is. Had to happen sometime tonight.

It was his looking up at her that had done it, he could tell. It had happened last year and now this year as well—though whether last year had also taken place by the oven, he didn't quite remember.

Everything slowed down for a second as Gigi returned her grandson's smile.

She gently took the mitts from his outstretched hand and leaned down to say, "Grandson . . . tonight and tomorrow? They wouldn't be the same without you here. It just wouldn't be the same at all."

"Thanks, G—"

There was a knock at the front door.

"Ah! That'll be Abigail from next door. I told her to drop by," Gigi told Henry, quickly smoothing his shirt. "That young lady was very excited to hear you were coming over tonight!"

Abigail? Abigail Kentworth?! What's she doing here?!

Henry had gone to school with Abigail for a couple of years and spent a good portion of that time trying to keep his cheeks from turning bright red every time he saw her. Fortunately, her father had been named as a board member at another school— one of New York City's best—and she'd switched over just this fall. The move had given Henry's cheeks a much-needed break.

"Go on now," Gigi shooed him toward the door. "You don't want to make her knock a second time."

Seriously? We're really gonna do this? D'you pick up some flowers you want me to give her too?

He could feel both his mom and grandmother watching as he made his way down the hall, his adrenaline level spiking with each step.

The doorknob silently taunted him: *Come on, turn me. I dare ya.* Henry stopped a foot from the entryway, not willing to take the dare yet.

Oh man . . . she is gonna look great. She always looks great. It's an indisputable fact. 'Specially if she's got the ponytail working. The blond *ponytail. Uh boy.*

Her looks were just part of the reason he'd always had a hard time figuring out why she even took an interest in him.

"Oh dear," he heard his mother say as she and Gigi moved into prime eavesdropping position a few feet behind him.

Henry waited another second before reluctantly opening the door, and—

Daaaaaaannnnng.

Sure enough, it was Abigail Kentworth, looking as great as ever. Ponytail intact, though tonight it had the added bonus of being nicely tucked under a winter hat and falling perfectly over her left shoulder. The white jacket she was wearing, along with the blue scarf and boots with some kind of fake fur around the top, didn't hurt either.

He could feel the first rush of crimson heading for his cheeks.

"Hey, Henry. Merry Christmas," Abigail said with a warm smile and appropriate spirit.

"Hey, Abigail," he replied with appropriate awkwardness, his nerves running at about 120 percent.

She held out a sparkling glass plate of homemade candy. "I brought you some fudge."

"Oh, cool, thanks . . ." Henry's tone was polite and carried just enough enthusiasm as he took the plate off of her hands.

"You're welcome. My mom and I made a whole bunch this afternoon."

"Oh . . . well . . . it looks really great. Really . . . fudgy."

Fudgy . . . is that even a word?

"Ummmmmmmm," Henry shifted gears. "Pretty amazing snowstorm, isn't it?"

Weather. Great. You couldn't come up with anything dorkier to talk about?

He did get the feeling that Abigail might be nervous too, since she was clasping her hands behind her back. Not that knowing this helped much. He'd have bet the contents of his grandmother's house and a few other houses on the block that his nerves swamped whatever nervousness she was feeling.

"Hey, Mrs. Babbitt," Abigail said, waving to the two women standing behind him. "*Both* Mrs. Babbitts! Merry Christmas!"

"Merry Christmas, Abigail!" Gigi nearly shouted, while Eloise, who seemed to look as if she knew how Henry was feeling, offered a smile and a slightly more subdued, "Merry Christmas to you too, Abigail."

"Come in, come in, dear," Gigi gestured, taking the plate of fudge from her grandson and putting it on a nearby table. "Henry wouldn't want you getting snowbound out there, would you, Henry?"

"Oh, sorry, no," Henry could feel the crimson in his cheeks turning a deep shade of burgundy. "Yeah, come on in."

Abigail stepped inside, the snow quickly beginning to melt off her coat, her hat, and . . . her ponytail.

Oh man, her ponytail. You kiddin' me? I'm the one who should be snowbound. Better yet, maybe I should just run outside and bury my head right into the snow.

It took little to no time before his grandmother's grand, grandmotherly plan became all too apparent.

"Abigail?" Gigi asked innocently enough. "Didn't your mother tell me you had something you wanted to ask Henry?"

What?!

"Oh, yeah, she uh . . . she did." Abigail fidgeted a little. "Soooo . . . there's ice skating over at Central Park in the morning," she said, her eyes going to Henry's. "I was kinda thinking I might go."

Gigi interjected. "No, no, no . . . I think you mean an ice skating *gala*, Abigail, don't you?" she corrected her. "Not just skating, but dancing and other holiday fun, yes?"

Henry could see his mother pressing her lips against her fingers, stifling a laugh.

Skating? Dancing? thought Henry in growing terror. *Sure, let's go ahead and mix sharp-edged steel blades with the tango.*

"Yeah, I think it is called something like that," Abigail replied. "And I do think they might have some dancing."

Henry could hear his grandmother trying to suppress a squeal behind him. "Oh, Henry, you must go!" she said to both of them. "It sounds like such a wonderful thing to do on Christmas morning! Don't you agree, Eloise?"

The look Henry saw on his mother's face was a little more complicated—as he knew it probably would be.

"Well . . ." Eloise chose her words carefully, already somewhat hesitant. "It's, umm, I mean ice skating can be dangerous, can't forget that, especially with the snow, right?"

"It's supposed to be over first thing in the morning," Gigi countered encouragingly.

"I know it is," Eloise said with a sympathetic look in Henry's direction, before turning to Abigail. "Abigail, hon . . . maybe if we could just wait to see how the morning looks, would that be all right?"

"Sure, absolutely. That's . . . fine with me," Abigail replied. She turned to look back at Henry.

"Yeah, that's prob'ly smart," he agreed, before deciding on the spot to toss cold water on the whole idea. "Might be kind of a long shot, though. I've got this cold that's really been bothering me for the last few days. Y'know how it is."

Now her cheeks were the ones turning red. "Oh, okay. Stuff's been goin' around, I know."

"I might just kind of hang out here," he said, hoping to strike the right tone. "But have a really Merry Christmas, okay?"

Abigail nodded. "You too, Henry. I understand," she said to him quickly, before making sure to also say to Gigi and Eloise, "Merry Christmas, Mrs. Babbitts."

"You too, dear child, you too," Gigi said warmly and then winked. "I'll have this plate cleaned and ready for pickup tomorrow morning, in case Henry's feeling better."

"Oh, right . . . and thanks for the fudge, Abigail," Henry knew to say.

"You're welcome." Abigail turned and waved, a fresh dusting of snow settling on her hat and shoulders. Henry waved back, watching her bouncing ponytail for a moment before slowly closing the door.

Gigi sighed and shook her head. "Ohhhh . . . Henry, Henry, Henry, what am I going to do with you?" she said, leaning down to look him straight in the eye. "You had the chance right there in front of you! Abigail came to *you*, even. What's the worst that could have happened?"

"Yeah, I know," was all Henry could think to say, throwing in a shrug to boot.

"All right, well." Gigi clapped both knees with her hands. "I know your grandfather's *very* excited to see you. He tells me he has something of utmost importance he wants to discuss with you upstairs."

"What is it?" Henry asked, curious at once—as was his mother, apparently.

"Is everything all right, Margaret?" Eloise asked.

"Yes, yes, everything's fine, dear," Gigi replied as she nudged Henry toward the stairwell. "He's very secretive about such things, you know."

"Remember what we talked about, Henry," Eloise reminded him with a knowing look.

"What did you talk about?" Gigi asked. Now she looked to be the curious one.

"Nothing important. Just . . ." Eloise looked pointedly toward Henry. "If your grandfather's tired, let him rest. You can talk with him later when we're all visiting."

Gigi sent him a wink. "Take your time. I'll call you when dinner's ready, all right?"

THREE

The Old Man

HENRY ALWAYS TOOK his time going up the stairs of his grandparents' house because of the story the climb told. Not the steps, of course, but the photos on the wall next to them.

They told the story of a lifetime. The life of Henry's grandfather, to be exact.

The cluttered wall was filled with old and perfectly framed photographs, most of them black-and-white. Not as a creative choice, mind you, but more because when eighty-year-old Carter Babbitt was given his first camera, black-and-white was the only choice. Henry had shaken his head for a week at that little snippet of information.

Each photo captured a chapter of the old man's amazing life, all the way up to his second-floor study. Each and every image featured the lean and lanky patriarch of the family proudly wearing one of his assorted hats, all of which put a spotlight on his unique personality. A Yankees baseball hat, a Sinatra-style porkpie cap, even the wide-brimmed cowboy hat Carter had purchased twenty years ago somewhere out in eastern Oregon.

The pictures at the bottom of the stairs showed him as a young dreamer in Boston, where he was well on his way to a career manufacturing high-quality fabric for clothing.

Whenever Henry asked how it began, his grandfather would simply shrug and say that he'd stumbled into it. Henry knew better, though. His grandfather had worked hard for everything.

A few more steps up were the first photos of Carter alongside a strikingly attractive woman of a likely self-proclaimed five foot nine, her eyes almost forced shut by the joyful smile on her face: Gigi in her younger days—already on her way to becoming a tenured math professor.

By the seventh stair, Henry's father had joined the picture. He looked to be only two years old, with his entire lifetime— short as it turned out to be—still in front of him.

Then there was the highlight of step eleven: a photo taken in the snow of Colorado. Nathan Babbitt with Eloise Lewis, joyously laughing during a piggyback ride on her future husband's back, both in their early twenties—Henry years away from becoming anything more than a twinkle in their eyes.

Until the fourteenth stair, right next to his favorite photo ever: Seven-year-old Henry standing next to his father and grandfather in front of the African elephants at the museum. The same exact spot where twelve-year-old Henry had stood, very much alone, just this afternoon. Three generations of Babbitts caught in the kind of sudden, joyful laughter that comes only once in a great while.

Under the elephant's watchful eye, right, Dad? It's what you always used to say to me when we were there together.

Henry climbed the last few stairs and discovered the old man's study door was open, but only by an inch or so. The dim light from within wavered onto the landing.

Carter Babbitt sure did love his candles. Whenever he'd see the bright, fake light emanating from things he called "newfangled," he'd frown and say that real knowledge was born with real light.

The phone in Henry's pocket rumbled and he looked down to see the trace of unwavering light his grandfather would most certainly frown upon. He pulled the phone out, just enough to read:

FIVE MINUTES! COME ON DOWN TO HELP WITH DINNER!

Henry sighed and clicked away his mother's message, then went a step further and turned off the phone entirely, which may have surprised the phone most of all.

Five minutes? He can barely start *a story in five minutes.*

"Grandson?"

Henry looked up. The door was still open only an inch or two. The old man's ears apparently were open much wider.

"Chief?" the young boy replied as he elbowed the door open and peered inside.

"Chief" was the name Nathan had always called his father. It was one of Henry's first words too, even though the "chh" at the front was tricky for a one-and-a-half-year-old to master.

"Ah! There you are," Carter said with a smile, candles burning on his desk. "I thought I heard you come in, along with a lecture about making a proper greeting on Christmas Eve."

"Oh . . . right," his grandson answered, knowing he was busted. "Guess I forgot both times. Merry Christmas."

The old man leaned back in his chair, pressing his fingertips against one another. He'd obviously trimmed his gray beard and mustache just for the occasion, and he looked especially sharp wearing his dark green Christmas fedora, the color of

which was close to that of his eyes. Henry had said on a few occasions that if Sean Connery had had a twin brother in *Indiana
Jones and the Last Crusade*, it would have been Chief.

"Merry Christmas indeed, young man," Carter smiled as
he leaned back. "I also heard Abigail mentioning tomorrow's
ice skating over at Central Park. With dancing, it seems."

Henry knew what was coming next.

"Seems like a nice opportunity lost, don't you think?" his
grandfather continued. "Skating, dancing, a pretty girl. Am I
missing anything?"

"No. No, I like Abigail," Henry answered, trying to get out
of it. "It's just that, with the snow and everythi—"

"Nonsense," Chief interrupted as he rose from his chair.
"Don't blame that on your mother. The only one to blame for
missing out on that is you. One of these days you need to stop
being so nervous about seizing life's opportunities. Of which
there are many."

Carter gestured toward the ancient leather chair Henry always liked sitting in. It was wide enough for two of him.

"Having said that, though," he admitted, looking for
something on his desk, "it is quite an impressive snowstorm
out there tonight."

"Yup, sure is."

*A downright nasty one, if ya ask Mom. And Dr. Riggins.
Maybe a few others.*

Henry surveyed the quirky office he'd loved since forever,
seeing if there might be anything new among the overflow of
artifacts from almost every continent.

There were old wooden boxes that held Chief's collection
of royal garments from ancient Egypt; century-old newspapers stacked next to an original golf club from St. Andrews,
Scotland; an enormous framed image of his grandparents sitting in the cockpit of Howard Hughes's giant aircraft from the

1940s: the *Spruce Goose*. Oh, and yeah, an *actually* dirty, worn first base from Yankee Stadium back from the Mickey Mantle days. One that the Mick, Joe DiMaggio, and countless other champs thumped their cleats onto a few thousand times.

"See anything new?" Chief asked as he turned to face him.

"Not yet," Henry answered, shaking his head. "Am I missing anything?"

With a smile, Carter held out the single item he'd been looking for on his cluttered and timeworn desk: a single sheet of paper, which even from a few feet away looked old. *Very* old.

"This," Chief said as he held it up, pinned between his thumb and forefinger. "This is what you're missing."

∽

Henry stared down at the old sheet of parchment, now resting in the middle of Chief's desk. It was covered with columns of small and faded boxes meant for dates, destinations, and perhaps a note or two about what had happened both then and there.

Except none of the boxes were filled in. All of them were dead empty, printed in a time that appeared to be—considering the crumpled coloring of the paper—long since gone.

"Okay," Henry ventured. "So, what exactly is it?"

"It's a ledger . . . for record keeping," Chief answered. "Late 1800s, I'm pretty sure. 1885, if you put me on the spot."

"How do you know that?" Henry asked with a suspicious look. "The 1885 part, I mean?"

His grandfather was smiling—and Henry knew why. Ever since Henry was old enough to form a question, Chief had encouraged him to be skeptical. It was a big-time motto of his: If you don't know something, ask. If you don't believe it, ask again.

"I want you to listen to me carefully, grandson," he quietly started. "And I'm going to need you to . . . what is it you sometimes say? Roll to it?"

"Y'mean, roll with it?"

"Roll with it, precisely." Chief nodded. "It'll all make sense in a few minutes, but all you need to know right now is . . . I have studied the story I'm about to tell you not for months, not for years, but for *decades*."

Whoa. This sounds serious.

"Tell me something, Henry," Carter continued after letting his intro take root. "Have you ever taken part in a scavenger hunt?"

Henry lifted his eyes from the ledger. "You mean one of those hunts where you get a list of things you have to find?" he asked. "Paper clip, box of raisins, that kind of hunt?"

"No. No raisins, no paper clip," Chief replied. "I'm talking about a scavenger hunt much, much bigger than that. I'm talking about the first scavenger hunt ever held. One that was filled with clues, puzzles, mysterious quests across the country, sometimes spanning the entire world."

The back of Henry's neck tingled.

Ohhh . . . this one sounds good. This one sounds epic even by Ol' Chiefy's standards!

He could tell that his grandfather was just getting warmed up, but that he'd also want Henry to hold his feet close to the fire.

"Whoa, whoa, whoa, Chief," Henry said with a small measure of disbelief. "You've spent decades studying the very first scavenger hunt?"

"Actually . . . there were three hunts," the old man amended. "Like I said, grandson, you'll need to 'roll with it' for a few minutes. Did I get it right this time?"

"You did. Good job."

"Thank you." Chief tipped his forehead appreciatively and then continued. "The first hunt was in 1883, the second in 1884, and the last in 1885. All starting right here in New York."

"See? I knew 1885 wasn't just a guess." Henry smiled at his grandfather.

"Of course it wasn't," Chief replied before letting his voice drop to a near-whisper. "And the one thing that each of those three hunts had in common? Every riddle, every clue . . . was put together by one mysterious, very secretive man who put his very own name on it."

He paused to heighten the revelation before announcing: "Hunter S. Skavenger!"

"Hunter S. *who*?" Henry asked.

"Skavenger. Spelled with a *K*, not a *C*. He was the richest man in the city, Henry. Perhaps richer than Rockefeller. And where his money came from? No one was quite sure."

Carter leaned farther across his desk, looking his grandson squarely in the eye. "That's because no one ever saw him. He was a man of industry, that much was known. But it was as if he were a magician! A sorcerer! A ghost of a man who had secret friends everywhere. And the only thing those friends knew—and I mean the *only* thing—was that if they were ever to talk publicly about him or his secret business dealings?"

Again, he stopped.

"What?" Henry asked, momentarily spellbound. "What would happen?"

"He'd disappear from their lives forever," the old man told him. "Just like a good many of the stories from those three elaborate hunts have now disappeared from history. Gone!"

"Wait a second." Henry's expression zipped back to skeptical. "I mean, if these hunts were so great, why wouldn't people still be talking about them?"

"Because no one ever won, that's why," Chief enticingly answered. "And by the way, I am a little concerned why you didn't ask why I'm still talking about it."

"No, no, no. Keep goin', Chief," Henry said with a smile. "I do like the start of this one."

"Good. Because the best part's still coming," Chief said with a tantalizing wink. "First, though, you need to know the rules of the hunt, which I've been studying for how long now?"

"Decades," Henry played along.

The old man's eyes twinkled as he walked over to the stack of ancient newspapers, taking the one from the very top.

"Skavenger placed an announcement in the *New York Times*, the Old Gray Lady." Chief always made a point of using the paper's nickname. He spread the brittle and yellowed paper out next to the ledger sheet. "See? It covered two full pages. The greatest hunt ever. A hunt that Hunter S. Skavenger himself would reveal the rules to, including the prize to be won, on July tenth, 1883, right here in Central Park."

"You mean right-across-the-street-here Central Park?" Henry raised an eyebrow, nodding toward the window that was now framed with snow.

"Right-across-the-street-here Central Park," Chief confirmed. "Thousands upon thousands, that's how many people showed up that morning."

"Even Skavenger? I thought you said no one ever saw him."

"They saw him that day. And he was every bit as mysterious and charismatic as everyone thought he'd be. He started off the hunt by reciting a single puzzling clue. For those who solved it, wherever it led them, a second clue would await, and then a third, and then a fourth . . ."

"When do we get to the paper clip?" Henry couldn't resist.

The old man continued without taking the bait, "Until finally—how many clues later, no one was sure—one person or one team would find the last clue. And if they, and they alone, could decipher that one final, all-important riddle? That winner would receive the grandest prize ever—worth more than anyone could imagine."

"What?"

"Skavenger's fortune, Henry! That's what!"

It was right at that very moment—with his story reaching its absolute crescendo, wind-driven snow dancing in the window behind him—that Chief sighed.

"What's wrong?" Henry asked.

Carter took in a deep and sad-sounding breath. "Like I said. No one ever won. He was there to start the hunt on July tenth, 1883. On July tenth, 1884. And on July tenth of 1885. And when everyone showed up the following year? The only one who wasn't there was Skavenger himself."

"Where was he?" Henry inquired as if on cue.

Chief struck a match to boost a couple of his struggling desk candles.

"Well, some felt the mysterious old recluse had simply grown tired of outwitting everyone," he said. "But there were others who felt there was a much, much darker ending to the story. A worse ending."

"What kind of worse ending?" Henry knew he'd fallen into asking the most rudimentary of questions, which always seemed to happen at some point during his grandfather's stories.

"That he'd met his demise at the hands of Hiram Doubt," Chief answered.

"Who?"

"Skavenger's old business rival," Carter replied as he blew out the match. He turned a few pages of the century-old newspaper on his desk. "This man here."

He pointed to an old photo, and Henry shuddered the second he looked at it. The man in the photograph looked

like something out of a nightmare—tall and gaunt with short
gray hair, deep sunken cheeks, and unwelcoming eyes that
somehow found a way to pierce through even the ancient
black-and-white.

He was flanked by four other equally haunting men, all of
whom wore black longcoats and top hats that made them look
even more menacing, each gazing at Henry with eyes just as
chilling as Doubt's. One in particular.

"You see the one just off his shoulder, don't you?" Chief's
eyes had accurately tracked his grandson's.

"Yeah." Henry almost swallowed the word.

"Doubt's closest and most trusted aide," the old man informed him. "And by far the most dangerous. His name was
Grace, of all things."

Thump, thump, thump, thump.

Eloise tapped her hand against the doorframe of the study
and walked in before Henry could reply.

"Sorry to interrupt you two. Merry Christmas, Carter," she
said with a smile.

*Uhhhhhhh . . . not the best timing here, Mom. We're gettin' to
the really good part.*

"Merry Christmas, Eloise," Chief replied with a patient
smile. "No bother at all. Henry and I have just been catching
up on a few things."

"Margaret says dinner's just about ready," she said. Henry
knew the words were for him more than his grandfather.

"Of course. We'll be right down," Carter promised.
"Five minutes."

"Tops, Mom. Promise." Henry nodded.

"Okay, five minutes. Fair enough." She sounded less than
convinced. "Don't want our Christmas Eve dinner to get cold."

"Nor do we, dear, nor do we. Merry Christmas, again. It's
good to have you here."

Chief politely waited for her to leave, then stayed quiet while the sound of her footsteps clicked down the stairs. Once everything was silent, he leaned toward his grandson once more. Henry leaned close as well, only to hear the old man say through a wry and teasing smile:

"Perhaps we should wait till after dinner. And not a word of this to either your mother or grandmother. This is our secret."

FOUR

Pumpkin Pie and the Tale's Ending

DINNER, AS HENRY knew it would be even before the first bite, was both terrific . . . and long.

Henry had been itching for an hour now to get back upstairs to hear the end of Chief's story. Yes, it would have been both impolite and a full-blown disaster if they'd stayed upstairs after Gigi proudly announced her prize meal of the entire year was on the table.

But they did have five minutes.

Five minutes in which Chief could have given him another piece of the story. Maybe two pieces, depending on how long the first one took for him to tell.

A hint of a smile crossed Henry's face as he realized that what he was thinking was ridiculous.

The old man, now sitting across from him on the other side of the table, had taught Henry that the only thing better than a good story told straight through was a good story that had a tormenting break somewhere in the middle of it.

Boy oh boy, did he ever nail that spot.

Henry looked over at his grandfather, who was looking back at him, Carter's fedora resting right next to his butter plate. There was still the tiniest of twinkles in Chief's eyes, the same twinkle that had told the young boy from the moment they stood to leave his office for Christmas Eve dinner . . .

That the two of them now had a secret. A secret on Christmas Eve.

"All right," Gigi said from the head of the dinner table, unaware of the silent conversation taking place. "I see empty plates all around. Who's ready for thirds?"

"Oh no. No, thank you," Eloise held up her hands to stop the onslaught of holiday delight. "Although, I do have to tell you, Margaret, that was the best turkey you have ever made."

"Really? Well, thank you, dear. You are so sweet to say that." Gigi beamed at the compliment. "I'm not so sure I haven't had a few others that turned out better."

Chief shot Henry a wink, motioning for him to please pass the mashed potatoes—intentionally drawing the suspense out at least one serving longer.

Fine. I can wait a little longer. Even though I already know this is the best story you've ever told me.

"Let me tell you something I'm not so sure of, dear," the old man slowly chimed in as if he'd heard the exact thought in Henry's head. "I'm not so sure Eloise isn't one hundred percent correct about this meal. What do you think, grandson?"

"Mmm, absolutely," Henry agreed. "Thirds comin' up."

The beaming look on Gigi's face now looked as if it might never fade.

"Oh please, you're all being far too kind." She reached for the uncut pumpkin pie at the center of the table and said, "Don't worry, Henry. I'm just getting it ready. Plenty of time for you to have your thirds or fourths if you'd like."

Henry looked at his grandfather again, concerned that the twinkle had just disappeared.

This was when the table had gotten a little quieter and a whole lot heavier last Christmas Eve. And the reason for that was simple. Henry's father had always been a slam dunk for two slices of Gigi's famous pie; on one memorable occasion, he'd even pulled off an incredible three-slice hat trick.

The one thing Gigi had done both this year and last, something Henry really appreciated, was not setting out an empty plate for his father. That always felt, at least to him, like something that should just be left for the movies. Besides, the sadness of such a gesture would have been too much for all of them.

Same as the year before, though, the silence at the table grew heavy. Henry thought the odds were good that Chief would be the one to break the silence, as he had last year, but surprisingly it came from somewhere else this time.

"So . . . Henry . . . Carter." Eloise nodded toward both of them. "It looked like the two of you were having quite the conversation just before dinner."

"Ah, yes," Chief said as he smoothed out his napkin. "I've been going through some of my old newspapers of late and found quite a few articles I thought Henry might want to share with Dr. Riggins over at the museum."

Ooooh, well played, Chief. I wouldn't have thought of that one. Short. Makes sense. Perfect.

Eloise looked somewhat relieved at the newspaper revelation.

"Oh! Well . . . that sounds great," she said with a look to-ward Henry. "You told Chief you saw Dr. Riggins just today?"

"Yup, sure did. Santa Claus. Space-time continuum."

Somewhere along the line, Henry had picked up—from Chief, naturally—the skill of smiling without smiling, which he was putting to good use right now. As was the old man, his once-again twinkling eyes sharing a look with Henry's.

"I think we may have found plenty for the good doctor to *hunt* through, don't you, grandson?" Carter put an ever-so-slight emphasis on the word "hunt."

"Oh, absolutely we did!" Henry answered, having picked up on it. "He might not have a *clue* about some of that stuff, but I'll bring him up to speed."

Chief winked.

Henry smiled.

Eloise and Gigi shared a suspicious look.

"All right, you two. What's up here?" Eloise asked, even though she was still wearing a smile.

"Up?" Carter replied, cranking up the innocence. "Nothing's up. Just a part of this one article that Henry and I both found very interesting. I'm sure Dr. Riggins will think the same."

"Henrrrry?" Eloise turned her head.

"Hmm? Oh . . . yeah, yeah, yeah. What Chief said."

"Mmm." She nodded, even though Henry thought she looked completely and thoroughly unconvinced.

The old man gave Henry a slightly mischievous look.

"Ladies," he announced. "If it's all right with the two of you, I'd like for Henry and me to take our pie up to the study before we open gifts. Two slices each, please. I have a few more things to share with him that I think the good doctor will find very, very fascinating."

❧

Four pieces of untouched pumpkin pie sat on the edge of the old man's desk, the snow now crisply pelting against the window as the story resumed. Henry listened intently as both the tale and the storm took a decided turn for the worse.

"Hiram Doubt was an evil man, Henry, and I don't say that lightly," Chief said with a lowering voice, the old newspaper photo staring up from the desktop below them. "He was nearly as rich as Skavenger, which is saying something, but then he lost nearly all of it. Lost it to Skavenger himself, who always found a way to stay ahead of him when it came to the business of industry."

"Sounds like Mr. Doubt might not have taken it too well," Henry speculated.

"No. No, he did not," Chief continued. "But the one thing Skavenger didn't know was that Doubt wasn't just evil, he was vindictive . . . dangerous."

The old man pointed to the photo again. "He surrounded himself with Grace and three other agents of darkness— shadowy men who carried out the very worst of his intentions."

"Carried out? You mean they actually . . . ?"

Chief gravely nodded. "Legend has it Doubt himself took part in that last hunt on July tenth, 1885. Made it to where the grand prize was hidden, and found himself face-to-face with his longtime adversary."

The old man leaned closer once again. "And that's where the great Hunter S. Skavenger finally fell victim to . . ."

"Doubt," Henry finished the sentence for him.

"Or so the story goes," Chief said with a shrug. "Me? I think the reason Skavenger didn't show for that next hunt was that he'd simply decided the puzzle wasn't meant to be solved. Which is the one theory that still captivates me after all these many decades."

Henry realized at that moment that his grandfather had once again shattered his skepticism—that his mother had been absolutely right just before they'd arrived that night.

His stories are *getting crazier! Beautifully, magically crazier!*

"I've waited a long, long time to tell you this, Henry," Chief said to him with a look that said as much. "I have something I want us to do . . . together. Same as your father and I did for years and years, neither one of us ever telling a soul, not even to your mother or grandmother."

Henry's face dropped at the mention of his father. Chief nodded.

"I miss him too, grandson, more than anything in the world . . . but this'll help, the two of us finishing it."

"Finishing what, Chief?"

His grandfather said the next handful of words as if they were the most obvious in the world.

"Skavenger's Hunt, of course! Finding the clues that must have been left behind. If nobody won, the riddles and puzzles are still out there. Right now, this very minute, here in New York."

Omigosh, he's right. Of course!

"Your father and I found fourteen clues—mostly small, easy things." Chief smiled as he continued with the story. "Like how every eighth word in some of Skavenger's riddles could be a key word. That was a fun discovery."

He took a deep breath, before finally nudging the old and yellowed sheet of ledger paper closer to Henry.

"But the one thing we never did find, was the one thing I found just two weeks ago. Something I could put my hands on." He nodded at the age-old, faded sheet.

"This?" Henry finally asked, not wanting to disappoint his grandfather.

"Two hundred and fourteen pages inside a book at the New York Public Library," the old man replied, sounding far from disappointed. "I'd bet my first base from Yankee Stadium it was Skavenger himself who put it in the old Astor branch."

"Okay," Henry tried his best to sound impressed. "Buuuuuut, back to my very first question again. What is it?"

The great man—who always had a story for every moment, an answer to every question—rose to his feet and triumphantly proclaimed:

"I don't know."

Henry looked at him, confused.

"Not an idea in the world." Chief shrugged. "Nothing. I don't have a clue what it is. That's what makes it so great!"

He rested his palms on each side of the ledger, the adventure-seeking smile returning as he added, "But there is one thing I do know, grandson. You and I are going to find out. That's the reason I decided to tell you all of this tonight. The discovery of the ledger sheet was only a fortnight ago. You're reaching an age where you can help with the search. And, perhaps most important, it's Christmas Eve."

The old man took in a much-needed breath before closing in on the end of his amazing tale.

"You and I are going to walk the streets of New York these next few months. Same as I did with your father for a long, long time. To try and solve what no one could more than a hundred years ago. Now what do you say to that?"

Henry answered the question with a growing smile as he pulled the ledger closer still.

"We map out our plan first thing tomorrow," Chief said with growing anticipation. "What better time than Christmas morning, yes?"

"Yes," Henry replied without a hint of hesitation. "Yes, yes, yes."

FIVE

The Ledger Sheet

HOURS LATER, SAME as every Christmas Eve, Henry stared up at the ceiling of his grandparents' guest bedroom with only the occasional blink, waiting to fall asleep.

Most years he lay awake because of the expectation and excitement for the morning to follow, especially those Christmas Eves more than two years ago when he knew that if he could just fall asleep, he'd soon hear the sound of his mom and dad calling for him to come downstairs.

Tonight, though, felt different. Really, really different.

Yep, this staying-awake business had absolutely nothing to do with whatever would be under the tree in the morning. Besides, he'd already opened two of his gifts: an authentic New York Giants hoody that his friend Jeremy-the-Jets-fan would hate, and an old pen that Chief later whispered to him was for the ledger—once they figured out what the darn thing was all about.

That's what was keeping him awake, of course.

The ledger.

And the story that came with it.

Henry turned on his side, as if that would help him get to sleep, and looked over at the bedroom door. It was open a scant couple of inches—his mother always kept it cracked so she could peek inside a handful of times each night. Even at home, she had to make sure her son was still breathing.

I'm fine, Mom. No worries, I'll be okay. Just need to find a way to get a little sleep.

He heard Christmas music softly playing downstairs. Just from the beat, he could tell it was Mariah Carey telling him that all she wanted for Christmas was, well . . . him.

Gigi liked to say she was an expert, or, as she politely urged Henry to call her, a historian of holiday music old and new. This was her favorite radio station—the one she'd tune to in the middle of November and leave on until New Year's, when the last "Merry Gentleman" had been put to rest.

Henry sighed and plopped his arms on top of the comforter, unable to stop thinking about the great Hunter S. Skavenger's story; of the unsettling description of Hiram Doubt and his Four Men of Darkness; of the legendary, though never-completed, hunts of 1883, 1884, and 1885.

And, of course, his father.

Henry had discovered only a few hours ago that Nathan's promise of adventure had its roots in the very story Chief told him. That it should have been the *three* of them walking the streets of the city searching for whatever undiscovered items Skavenger had placed. A secret the three of them would have tried to hide from Gigi and Mom while asking for another piece of pie around the Christmas Eve table.

I just wasn't old enough yet. They were waiting on me.

None of those things could ever be changed, of course. Henry knew that much. But the thought of adventure had been revived tonight by Chief's promise.

A promise that the two of them would figure out what that ridiculous piece of ledger paper was all about.

Yeah, but seriously, what is it? Even Chief doesn't know, and Chief knows everything! Is it really one of Skavenger's clues? The first one? The last one? Maybe it's nothing . . . maybe it's just a bookmark in a book.

Henry tossed the covers aside. Maybe there was something in the story he'd overlooked or forgotten. Or, most tempting of all, maybe there was something on the ledger sheet he hadn't seen. Maybe they just hadn't looked closely enou—

Wait a second!

Henry remembered he'd once watched an old detective movie with his father in which the hero closely studied a piece of paper with a magnifying glass, seeing the imprint of words written on a sheet that had once rested above it. Henry and Nathan had laughed and laughed at how serious the detective seemed to be.

"Y'see? Y'see?" his father had mocked the actor's stilted delivery. "Detective, this is now hard evidence! It can be admitted in a court of laaaaaw!"

Even now, Henry smiled.

Maybe that was it.

Maybe if he studied the ledger sheet closely enough, he'd find something he could show Chief in the morning; a Christmas gift of his own to kick-start the detective work for both of them.

He eased his way out of bed and tiptoed toward the door, being careful when he peeked out—in case his mother was on her final approach, ready to peek in.

The hallway was empty.

Henry stepped out, the music from downstairs barely loud enough to dampen the sound of his footsteps. He leaned his head around the edge of the hallway at the corner . . . the one that turned and led directly to his grandfather's study.

The door was open, but only by the couple of inches he'd found it earlier that evening.

A layer of full-moon blue drew a line across the floor toward Henry's feet, and for a half second, he was sure the old man would be in there, surrounded by candles blazing their light.

He wasn't, though. The study was empty.

And Henry made his way in without a hint of a sound.

He looked toward the desk, dark but uncluttered, which meant he'd have to actually find the ledger sheet, wherever it might be. Knowing Chief, it could be anywhere; maybe even tucked inside one of the hundreds of books lining the shelves or stacked high on the floor.

Next to page 214 prob'ly.

Or over by the newspapers.

Or under the first base from old Yankee Stadium.

Or anywhere.

Henry decided to start at the desk, his eyes jumping to the old green banker's lamp an arm's length away—fake light absolutely, which meant nothing good could ever possibly come from it.

The lamp probably wouldn't even work, he figured, given how much Chief relied on candles. If it did, though, it might spill light into the hall and straight under the door of his mother's guest room.

Risky. Risky, risky, risky. But . . .

Gotta do it.

Ever so gently he tugged at the small, old chain hanging next to the bulb and the lamp flared bright.

Henry held his breath for a half moment, certain he was about to hear the turning of a doorknob, the steady rhythm of his mother's footsteps, or some other sound that would quickly be followed by "Henry? What's up? It's the middle of the night. You feeling okay?"

There was nothing, though.

Nothing except for the scratching sound of Henry opening the desk compartment, revealing the junk drawer to beat all junk drawers. He shook his head, quietly moving aside the countless old letters, several of which were tucked inside brittle, old air-delivery envelopes, the familiar red-and-blue stripe around their edges.

Australia.

Brazil.

London.

Istan—

The ledger sheet!

It was right here. Not inside a book, but instead, underneath a letter from some guy named Dewey McElroy, postmarked 1947.

Henry quietly pulled out the old ledger and placed it under the light. The only sound came from the downstairs radio, which was now quietly informing the entire house that it was beginning to look a lot like Christmas.

Henry pushed the lamp cover a smidge higher to better highlight the old sheet of paper, then spent the next few minutes holding it upways, sideways, and longways, before reaching the conclusion that . . .

Zero. Zip. Nada.

He muttered under his breath, though very much out loud, "Well, guess I'll wait till tomorrow to solve the Great Skavenger Hunt of eight . . ."

Henry barely whispered the first syllable of the year before a long-faded numeral . . . 8 . . . slowly began to scrawl itself onto the paper, without a hand or pen guiding it. Right there, in the old empty box where the date would've been recorded, the inked number quickly deepened into a dark and brilliant black.

Waaaait . . .

. . . wait wait wait wait wait wait wait wait wait wait.

His actual voice had fallen silent even before saying the rest of the number, because he couldn't say the rest of the number. Not with an *eight* now clearly, unmistakably visible on the age-old ledger paper.

Not a computer-looking eight, or a typewritten eight— even though the only typewritten eight Henry had really ever seen had been on his computer.

This was a handwritten eight. Gliding onto the paper as if it had been written in that same moment by the hand of a ghost.

"Whoa, whoa, whoa," he finally managed to murmur as he tilted the lampshade even higher to see if his eyes were playing tricks on him.

Nope. No tricks.

8

It was there. Right there. In black and white . . . well, black at least. And all he had done, just before the number had somehow appeared, was to say that Skavenger's Great Hunt of—

Hold on. You said it. You said it out loud. You started to at least.

"Eighteen," Henry whispered, making certain this time to say the entire word.

And just as the first number had appeared in the date box of the ledger, before his voice had stopped and faltered, the second numeral now followed suit.

18

The ghostly ink soaked its way into the old paper, slowly and hauntingly. Written in that very moment in letter-perfect handwriting. The elegant style of writing reserved for the year . . .

"1885," Henry hesitantly added. Out loud.

Another eight and a new five began to spill onto the page. It was quiet enough that he could actually *hear* the scratching sound of an old pen as the full year appeared.

. . . *shhccrriisstttchhh . . . shhccrriisstttchhh . . .*

1885

The back of Henry's neck tingled cold, his thoughts instantly jumbling into nothing more than a steady, uninterrupted stream of:

Holycrapholycrapholycrapholycrapholycrapholycrapholycrap.

Until, for whatever reason, the smallest flicker of curiosity decided to fight off the adrenaline and bubbling panic rushing through his body.

Perhaps it was Dr. Riggins and his never-ending fascination with questions that begged for an answer. Maybe it was Chief, who taught him that if he didn't know something he should ask. And if he didn't believe it, he should ask again.

Maybe one of those things was the reason why Henry was still sitting right there in the old man's chair, staring at the suddenly very mysterious piece of ledger paper below him.

Wait, hold on here a second. I say it and it shows up? I say 1885 out loud and there it is? I said 1885 a couple of times when Chief and I were talking. I'm sure I did. So why now? What the heck's even going on here?

He stared at the number for another good long minute. Maybe two.

The practical side of Henry Babbitt's brain usually won most of these arguments, if not all of them. He got it from his mother. And right now that practical side was telling him: *All right. Enough with all this "saying 1885 out loud" business. You fell asleep, okay? You're dreaming. Simple as that.*

He rubbed his eyes and then closed them tight. Really tight. It was a trick he'd figured out a few years ago as a way to help him get out of nightmares.

Close my eyes as tight as I can, long as I can, and I'll wake up.

Henry kept his eyes shut for longer than was usually necessary; longer because the rolling, tingling sensation that was always there as he'd slowly wake up was missing this time.

He opened his eyes.

1885

Still there.

Still impossible.

Somehow, the ink had already faded enough that it now actually looked as if it had been there for well over a century. Henry rubbed his thumb right on the date—gently at first, but then hard enough that he worried for a second the old paper might rip in two.

The ink didn't smear in the least.

Henry hesitated again for what felt like forever—wanting, but terrified, to say the one word he knew made perfect sense.

Tick, tick, tick, tick . . .

It was as if the clock on Chief's desk was tapping him on the shoulder, reminding him that he was now officially wasting time. Nudging him to either say it out loud or keep his mouth shut.

Or maybe I should just go get Chief. He won't be mad. He'll be excited. He'll know what to do.

But instead, Henry Babbitt took in a deep, uncertain breath, unable to resist.

"July," he finally said out loud.

. . . shhccrriisstttchhh . . . shhccrriisstttchhh . . .

JULY

This time he didn't wait, finishing the date with the only item left missing.

"Tenth," he quietly said. Out loud, just as he had bef—

WHUMP.

It was in that moment that something clearly happened, though what that something was, Henry didn't have a clue. The sound that followed his saying the word "tenth" wasn't so much a sound. It was a feeling. Almost like the quick change in the air one felt during the strongest of summer thunderstorms. An electric sensation.

What happened after that, though, was entirely clear— despite that it was also completely and totally unexplainable.

The brand-new laptop computer on the far corner of Chief's old desk, the one he used more as a paperweight than for anything else, slowly began to fade away, until it disappeared entirely.

Gone. Vanished.

What? No.

This week's short stack of newspapers followed suit, quickly evaporating from Henry's sight.

The newer books on the old man's shelves began to fade away as well, vanishing within seconds. The pens on his desk. The Derek Jeter–autographed baseball in its small glass collector's case, disappearing like a soft grounder into the Hall of Famer's glove.

No, no, no.

One by one, as if in mind-boggling exact order, the contents of Chief's study grew transparent and then became . . . nothing. Nothing at all. Henry could both see and hear the stack of Old Gray Lady editions thumping its way shorter and shorter.

The banker's lamp on the desk eased its way from white light to gray and then black, followed a heartbeat later by the wicks on each of the old man's candles unexpectedly and eerily crackling to life as the gentle, soft hum of electricity faded with a steadily slowing *whooooooosssshhhh*.

No no no no no no no no no no no no no no no no no no no no no.

KUHTHUMP!

Henry plopped straight onto the hardwood floor, landing right on his rear. Chief's chair, the one he'd been sitting on, was now nowhere to be seen.

The desk was the next thing to go.

The first base from Yankee Stadium was already fading.

And the golf club from Scotland? It was still there, but it was now on the floor because the one thing that had always held it up, Henry's favorite leather chair, wasn't there anymore.

Henry pushed himself up to run toward the door, tripping and falling right on his face as his foot got tangled in one of the royal garments from ancient Egypt. The only thing that had made his fall even possible was that the wooden box that had protected the delicate items for decades had also vanished. Those garments had never been out on the floor before, until right now.

"CHIEF?! MOM?! GIGI?!" Henry yelled out, repeating each name even louder as he ran into the hallway, seeing that everything in the corridor and on the landing was absent. It was as if a moving company had finished three days of work in the span of three minutes.

"MOM? CHIEF?" he shouted over the bannister. But the only sound Henry heard was his own voice, which had recovered enough to drown out the music playing downsta—

He stopped.

There's no music playing downstairs. There's not even a crackle. Because you know there's not gonna be a radio down there.

Henry raced down every step with barely a glance at the wall now barren of any and all photographs. Once on the main level, he stopped long enough to glance into the dining room—emptied of all its furnishings as well as the usually long-lingering aroma of Christmas Eve dinner.

Gone. All of it.

But it was when Henry stumbled into Chief's and Gigi's great room that he noticed something else was already well underway. Something almost as unsettling as the past three, probably now four, minutes.

Everything from the fourteen-foot-tall Christmas tree to the stunning artwork, even the hardwood floors, had been erased from the vacant room. Until . . .

A much, much different collection of furnishings slowly began to appear. Almost all of it looked Victorian in design, despite the fact that each piece looked as new as if it had just been purchased yesterday. Oak cabinets proudly stood against the wall, dark red tables covered with bright white linen were placed in each corner, and the room itself was now illuminated by brass lanterns slowly coming into view, both on the walls and on the side tables.

Henry even felt a tingle rippling over his own body; a chill that made it seem as if something had just changed about him as well.

This is crazy, this is crazy, this is . . .

Henry couldn't catch his breath. How could he? Everything that was in the house he'd known for so long was now gone, all of it eerily replaced by *what*, exactly? From when, from where, from what?

"MOM? CHIEF? GIGI?" Henry called out once more, but even as he did, he knew there wouldn't be an answer. Just as he knew—

Wait.

Something was different about the main window in front of him.

It wasn't just that Gigi's prized window coverings were gone, replaced by Victorian drapes. It was what he could see beyond the window, through the inch-wide opening in the curtains. Light. Henry cocked his head and stepped closer.

The snow can't be that bright, can it? Wait, no. It's not that it's bright. It's that it's . . .

Something was wrong. Something with the color of the moonlight that was piercing through where the drapes were bunched together. Instead of being a sparkling white, it was almost . . . yellow.

Clip, clop, clip, clop . . .

What the heck? What the heck is that? He was right on the verge of panic.

In the same way the objects inside the house had slowly been appearing, now there were sounds outside that were slowly rising. Sounds that made zero sense at half past whatever in the middle of Christmas Eve night.

Clip, clop, clip, clop . . .

Clip, CLOP, clip, CLOP . . .

CLIP, CLOP, CLIP, CLOP . . .

Henry gulped.

Okay, okay. Calm down, just think it through. Everybody's still in bed. You fell asleep in Chief's study. That's the only thing it can be. All the excitement of Christmas, the talk you had with the old man, it all just—

CLIP, CLOP, CLIP, CLOP . . .

No matter how hard his head tried to tell him he was asleep, Henry felt wide awake.

Nothing makes a noise like that in the middle of Christmas Eve night. NOTHING.

Just then, with the room steadily brightening from not only the lanterns but the general warmth and humidity that certainly didn't come with midnight in December, Henry heard . . . a voice.

A voice he didn't recognize coming from far upstairs, deep in the master bedroom.

"George? Emily?" a man's deep and resonant voice called out. "Your mother and I are ready to head to the park. We're already late, and we don't want to miss anything."

"Okay, Papa!" a young boy's voice answered.

A rush of near-terror flooded through Henry's veins. He looked up and over his shoulder, seeing no one. Yet.

George? Emily? Who's George and Emily? Who's Papa?

Henry reached for the knob, turned it, and quickly pulled the front door open. And that's when the warm air of a summer morning brushed against his face.

SIX

1885

HENRY TOOK ONE step outside, but then couldn't take a second. That's because the clip-clopping sound that had lured him through the front door of his grandparents' home was coming not from one horse-drawn carriage, but dozens and dozens of carriages moving through the snowless and bone-dry streets.

All right . . . stop. Stop, stop, stop. Close your eyes again. Now. Tight! All a dream, all a dream.

Henry closed his eyes again, but it was difficult because of the noise of the horses and voices and all sorts of other things invading his ears from all directions.

CLIP, CLOP.

"Hey!"

"Little Arthur, don't stray now."

Henry opened his eyes again. His completely disbelieving eyes.

The number of horse carriages was the first thing that got his attention. Sure, he and his father had seen plenty of the ones that tourists paid top dollar to take a slow lap around Central Park in, but these carriages were different.

These horses were sturdy and strong. The black carriages they pulled were shiny and spit-polished, all of them with a distinct sense of purpose.

Okay, okay, okay, okay, okay. It's New York. It's not my New York, but it is New York. That much I know.

Central Park stood right across the brick-laid street in front of him, but the towering old trees—the "Guardians of the Park" his father used to call them—were much, much younger and noticeably shorter.

Not to mention they didn't have snow on them, or that it felt like it was seventy degrees and it wasn't nighttime.

There wasn't a car in sight. Dozens of young kids—girls in summer hats, boys in sharp suits—ran across the road, their parents yelling for them not to run in front of the horses. The children would turn and laugh, ignoring the advice, and their parents would call out again with only the faintest of concern.

Henry felt hypnotized for a moment. Trying to work through the unworkable. Think through the unthinkable.

The powerful streetlights were unfamiliar too. New, yet old. Almost all of them gas-fueled, only a very few electric.

New York. *Old* New York.

A good many of the men in sight wore silky black top hats; the women rested parasols on their shoulders; and a band of trumpets, trombones, and tubas could be heard playing some-where close by.

A dream, a dream, a dream, still a dream . . .

Henry kept trying to convince himself, but it was getting more difficult with every moment. Each horse-drawn carriage, each vision, was trying its best to reassure that all-important corner of his brain: the corner that sorts out what's real from slumbering fantasy.

But there was something getting in the way. Something allowing a crest of fear to rush in like cold water through an already frigid faucet.

Nope, doesn't feel like a dream. Stuff's too clear.

Things are . . . I mean, look at that leaf . . . look at that wheel. . . it's all sharp and in focus. . .

Henry whipped around and lunged at the front door, forgetting for the moment about Papa and George and Emily, only to discover that the door had closed on its own and was now locked tight.

"No, no, no, no, NO, NO, NO!" Henry now yelled the words, his heart suddenly pounding. He gave a hard twist on the doorknob, pushing and pulling, but it wouldn't budge.

Locked. Tight.

"C'mon, c'mon," he pleaded to himself, thumping on the door as loudly as he could.

"MOM!! CHIEF!! GIGI!!"

"Everything all right there, laddy?" a voice with a thick Irish accent called out from behind him. Henry turned to find a carriage driver looking his way with mild concern, his chestnut-colored horse snorting impatiently.

"Not often I see a screamin' young snapper callin' for his ma or his . . . who was it? His Gigi?" the driver half laughed through a mustache that covered his entire upper lip.

Henry was too shaken to reply. He drove his hand into his pocket . . .

All right. Okay. Phone. Call. Key.

Wait, c'mon . . . you've never even had *a key for . . .*

His hand froze. Not because of the key that wasn't there that he now realized couldn't have been there.

It was because of something else entirely.

"Up the yard with ya then!" The carriage driver shook his head, snapping the reins and heading away.

Henry looked down at the raggedy old coat he was now wearing—a brown and shabby jacket that had never been on his shoulders before. Gone was the gift of the New York Giants hoody he'd gone to sleep wearing, along with his favorite pair of baggy sweats—all replaced with a full set of clothing he'd never seen before.

It's what I felt. When everything was appearing inside. That was it. What *is going on?!*

He plunged his hand into his other pocket, stopping as he felt something crinkle against his sweaty palm. He grabbed it and pulled it out.

It was the ledger sheet.

The ledger sheet that he now realized had somehow, incredibly, improbably, brought him back to . . .

July 10, 1885.

Henry took in the date as he looked at the box that had somehow been filled in only minutes ago. The ink that had looked faded in Chief's office was now growing darker and seemingly newer by the second.

Now being joined by something else.

Words gracefully began to scroll into the ledger's first empty destination box.

CENTRAL PARK, NEW YORK

And once those words appeared, another set began to show up in the largest empty box, right at the very top. These words, however, weren't being magically written in the moment by a ghostly hand, but were simply reappearing—as if the ink they'd once been written with had faded to nothing and was now finding new life.

The message read:

TO WHOEVER HAS FOUND THIS PAGE FROM MY
LEDGER: FIND ME. THERE IS A WAY BACK. OR
FORWARD. BUT KNOW THIS TOO—WHEN THE FINAL
EMPTY BOX OF THIS SHEET IS FULL, SO ENDS
YOUR ADVENTURE. WHATEVER THE DATE AND
LOCATION, THERE YOU WILL STAY. FOREVER.

Henry realized that he hadn't taken a breath—and that the
next one would have to wait as well.

SINCERELY, HUNTER S. SKAVENGER

"Wait, what?!" Henry muttered as his thoughts went into
overload.

*Ledger . . . Skavenger . . . horses . . . clop . . . calm down . . .
Mom . . . need to settle down . . .*

The front door of his grandparents' home opened behind
him. A barrel-chested gentleman wearing a finely tailored brown
suit, along with his strikingly beautiful wife wearing a long em-
erald green dress topped with a peacock feather hat, stood in
the open door with their two young children, dressed much
like the kids Henry had just seen running across the street.

George. Emily.

"Excuse me, young man," the gentleman sternly said to
Henry. "What are you doing standing on my front step?"

Papa.

"Oh . . . I . . . just . . . well . . ." Henry spluttered the words
out. The gentleman gestured for his wife and children to head
down the steps while he finished the conversation.

"Away with you. Now!" Papa's voice carried a threatening
tone as he locked the door and checked it at least twice. He
waited for Henry to abandon the steps, every last one of them,

before walking over to join his family. The four of them crossed the street, the reprimanding gentleman looking back over his shoulder more than once.

Henry stood on the edge of the cobblestone street, at a complete loss as to what to do next. The clock had somehow been turned back more than a century, and the closest thing he had to a home had just been locked tight by a man he'd never seen before.

His hands trembled as he looked back down at the ledger, still in his hands, before a young, hard voice yelled out a short distance away from him.

"MORNING EDITION! READ ALL ABOUT IT!"

Henry turned to see a boy of maybe ten—a newsboy, he guessed—hawking papers from a nearby corner. His ink-stained hands held a *New York Times* aloft, his hair much too thick for his cap.

"Ya got one there, Billy?" the kid shouted, already winding up to toss a paper to someone over Henry's shoulder.

Henry slipped the ledger into his pocket and turned around to see a nodding fellow hawker making a sale, even though he'd run out of copies.

Wup wup wup wup wup wup . . .

Henry could hear it flying through the air, right up until it smacked him in the back of his head.

"Owwww." Henry reached up to where the newspaper had thumped him, then watched as it fell to the ground and rolled open to the biggest front-page headline he'd ever seen.

SKAVENGER'S LATEST HUNT BEGINS THIS MORNING!

Henry reached for the paper in a heartbeat, his already-jumbled mind latching on to the announcement that stretched across the entire banner. The words were all in perfect order, unlike the crazy mess inside his own newspaper-whacked head.

"SKAVENGER'S THIRD HUNT BEGINS THIS HOUR! CENTRAL PARK ABUZZ!" he heard the first newsie cry out to no one in particular, while his fellow hawker walked over to Henry with an impatient look on his face.

"Hey, Ace!" the newsie said, rapping the fingers of one hand into his palm. "Ya read it? Ya owe me a nickel."

"Just a second," Henry was quickly scanning the front page.

It's the New York Times, *all right. The Old Gray Lady. All the news that's fit to print from . . .*

His eyes popped up to the date.

"July tenth, 1885," Henry whispered to himself—or so he thought. Apparently, he'd said the words loudly enough that the young news-hawker had overheard.

"What'd you think it was? Christmas Day?" The newsboy shook his head, snatching the paper back. The noise leading into the park was now growing louder—men, women, boys, and girls all streaming onto every path they could find.

"No, no, no." Henry reached for the paper. "I gotta see that, you gotta help me here!"

"I? Me? Gotta help you?" the newsie scoffed as he turned to walk away. "You got a nickel? We'll talk. If you don't, scram."

"Wait, wait! Where can I find Mr. Skavenger?!" Henry shouted to him, now desperate. "I gotta find him right now!"

The boy spun around.

"Oh, so no nickel *and* no idea what's goin' on." He rolled his eyes. "Follow the crowd, wise guy. You wanna get close enough to hear, ya better get movin'."

And with that, he rolled up the paper, tucked it under his arm, and was gone for good.

Henry stood on the edge of the brick road that was Central Park West, not knowing what to do.

Skavenger's third hunt. Today. Wait a second . . .

Henry reached into his pocket again, whipping the ledger sheet open with a flick of his wrist. The words were still there. Only one of the precious destination and date boxes had been filled:

JULY 10ᴛʜ, 1885, CENTRAL PARK, NEW YORK.

Up at the very top, though, in even brighter black ink than just a moment ago, were the most important words of the entire message. . .

FIND ME. THERE IS A WAY BACK.
SINCERELY, HUNTER S. SKAVENGER

There. Right there.

There's a way for me to get back!

Quickly, Henry rattled through the things he knew—or at least the things he thought he knew. Chief's and Gigi's house wasn't Chief's and Gigi's house—not yet. He had no phone. No way to let anyone know what had happened to him. No way to let his mother know he was . . .

Oh no.

No, no, no. She's gonna wake up soon . . . and I'll be gone.

Henry was already backing up toward the street, his only hope somewhere behind him in Central Park. He had to get to Skavenger while he was still there, before the legend himself was gone, before . . .

He turned straight into the path of another oncoming horse-drawn carriage. "Hey! *Oglądać się!*" a Polish driver angrily shouted as he pulled his nickering draft horse to a not-so-sudden halt.

"Sorry!" Henry managed to call back, still scampering. A small smile grew on the carriage driver's face—he was obviously aware of what was going on this morning along with everyone else in sight.

But there was no smile on Henry's face as he sprinted hard into Central Park, through the ever-growing flood of men wearing top hats and women carrying parasols.

Skavenger. Gotta talk to Skavenger.

Which, he could tell with one look around, was the same goal everyone else had too. Thousands and thousands of hunters were crowding into Central Park, with a lot more on the way.

The trumpets and trombones sounded brighter now. Closer. And in an opening in the crowd up ahead, where an enormous stage had been constructed, rising high above the summer-battered ground, Henry finally heard the announcement that was so important for him to hear.

"Ladies and Gentlemen! I present to you—MR. HUNTER S. SKAVENGER!"

SEVEN

Skavenger

CHIEF'S CLAIM THAT there had been thousands and thousands of people in Central Park that day turned out to be absolutely true. There wasn't just one brass band playing—there were at least a dozen. Hot air balloons were stationed here and there, apparently ready to help a hunter or two with a quick escape once the first riddle was announced.

Henry waded into the back of the enormous gathering. He passed one team of hunters that looked like a nineteenth-century quartet of Dr. Riggins-types; another group that was made up of flag-waving Canadians, their pencils already poised for whatever was about to be said; and even a trio of priests with rosaries around their necks.

The crowd of onlookers suddenly roared as Skavenger finally stepped up to the elevated riser at the front of the stage, every inch of it decorated with red, white, and blue bunting. He wore a thin black suit that fit his lean frame like layered feathers on an eagle, accented by a bright red shirt and a pure-black tie.

There was no top hat on his head, no hat of any kind, for that matter. His hair was combed back and shiny gray, which gave him a commanding look; as did the buttons on his coat, which sparkled like diamonds in the morning sun.

Skavenger offered the throng a proud and confident smile as he held his hands out wide—dispelling the notion that a secretive and private man could not be a pure showman.

As Chief had guaranteed Henry during the telling of his tale, Skavenger looked both mysterious and charismatic.

Henry, though, was stuck at the back of the crowd, with no easy way of moving any closer.

"Fellow citizens of New York!" Henry heard the booming voice as he started wedging his way through the gathering. "Fellow citizens of the WORLD! I welcome you once more to the greatest of adventures."

The crowd erupted as one, raising their arms to cheer. Henry took advantage of the moment to dart below a good many of them, stopping when he heard the voice again.

"The rules of the hunt remain elementary," Skavenger announced as Henry tried to perch up for a better view.

"Solve the first clue, solve the second, solve them all," he went on to proclaim. "But to that one person or one team that solves the final clue, after a perilous journey—a QUEST!—that shall take them far and near . . ."

Henry's tiptoes were already aching.

". . . I offer THIS!"

With a grand flourish, Skavenger gestured toward an enormous canvas that had just unfurled across the stage. On it was an artist's rendering of a spectacular bank safe—the etching detail so precise even Henry could see it.

"A fortune both enormous and incalculable!" Skavenger boomed through the cheering as two top-hat-clad gentlemen moved to each side of the painted canvas. "A prize that has been both witnessed and certified as authentic by these fine men. Two of New York's most reputable and honorable bankers!"

The thunder of approval lasted long enough for Henry to move closer than even he'd expected.

One more quick shot to the right, whip through there, and I'll be—ummmph—

"Hey! Lunkhead!" A hand latched tightly onto his collar. Henry turned—or, more accurately, was turned—putting him face-to-face with a scruffy, sharp-eyed boy he guessed was at least two years older than him.

Worse yet, he was four inches taller and wider.

"What's the hurry?" the boy demanded with a no-nonsense smirk, before stealing a quick glance toward the stage over Henry's shoulder.

He wore roughly the same kind of clothes as the Brooklyn newsboy, except they were just that: rougher. The boy's brown trousers were held up by green suspenders that looked as if they'd been pulled out of a gutter—and not recently. Same thing applied for the gray cap covering his reddish, poorly cut hair. The only thing that didn't hint at an apparent lack of money were his eyes: green in the middle, brown on the edge, but whip-smart in their attentiveness throughout. As if they never missed a single thing.

"C'mon, dude," Henry replied, trying to squirm free. "I just couldn't hear what he was saying."

"Join the crowd," the boy grumbled under his breath, smirk still intact. "And what did you call me? *Dude?*"

Oh boy. Careful what you say. Who knows what "dude" means in 1885, right?

Another boy, who looked closer to Henry's age and thankfully not much bigger, stood nearby, frantically scribbling down notes barely an inch from his patched-up spice-colored vest. His writing was actually frantic enough that the frayed hat resting on his dirty-brown and somewhat trimmed hair was threatening to fall off at any second.

"Whatta ya say, Ernie?" the boy holding Henry in midair asked the other. "Got ourselves a bootrag says he can't hear."

Ernie, peering over his long nose through what looked like hand-me-down frameless glasses, replied without so much as a glance, "Yeah, well, he's not the only one who can't hear. I'm tryin' to write all of this down, remember?"

The boy wearing out Henry's collar finally let go. "Stay put," he said as he pointed a threatening finger at him. "We've been here for hours, what's fair is fair."

Henry would have had trouble getting much closer anyway—right now, at least. He figured he was a football field away from the stage, maybe more.

Ernie, in the meantime, was repeating each of Skavenger's words out loud. "I . . . offer . . . this. Fortune. Enormous. Incalculable."

The man in front of him turned and glared. "Shhhh, quiet!"

"Aw, quiet yourself," Ernie shot back. "I'll pipe down when there's somethin' to hear."

Thousands upon thousands of eyes were locked on Skavenger as he looked out over the tightly packed multitude.

"And so," Skavenger decreed as Henry heard the undeniable scratching sound of thousands of pencils landing in unison onto notepads, "I hereby offer to those here, a call!"

Ernie wrote the words down as quickly as Skavenger said them.

"One that can only be heard by the great explorers like Lewis and Clark. Who number here in the thousands, same as in 1804, searching distant territories for new adventure!"

Henry heard the shushing man say to the woman next to him, "Clark. Distant territories."

"And now," Skavenger held his hands wide again. "Let this adventure begin! Good luck!"

Central Park nearly shook, so deafening was the response. The man in front of Ernie jabbed his pencil onto the paper he'd been writing on—the unmistakable motion of an exclamation point.

"I've got it, I've got it, follow me." He kept his voice low, excitedly reaching for the woman's hand. They quickly disappeared into the crowd.

Now's your chance. Go! Go!

Henry tried to make his move, but got stuck right off the bat. The crush of thousands of New Yorkers and citizens of the world swirled in every direction around him.

Gotta get to him. Just . . . okay . . . where'd he go? Where is he?

Henry jumped up just high enough to spot the creator of the Great Hunt moving to the right-hand side of the stage, but he was still a whole football field away. He jumped again and saw Skavenger in his bright red shirt heading for something . . . heading over to . . .

He's gonna get off the stage. On that side. Over there!

Henry ran as quickly as he could, which wasn't as quickly as he needed. Half the crowd was heading one way, the other half the opposite. It took more than a few precious seconds before Henry was able to finally find his first good opening and rushed through it, weaving past scattering and hopeful hunters.

Until he was blocked again. He rose onto his tiptoes for yet another desperate glimpse.

Skavenger was surrounded by what had to be security—two dozen men at least, probably more—ready to lead him off the stage. Henry jumped, but couldn't see Skavenger's destination. He jumped again.

His horse carriage. There!

Henry could get there, he knew he could. It was close enough now; all he needed to do was head that way just a little bit more and . . .

I can show him the ledger. I can find my way back!

But an unexpected cluster of hunters rushed right in front of Henry just then, completely blocking his path as they loudly shouted out: "Mr. Skavenger! Mr. Skavenger!

C'monnnn, no, no, NO!

His legs were running short on gas, but Henry jumped one last time as high as he could, barely catching a glimpse of Skavenger. He was right there—approaching the carriage that was now so close.

"Wait! Hold on! Over here!" Henry yelled. A narrow path opened to one side and he dashed into it, now able to see the polished wheels and the immaculate midnight-black sideboards.

The carriage was now very close.

But it was also the carriage that Skavenger was now climbing into, waving to the crowd before ducking his head and moving in to sit down inside. The outstretched arms of his security team kept the starstruck hunters from approaching even one more inch.

"MR. SKAVENGER!" Henry shouted. "MR. SKAVENGER! OVER HERE! I NEED TO—"

"Back up, young man! Now." A stout security man fixed him with a steely, no-nonsense look, just as Skavenger turned his head and locked eyes with Henry.

He sees me!

"MR. SKAVENGER!" Henry yelled, his best chance yet, his only chance. "I'VE GOT THE LEDGER SHEET! THE ONE YOU LEFT! YOU SAID THERE'S A WAY . . ."

But the driver had snapped the reins and the pristine carriage was now slowly pulling away. A somewhat curious look remained on Skavenger's face for another second or two, his eyes staying with Henry as the glittering wheels gathered momentum.

"MR. SKAVENGER! WAAAAAIT!"

But the only response Henry heard was the sharp clip and clop of the enigmatic man's black horses and the rolling sound of his departing carriage, which was now blocked by the convergence of hunters wanting to watch him leave.

Henry's shoulders sagged as the sound of the horses faded into nothing, leaving behind only the growing buzz of hunters jabbering over the puzzle Skavenger had left for them to solve.

For Henry Babbitt though, Hunter S. Skavenger hadn't simply left. No, it was far, far more lasting than that.

Hunter S. Skavenger was gone.

ભ

Henry trudged his way through the still-crowded, still-excited park, even though he didn't feel the activity in the least. Instead, he found himself feeling something all too familiar.

He felt alone.

All right, so . . . what now?

That was one of, oh, only about a million questions Henry was busy asking himself. His distant eyes were fixed on nothing more than the torn-up turf a few feet in front of him—the shredded papers with misspelled words written on them; the occasional group of hunters running in tandem, seemingly convinced they had the answer to the legendary figure's first riddle.

The wild panic he'd felt only an hour ago had faded a little. Not all of it, of course, but a good amount had been dampened by the sobering sight of Skavenger actually seeing him, actually locking eyes with him—only to be followed by the finality of his carriage not stopping or even slowing down.

Which brought Henry right back to his first question.
What now?

He lifted his head, slowing to a stop as he heard two familiar voices squabbling just a short distance in front of him.

"Come on, pal, hurry it up!" the collar-grabbing boy barked
at Ernie, snapping his raggedy green suspenders apparently out
of habit. "Look at everyone! They've already got it figured out!"

Ernie glanced up at the hundreds of people pursuing the
first clue, which Henry could tell was doing nothing to help
the young hunter with his own detective work.

"Lewis. Clark. 1804," he said, waiting for something to
click. "1804. That's the year they started their expedition."

"Right, right, right. Distant territories, something about
new adventures," the other boy offered, hoping to provide
inspiration.

"Yeah, yeah, I know, Jack." Ernie sounded impatient with
himself. "The distant territories of the west."

Neither of them had noticed Henry yet.

Ernie's pencil tapped over the words as Jack paced back
and forth. "Holy smokes, Ern," he whispered loudly enough
that Henry could easily overhear. "If we don't come up with
something right here, right now, we're gonna be out of this
before we ever—"

"Clark might not be William Clark," Ernie noted with
a sharp tone. "It could be a different Clark. What if he's
Edward Clark?"

"Who the heck's Edward Clark?" Jack leaned closer to ask.

"He's the guy making all those sewing machines. He had a
partner." Ernie snapped his fingers, trying to place the name.
"C'mon, c'mon . . . his name was Ringer, Linger, SINGER!
That was it. Singer. They went into business together a few
years ago."

"Yeah? So?"

Henry inched closer to listen, neither boy paying a sliver of attention to him.

"So Edward Clark isn't only about sewing machines." Ernie rubbed his forehead. "He's been building stuff, all these new buildings. They're all over the city."

Ernie looked at his notes, his hat once again threatening to fall from his head. The worried crease between his eyes had grown too tight for Jack's liking—right up until it disappeared.

"Distant territories!" Ernie shouted as he circled the words. "The ones out west! It's the Dakota. The Dakota Apartments. He just finished it!"

Jack fixed Ernie with a skeptical look. "Skavenger put his first clue right here next to Central Park? Is that what you're telling me?"

"Looks that way," Ernie grinned. Jack clapped him on the back, noticing Henry eavesdropping in the same moment. "Don't even think about it, pal," he warned. "You go your way, we'll go ours."

The two boys headed off in the direction of the Dakota as Henry glanced up at the building's proud gables and steep-pitched roofs, already visible over the park benches edging West 72nd Street.

It was a place he'd seen countless times before—but not like this.

Look at it. It's brand new! They must have just finished it.

Henry had listened to every word the two boys had just said, which, unfortunately, reminded him that in the chaos of the announcement, he hadn't taken down a single word of the first puzzle himself. He'd been too busy trying to figure out a way to get to Skavenger.

Now that he'd missed out on that tiny little detail . . .

Chief said he'd learned something important about the clues. He and Dad. What was it? The thing he said they discovered about the words. Oh yeah! Right!

His eyes scoured the ground, searching for a left-behind scrap of paper that might have the puzzle written on it.

Gotta be one around here somewhere. It's a long shot, yup, but it is a shot at least. There!

Henry grabbed a crumpled slip of paper and unwadded it. Blank. Nothing.

Guess it's more of a really, really *long shot. Being as I'm in 18-freaking-85, and I don't know a single person or anything about the ci—*

Henry whipped his head up. Jack and Ernie were already almost out of earshot and moving quickly.

"Hey! Wait!" Henry called out to the two boys. Jack and Ernie kept right on going, without even a glance back.

"I THINK IT COULD BE SOMEWHERE ELSE!" he shouted loudly enough that the two of them, along with about a hundred other hunters, turned to look.

Luckily, Central Park was still enough of a frenzied mess that Henry was able to kind of disappear as he hurriedly worked his way over to Ernie's side, which was the much safer side of the two boys, he figured.

"I told you to scram, remember?" Jack growled at him.

"No, no. Whatta ya mean, it may be something else?" Ernie ignored his hunting partner, whipping out his notebook just in case.

"Skavenger puts key words into each of his clues," Henry told them, struggling to keep up with the speed-walking boys. "Least that's what I heard he does. Every eighth word is a clue within a clue."

Both kids came to a sudden stop, as did Henry.

"Who the heck says that?" Jack cocked his head and asked. It was now fairly apparent the smirk was pretty much etched onto the older boy's face.

Henry wisely chose not to answer, turning to Ernie instead. "You wrote down every word, right?"

Before he could answer, Jack stepped closer to Henry. "I asked you a question."

"Hey, Jack. Let him finish," Ernie interrupted, suddenly looking curious. He flipped his notebook open like a cop ready to display his badge.

"Read the eighth word," Henry managed to say, realizing he was now short of breath. "The eighth word of the clue."

Ernie eyed him suspiciously, but he also held up a hand toward Jack, silently asking for a few more seconds of patience. He waited for a lengthy parade of Dakota-bound searchers to march by before his eyes returned to Skavenger's announcement.

Henry could tell Ernie was silently counting.

"'Call,'" he finally said. "The eighth word of what he said was 'call.'"

"And the eighth word after that?" Henry asked excitedly.

"This is all a joke," Jack huffed while Ernie counted. "I'm headin' over to the Dakota myself."

"'The,'" Ernie announced as he circled the word. "'Call' and 'the' are the first two words."

Jack stopped and turned, right in time to see Henry gulp. The next word was either gonna make sense or put the whole thing on a direct path toward gibberish.

Ernie, though, was already tapping eight words ahead. The tip of his dull, fractured pencil stopped a second to write down the next word, before quickly sprinting forward again.

"'Number.' Call the number."

Whew.

Tap, tap, tap. "Call the number 1804 . . ."

A smile started to spread wide on Ernie's face.

"Call the number 1804 NOW!" he announced to Jack with stunned disbelief. "It's a telephone call!" he nearly shouted. "Skavenger wants us to use a telephone."

"COOL! We can use mine." Henry, purely by reflex, reached into his pocket for his cell phone.

Uh oh . . . right . . . no phone.

"Whatta ya mean, we can use yours?" Ernie laughed. "Your family got enough money they got their own phone at home?"

"Sorry, my bad. I mean, never mind," Henry tried to cut his losses. "But you only said four numbers, what about the rest of 'em?"

The boys looked at him with the blankest of blank expressions.

"What do you mean, the rest of 'em?" Jack still looked more than willing to throttle Henry. "You only need four numbers to make a telephone call, genius."

Ernie closed up his notebook and tucked it away. "There's a telephone exchange not far from here, a block away from Hell's Kitchen. My aunt works there."

Telephone exchange? What's a telephone exchange?

But Jack's hard gaze had yet to move off Henry.

"Hey, tough guy." Ernie rolled his eyes at Jack. "'Nuff with the staring. Whatta ya wanna do?"

"I wanna know where he came up with that every-eighth-word thing, that's what I wanna do. We've done this hunt twice, and I never heard of that before."

"Look," Henry tried to reassure him. "I'm not trying to horn in on this, okay? The only thing I want is to talk to Skavenger, that's it. Whatever prize there is, that's for you guys. All right?"

"Oh, so you don't want nuthin'." Jack sneered. "You got a bridge you want to sell me too? They got one only a couple years old in Brooklyn."

"Jack," Ernie tried one last time. "Look around. See everyone runnin' everywhere? We gotta decide. Dakota or telephone call. My vote's telephone call, those words make too much sense."

Jack popped his suspenders again, moving from one to the other. Henry held his breath, waiting for the collar wrangler's decision. If these guys didn't help him get to Skavenger, he didn't know what he'd do.

Finally, Jack took a breath and said, "All right, but if we make this telephone call and nothing happens? You won't be talking to Skavenger, you'll be talkin' to me, okay?"

Henry gulped again. "Okay."

Jack turned on his well-worn heels and began to walk away from the Dakota. Henry followed, second thoughts already bumping around in his head.

Whatta ya gettin' yourself into here? Headin' off into 1885? 1885! Walking behind some guy who wants to take your head off?

Ernie fell in step next to Henry and held out his hand. "Ernie Samuels," he introduced himself.

"Henry Babbitt," Henry replied as they shook. He could see that his name prompted a curious look from his new acquaintance.

"No kiddin'?" Ernie grinned. "What a coincidence."

Henry looked over at Jack, who didn't appear interested in exchanging pleasantries, even though his next words helped explain why Ernie was grinning.

"Call me Jack," the kid with four inches on Henry said matter-of-factly. "Jack Babbitt."

EIGHT

Hazel in the Kitchen

BABBITT? BABBITT? SERIOUSLY?

Henry's head spun as he followed the boys through the area of the city that was already called Hell's Kitchen. He wasn't sure of the exact year his great-great-grandfather had been born, but the math sure felt right.

His father, Nathan, was born in 1965. And if Chief was almost eighty-five, he would have been born around 1927.

No, wait. He *was* born in 1927. He said it was the same year as the Yankees' big-time Murderers' Row team.

Henry stepped right into an unexpected gift left behind by one of the Kitchen's many stray dogs—just one of the countless things that made Old New York a lot different from Henry's New York.

Almost everywhere they'd gone since Central Park had been impressively awful. No internet, no subway, no cabs. Just lots and lots of walking.

Worst of all? Crapping dogs or no crapping dogs? The city reeked.

Chief had told him a few years back that New York usually smelled like week-old beef with broccoli. 1885 New York was the same—multiplied by about twenty.

"Oh man," Henry muttered with disgust, scraping his shoe in the dirt. "I hate it when people don't pick up their dog's crap."

"Why would anybody pick up dog crap?" Ernie glanced at him as if he'd sprouted an extra head.

Henry was smart enough to let the question go unanswered, choosing instead to get back to the family math.

Okay, there's Sam, Chief's dad. He was prob'ly born twenty-five, maybe thirty years before 1927, so that would be liiiiiike 1897 or so. Sam's dad was, yup, none other than Jackson Babbitt, who woulda prob'ly been born in the early 1870s.

The year 1885 was the year Henry had stumbled into, and the Jack Babbitt walking in front of him—scruffy, suspenders, trouble—looked no more than fourteen.

Chief never really talked much about his grandfather. Evidently he'd had a "somewhat checkered past," is how he put it. Whatever Jackson had done, Chief didn't sound too proud of that particular branch of the family tree.

"You sure your aunt's gonna be there?" Jack curtly asked Ernie. "When's the last time you saw her?"

"I dunno, what's with the guff? It's not like she tells me her work schedule."

"Stop bein' a smartass," Jack warned him. "I don't have time for smartasses right now." He nodded at Henry. "'Sides, I've got one more than I need right here. My new prayin'-that-he's-right, long-lost relative Babbitt."

Does he ever cool off? Henry thought to himself. *Even for two or three minutes maybe?*

It was late morning by the time they reached the north end of the Kitchen. Henry got the feeling this might be the poor section of the neighborhood—which, if true, would have been saying something. Almost all of the upper windows were open and draped with wet, faded clothes. Being July, he knew they'd probably dry quickly, but it was a smart bet none of them would smell summertime fresh.

Ernie stepped over a bulging crack in the sidewalk and pointed at the small metal letters on the building in front of them.

"Eighty-two. This is it," he declared with a quick nod.

"You sure?" Jack wondered aloud, giving the dismal neighborhood a quick once-over. "'Cause if it is, we're the only ones who thought of coming here."

He was right. The street was dead empty except for an old man rummaging through garbage and a stray dog leaving another potential booby trap for Henry's other shoe.

Ernie shook his head.

"This isn't the only place in New York you can make a telephone call, Jack," he pointed out. "They got four or five of these places now."

Four or five places you can make a phone call? Wow. No more Dark Ages here.

Jack rapped on the door with the back of his hand. "Yeah, it'll never last. What are they gonna do? Build a telephone exchange on every street corner?"

Well, Mr. Odds-On Great-Great-Grandfather, you're pretty much right on that. Put your money on 'em leapfrogging that little obstacle, though.

Ever since Henry had learned Jack's last name was Babbitt, he'd been sneaking looks to see if there was a family resemblance—which was absolutely there, clear as day.

Jack was tall and thin, but with wider shoulders than you might expect on his kind of frame. Probably explained why his constant suspender snapping was so darn loud. It was the same build as all the Babbitt men.

"Every eighth word." Jack shook his head as he knocked on the door again, shooting a glance in Henry's direction. "Lemme tell ya somethin', lunky-boy. Fifteen minutes from now I might have eight *really* good words for you."

Henry gulped. *Long as one of those eight words is "run," I should be good to go.*

A woman in a plaid black dress opened the door. She wore a white apron tightly double-knotted around her waist and looked as if she hadn't smiled in a decade.

"May I help you?" she asked. There was a thin operator's headset running across her black hair, and her eyes looked like they were born with frown wrinkles surrounding them.

"Yes, ma'am," Ernie replied as politely as he could. "Is Hazel Samuels here today?"

"Whether Hazel Samuels is here today is Hazel Samuel's concern. Not yours, thank you very much."

The door was nearly closed before Ernie quickly added, "Ma'am, please. I'm her nephew," he informed her. "She's my father's sister."

Henry was sure she had a ruler tucked somewhere in her apron and was about to whack all three of them with a single swing. Instead, she leveled a hard gaze on Ernie for a few uncomfortably long seconds.

"What message would you care to leave her?" she asked, letting out an exasperated breath.

Ernie mustered up his finest sad expression. "It's a message from my father, ma'am."

"That's right, his father, ma'am," Jack chimed in, trying to help. "It's very serious. We came all the way from Brooklyn to tell her."

"From Brooklyn," she replied suspiciously. "All the way to the Kitchen."

Henry spotted Ernie busily studying whether his shoelaces might unravel.

"Well," Jack sadly uttered. "Almost Brooklyn."

❧

Hazel Samuels wore the same black dress and white apron as the woman who'd answered the door, but Henry noticed she was also wearing something else: the thinnest of smiles.

Whether that meant she'd help them was another question, but it was more than the other fifty women working in the wire-strewn room were wearing. Each accepted phone call after phone call on their cable-filled connection boards with a clipped rhythmic chorus of "yes, sir" and "thank you, ma'am."

Henry couldn't help but look around the bustling room. Gigi had once shown him an old rotary phone she had in storage, the kind with a round dial that you spun and it went *chuk chuk chuk chuk chuk chuk*. That would have put this technology to shame.

This is where phone calls happen? Looks more like a spaghetti factory. What do they use to send texts? Ravioli?

Jack gave Henry a quick elbow in the ribs—either to tell him to pay attention or just because he liked to elbow people.

"An important message from your father," Ernie's aunt said in between telephone calls. "That was what you told her?"

Ernie nodded like he knew he was in trouble. Hazel—who really did look like someone who would have that name, complete with a dipping nose that gave her the look of a hawk—rearranged a set of cables, keeping the handful of New Yorkers with the means of making a call talking to each other.

She was placing calls with not ten digits, not seven—but *four*, as Henry had already found out the hard way.

"Hello, this is operator forty-one, let me connect you with Queens 1468," she said before pausing. "Yes, I'll check back in five minutes to see if you need more time."

Cable connection in. Cable connection out. Impressively fast, Henry had to admit.

Hazel turned her attention to Ernie. "Ernest, how dare you use your own father as an excuse to come in here. Being as you can't."

Henry whispered out of the corner of his mouth to Jack, "What does she mean, he can't?" He hoped Hazel hadn't overheard, but he'd forgotten she was in the business of listening.

"Because his father," she snapped at Henry, "who was my husband's brother, God rest his soul, has passed on. That's why. As has Ernie's mother. Any other questions?"

Henry shook his head.

"Perhaps if you accepted more of our offers to help," she quickly resumed laying into her nephew. "Perhaps if you stayed out of the Juvenile Hall for at least a month, you wouldn't be greeted with so much suspicion. You still have family, Ernest, a family who wants very much to help you. One you ignore far too much."

"Sorry, ma'am." Ernie looked down, his hat ironically in his hands. "Oh, and please say thanks to Uncle Phil. He gave us some food this morning from the restaurant, out in the back alley, enough for two or three days. Really appreciate it."

He thumped the bag on the floor that had been draped over his shoulder since Central Park, but Aunt Hazel was having none of it.

She jammed a phone jack into an open router. "Operator forty-one, how may I help you?" she asked with a harsher tone than usual.

Hazel was able to shield *some* of the hurt Henry saw on her face, but not all of it. He'd become an unfortunate expert on that subject following his own father's death.

He glanced at Ernie, who shook his head in a manner that clearly said: *Don't worry, lemme handle her.*

"Connecting you to Manhattan 0855. Go ahead, ma'am." Hazel pressed the four numbers before asking Henry, "And who are you, young man?"

Henry glanced at Jack and Ernie, unsure of what to do.

"Don't look at them, look at me," she demanded.

He hesitated, which he figured might not help. "I'm, uh, I'm Henry Babbitt, ma'am," he answered her.

"Henry Babbitt . . . really?" she replied. "Jackson, you never told me you had a brother."

"He's not my—"

"One of the many things you've never told me over the years, I'm sure," Aunt Hazel interrupted, before turning her rapidly cooling eyes back to Henry.

"Well, Henry Babbitt. Being as I will not get the truth out of these two hooligans, I'll ask you." Henry gulped as she put him on the spot. "What are the three of you doing here? And if you lie to me, trust me, I'll know."

Ernie tried to help out. "Aunt Hazel, we just met Henry this morning, and—"

"This Henry? The one to whom I just asked the question? The one to whom the question was directed? That Henry?"

"Yes, ma'am." He nodded.

Henry could tell he was on his own. Hazel clicked a switch to check on a call before putting him back on the hot seat. "You were about to say, young man?"

"Oh, well, yes, ma'am," he stumbled, praying another telephone caller might help him out. The singsong chorus of polite operators provided the only background as Henry began to fidget.

"Yes, ma'am, what?" Hazel was growing impatient.

Henry hesitated again. For whatever reason, aside from the fact that he had to say something, he told her, "We need to make a telephone call, ma'am, because we think it's a clue in Mr. Skavenger's Hunt."

Without looking, Henry could tell Jack was holding back from belting him on the spot. He likely would have, he guessed, except for the fact Aunt Hazel was sitting between them.

"Ah haaa, Mr. Skavenger," she said with cynical exasperation. "I should have guessed. These two wasted almost all of last summer trying to find even one clue. Isn't that right, boys?"

Jack answered her with a level of courteous respect that surprised Henry. "Well, ma'am," he said, "we thought we'd found the first one last year, but I guess we didn't."

"This is operator forty-one again," Hazel interrupted Queens 1468, "would you like five more minutes, sir?" She listened and then replied, "Very good, thank you," before ending the call.

She casually asked the boys, in a very offhand manner, "And why would you need my help with a clue to this year's hunt? An incorrect clue, I'm sure."

Henry had to hide the smile tugging at his cheeks, because he'd just seen Ernie's aunt soften. Now there was a certain gleam in Hazel's eye, illuminated by the dim light just above her station.

I know that look. Tryin' to make it seem like she's not even interested. She wants to see it for herself!

He jumped at the chance.

"Well, we, uh . . . we need to place a telephone call to 1804," Henry answered her. "Those are the numbers, ma'am. Just . . . those four."

He could feel Jack's silence telling him to quit. Now.

Unfortunately, the gleam in Aunt Hazel's eyes faded as quickly as it had appeared. "Well," she told them, "at least you won't waste as much time as last year."

"But . . . what do you mean, ma'am? Why not?" Jack wasn't sure if good or bad news was about to follow.

"Because, Jackson, there *is* no 1804 in New York," she answered him evenly. "They added new lines this spring, but they only go up to 1500."

Hazel pulled out any and all cables that weren't being used for a telephone call at that moment, which gave Jack more than enough time to glare daggers into Henry.

"I need to get back to work, Ernest," she said to her nephew, wrapping up the conversation. "We have room for you anytime you'd like, and I do mean anytime. Now if you could please show yourself out, I would appreciate it."

Ernie simply nodded at first, before deciding to quietly say, "Yes, ma'am. Thank you, ma'am." He tipped his head toward the exit to let the boys know it was time to go.

Jack nodded, then delivered a look to Henry that told him that while the conversation might be over here, it would sure as heck be starting up again once they got outside.

Henry figured that was good enough reason as any to stay exactly where he was for as long as possible, but it wasn't the only reason.

We can't just leave. No! We gotta at least give it a try.

"Ma'am, if you could please just *try* to make the call," Henry asked. Even Jack looked surprised that he'd decided to speak up.

Hazel sighed and looked at Henry with a small amount of sympathy. "What did I just tell you, Henry Babbitt?"

"Yes, I know." He nodded. "But . . . just one try. That's all we're asking. Just one."

The steady hum of voices in the telephone exchange grew louder as a sudden rush of phone calls rolled in.

"Good afternoon, ma'am, how may I help you?"

"Yes, sir, five more minutes."

"Hold, please, I'll connect you."

For a long moment, Aunt Hazel said nothing, instead choosing to organize her cables for the wave of calls Henry figured would likely spill over to her board any second now.

"It'll only take a minute, ma'am. Please?" Henry knew his voice was dangerously closing in on the annoying sound of pleading. Just as he feared, a new telephone call popped up on Aunt Hazel's board, followed by another right after that.

Cable in, cable out. Cable in, cable out.

The boys waited—and hoped.

Hazel Samuel's steady indifference, though, continued—lasting through the connection of Manhattan 1201 until finally coming to an end when she nonchalantly asked, "1804 what? Manhattan? The Bronx?"

Henry didn't have the faintest, but apparently Jack did.

"Which one's farthest west?" he asked Ernie. "That's the direction those Lewis and Clark guys were goin', yeah?"

"Right." Ernie's eyes widened. "Right, right, *right*."

Hazel, though, kept things firmly in check. "Staten Island is farthest west," she answered. "But they don't make any calls there yet."

"All right, so it's Brooklyn then," Jack seemed to know. "The 1804 that's the farthest west."

"Of course!" Ernie grinned from ear to ear, tapping his aunt on the shoulder and pointing at the connection board. "Aunt Hazel, where's that button that lets us all hear?"

Hazel had already pushed the switch allowing her to hear a call through the tiny speaker. She tapped the blue button for

Brooklyn, then pushed the presumably dead buttons of 1 – 8 – 0 and . . .

4.

Silence followed.

For way too long, it seemed to Henry, as the growing murmur of late-afternoon calls surrounded them. There was no sound of a ring, no sound of a connection—only a quiet humming that confirmed Aunt Hazel's earlier suspicion.

There's nothing there. Nothing.

"Sorry, boys," she said with what sounded like genuine disappointment. "At least we gave it a ch—"

The small speaker rumbled with a distant, wavering ring.

Brrrrrrt brrrrrrt.

Aunt Hazel gasped.

The phone rang through the tiny speaker, which was no larger than a poker chip. All four huddled closely around the speaker to listen. Before there was a third ring, a crackling sound came from the other end.

For a second, Henry thought it sounded like the old recordings of the space missions Dr. Riggins had played during his lecture on the moon landings. Right before Neil Armstrong had said to the world: "That's one small step for man . . ."

"Congratulations."

The voice that had just pierced through the crackling telephone connection wasn't the first man to walk on the moon. It was distant, yes, and somewhat hard to make out, but Henry knew it was the same voice he'd heard that same morning.

Skavenger.

"Congratulations to you for solving the first riddle of my greatest hunt ever."

In an instant, Aunt Hazel turned down the volume to keep the conversation as private as possible. Her hand trembled as Hunter Skavenger's voice scratched through the small speaker.

Except it wasn't a conversation. It was a recording.

"I'm speaking to you now courtesy of my good friend Thomas Edison—on his talking machine, the so-called phonograph," the charismatic businessman's voice intoned.

One of Riggins's Three Big E's! Henry thought with excitement. *Thomas Alva Edison!*

Hazel turned the speaker down a notch more, apparently still worried someone else in the room might overhear. Fortunately, the stations on each side of her were empty.

"Now, for the NEXT step in your quest," Skavenger's recording continued.

"Ernie!" Jack snapped his fingers and Ernie nodded, flipping open the journal to scrawl out whatever words were about to follow.

"The GRANDEST of times awaits the man who follows the track to his own heart," the steady voice of Skavenger slowly revealed.

The telephone recording then paused as if to let Ernie catch up with his writing.

"Once there, seek out the very greatest of these. There your journey shall be unlocked, but only by a second. And only before midnight. Congratulations again, and the very best of luck to you," his recorded voice wished them as the connection dropped.

"Mr. Skavenger?" Henry tried getting his attention, despite knowing there really wasn't anyone on the other end—just a hum of nothingness warbling through the tiny speaker.

Nobody said a word for a long moment.

Henry didn't know what the last minute had meant to the others surrounding the small speaker, but it was starting to sink in for him.

I just helped solve one of Skavenger's clues.
We're in this thing!

I'm in this thing!

Henry's hand plunged into his pocket to make sure the ledger was still there. It was, and wisely he let it stay there, resting among the lint. He just wanted to feel the only other link he had to Skavenger besides the scratchy connection they'd just heard on an 1885 telephone line.

Holy smokes, what would Chief think right now? What would Dad have thought? I solved one of the clues they wanted to solve but never could!

Aunt Hazel was the first to finally speak up, almost whispering with a tone of wonder in her voice, "I guess there's an 1804 after all."

Henry glanced over and saw that Ernie was already counting out the words of the puzzle.

"One . . . two . . . three . . . four . . . five . . . six . . . seven . . . eight. WHO!" he quickly deciphered. His pencil tapped along, finding the next word, and then the word after that, until he was able to reveal the sentence in its glorious entirety.

"Who once these only!" Ernie triumphantly declared, followed by the not-so-triumphant follow-up question, "Who once these only? What the heck's that mean?"

"Means the eighth word doesn't work every time, scroochbrain." Jack rolled his eyes. "Read it again, the whole riddle."

Ernie cleared his throat and slowly read it out loud. Though not too loud.

"The grandest of times awaits the man who follows the track to his own heart. Once there, seek out the very greatest of these. There your journey shall be unlocked, but only by a second. And only before midnight."

Henry was already thinking, but the only thing he knew for sure was that he could feel Jack's eyes on him.

"All right, fellow Babbitt, I'd say you've earned your keep," Jack grudgingly acknowledged. "For now at least."

He took a step closer, his thumbs in prime suspender-snapping position. "Whatta ya think?"

What do I think? Like . . . ten seconds after hearing Skavenger's riddle, what-do-I-think?

"Ummmm, well . . ." Henry hesitated, apparently much too long for Jack's liking.

"Well . . . what?" Jack demanded, snapping his left suspender and then his right. "You figured the last one out, let's see if you can get this one too."

"He doesn't have to," Ernie said, his eyes twinkling as they looked up from the journal in his hands. "I think I already have."

NINE

Grand

WHEN ERNIE TOLD them where he thought the next clue might be, it took Jack no time to rattle off directions. His memorized directions, of course—which weren't the same as those Henry's phone would have offered if he'd actually:

had his phone,

it worked, and

had access to GPS.

None of these things were available, though. Not in 1885.

Instead, they cut through two alleys, worked their way over a fence, climbed the next fence after that, then went down 49th Street a few blocks to a really short shortcut.

"Now all we gotta do is head south along the train tracks," Jack told the boys as they turned a corner leading to what Henry knew would be . . .

Park Avenue? With big ol' train tracks? Not a chance.

Sure enough, though, when they turned onto Park Avenue and started walking, there were railroad tracks right smack-dab in the middle of the avenue.

Henry had walked this same street with his mom just a couple of days before Christmas Eve. He'd seen about a million cars and cabs, storefronts loaded up with decorations, and about a hundred streetside trees glowing with white holiday lights.

Buuuuut lemme think. Nope. No train tracks down the middle *of Park Avenue.*

That, he was pretty sure, he would have remembered.

During the walk, the three boys had nibbled on some of Uncle Phil's leftovers. Ernie was right; they'd have enough food for a day or two. That was the good news. The not-so-good news was what they'd have enough of: meat that seemed to be a loose version of roast beef, a few squishy apples, and a couple loaves of moldy sourdough bread.

Now that they were getting closer to their destination, Henry could see Jack watching for other hunters who might be following the same path. If a pedestrian unknowingly walked past Jack, the suspender-snapper would immediately lengthen his own stride, which forced Ernie and Henry to follow suit.

Fortunately, the aroma of Old New York was a little closer to present-day New York in this part of town, Henry noticed. Not like the stench-fest he'd encountered in Hell's Kitchen.

He loved this aroma. This aroma actually was an aroma. Not an odor.

It was the kind of aroma he remembered from—

"Henry?"

He felt a tight, pained smile grow on his face.

"Henry? Do you know where we are right now?"

Clear as the morning sky on so many of those countless walks, the sound of his father's youthful voice surged back to Henry. No echo to it. Just . . . there.

"Mad Hatter!" Henry's five-year-old self answered.

His father looked down, shooting him a wink. "Mad Hatter, Manhattan. You got it. But do you know where in Mad Hatter, Manhattan, we are?"

"Ummmmm," young Henry shook his head.

"Y'know something? For just a second there, neither did I. How great is that?" his dad replied. "The minute you don't know where you are? That's when the adventure begins. The real adventure."

Still clear as could be, Henry remembered his father, who would be gone only a few years later, reaching for his hand.

"Let's go find that adventure, Henry. Whatta ya say?"

A jolting shove in the back of his shoulder brought a sudden stop to the memory.

"Hey, Molasses," Ernie chided him. "Little faster wouldn't be a problem."

Henry picked up his step a bit, his thoughts now drifting for a moment to the family he still had—the family he'd left on Christmas Eve night. A sick feeling started to percolate in his stomach.

What's Mom even thinking right now? Loses Dad not even two years ago, wakes up on Christmas morning and discovers her only son's . . .

Gone.

He swallowed back the emotion, as he already had a few times that day.

She's gotta be a wreck. Gigi too, and Chief.

"What's on your mind there, Babbitt?" he heard Ernie ask. "Ya been kinda quiet. Got a funny look on your face too."

"Nothing," Henry replied. "I was just thinking about someone."

"Yeah? Who?"

Henry tried not to say anything that might get him into trouble. Something that wouldn't fit in 1885. He didn't want Jack threatening his collar again.

"My father, for one," he answered, figuring that couldn't raise any suspicions.

"What about him?"

Henry held back for a second before answering. "He would've liked this. The hunt. Trying to figure all this stuff out."

Jack was close enough that he'd overheard, even though he was preoccupied with directing the sun's reflection from his suspender clasp onto the train track below.

"What do you mean, *would* have?" Jack said as he walked along, starting to lag behind a little bit.

"He died a few years ago," Henry replied. The words usually had a way of stopping most conversations.

Not this one, though.

"Hmmph, figures," Jack said. "Looks like no fathers all the way around here."

For a moment, the three of them just walked and said nothing, following the uneven rail line splitting the avenue into fourths.

"Yeah, well, ya wanna know what I think?" Ernie yelled out with fresh hope. "Who better to win Skavenger's Hunt! Come on, think about it. The smartest people in the world are at the Dakota right now, and you know what they're gonna find? Huh?" He raised his arms into the air, victorious. "NUTHIN', that's what!"

"Slow down, Chuckaboo. We got a lonnnnnng way to go," Jack shot back.

A horse-drawn carriage rolled past, faster than most, and Jack ran over to see if a would-be hunter was inside. The passenger, a woman holding her sleeping child, saw Jack approach and a suddenly fearful expression spilled over her face.

"Faster please, William!" Henry could hear her urging the carriage driver, who promptly snapped the reins.

Burning humiliation on his face, Jack shouted at the flee-
ing carriage, "Hey! HEYYY! I wasn't gonna do anything, lady!"

He made a rude gesture with his hands. "Go ahead!" he
yelled for good measure. "Think what ya want!" He kicked the
ground in frustration.

Ernie used the moment to quietly tell Henry, "Jack hates
that. Folks take one look at him—at us—just like that lady
did right there? All they see are the scruffy clothes, hats falling
apart, no money. They always think the worst. Like we're gonna attack 'em or somethin'. Bet you've seen it before too."

"Yeah, sure." Henry thought it best to agree.

For the first time since they'd hit Park Avenue, he noticed
the aroma slowly becoming an odor again. A smoky stench that
he guessed came from the trains that used the very tracks they
were walking on.

"Y'know somethin'? My father woulda liked this too,"
Ernie said to him. "Not Jack's yellin' so much, but the lookin'
for everything."

"What happened to him?" Henry asked. "I mean, if you
don't mind me asking."

"Nah, I don't mind," he said with a shrug. "He and my
mother . . . they walked into Five Points one day hopin' to
spread the word of God." He looked down at the tracks. "They
didn't spread it for too long."

*Five Points. Chief told me about that place. Big-time gangs, a
boatload of crime, all the . . . how'd he say it? Oh. The "unsavory
business practices." That was it.*

Henry cautiously pushed a little further, trying his best to
remember the exact details of Chief's history lesson. "I thought
all the problems in Five Points were over."

Ernie held his tongue for a few strides. "Nope, just ask my
folks," he finally answered, then shook his head. "Only thing

they wanted to do was talk to people about God. Me and Him ain't exactly been on the best of terms since."

Ernie pulled out his journal and opened it. For the first time, Henry noticed it was loaded with words on nearly every page.

"All those pages are just from the hunt?" he asked.

"Well, not all of 'em," Ernie answered, fanning the pages from front to back. "A big part is this book my mother was writin' 'fore she couldn't no more." He tucked the journal back inside his tattered coat, before bitterly adding, "It's a piece of crap."

Ernie looked up and nodded toward the massive building now coming into view.

"There it is!"

☙

The first thing that struck Henry about Grand Central Depot was that it wasn't Grand Central Station.

Grand Central Station, which he'd been in more times than he could count, was almost a palace. It was enormous. Huge. Whatever word you had for "big" would work just fine.

Grand Central Station had that amazing ceiling that looked like it belonged in Italy somewhere. It had the "Whispering Gallery" over by the Oyster Bar—where the acoustics did this funny thing where you could whisper something on one side of the room and someone else would hear it way off in a faraway corner. And that wasn't even bringing up the legendary brass clock that was worth about a gazillion dollars.

As far as Henry could tell, about the only thing Grand Central Depot had in common with the not-even-built-yet Grand Central Station was that they were in the same exact spot.

Also, the smoky stench had reached a new peak here. There were steam trains all over the place—and steam trains, Henry had now learned, used coal. Lots and lots of coal. He could have sworn at one point that ash was actually falling from the sky.

Horse crap everywhere, ash blizzards, stray dogs doing what they gotta do . . . ugh.

Ernie had also told him during the walk that the Depot had been built a good while back by Cornelius Vanderbilt, and that it had been a smart investment for the New York rail tycoon because he was just that: a New York rail tycoon. In a word, the railroad business was booming.

After Vanderbilt died a few years back, his grandson took over the family biz and decided that the Depot—while really, really big . . . and smoky—was hopelessly undersized given the crush of passengers using it every day.

So, plans were now in the works for a new terminal—Grand Central *Station*—the one Henry knew so well from his time.

There were two other things Henry had learned in the last hour. He discovered the first, very important, piece of information when they'd arrived at the Depot, and he'd checked the ledger sheet in his coat pocket.

The first destination line still held the ghostly-inscribed entry of CENTRAL PARK, NEW YORK, while the line below had since been filled with TELEPHONE EXCHANGE, HELL'S KITCHEN, NEW YORK, and the third line now read GRAND CENTRAL DEPOT, NEW YORK.

His eyes went back to Skavenger's message at the very top.

. . . WHEN THE FINAL EMPTY BOX OF THIS SHEET IS FULL, SO ENDS YOUR ADVENTURE. WHATEVER THE DATE AND LOCATION, THERE YOU WILL STAY. FOREVER.

Luckily, a good number of empty ledger boxes remained. Whether Henry could find his way to Skavenger before the last one was filled, he didn't have a clue—which, as it turned out, was the second thing he'd learned: the clue itself. The one

Ernie and Jack were arguing about right now across the street from the Depot's main entrance—the highlight of which was a massive and spectacular clock directly above the words NEW YORK & HARLEM R. R.

"Listen to it again, Jack, okay?" Ernie suggested, his finger aimed at the huge Victorian-framed timepiece as Henry walked closer.

"I don't need to!" Jack replied, snapping his suspenders. His patience looked to be long since gone.

"Well, you're gonna listen, to the important stuff at least," Ernie snapped back, holding his journal with one hand while pointing with the other—a pose that made him look like a southern preacher.

"GRAND! TIME! TRACK!" he continued with his sermon, popping the journal shut. "Grand Central Depot! The clock! The track for New York and Harlem. The track to his own heart, Jack! It's all right here!"

"That's not the only thing that's here." Jack shook his head. Now it was his turn to point: at the impromptu gathering of about a dozen fellow citizens of New York, or fellow citizens of the hunt, all of whom had apparently made the same phone call to Skavenger that the three boys had made earlier, along with making the same exact guess about the Depot.

Right now those dozen or so hunters were searching everywhere from the horse carriage valet to the street-side benches. They were trying—and failing miserably—to look discreet.

One pathetic guy had even placed a ladder against the brick facing of the entrance, an easy fifty feet below the clock's face, but much closer to the street-level cop patiently tapping his baton between two of the rungs.

Whoa . . . that's a cop? The one with the big ears and the funny-lookin' hat, carrying a baton? I thought those kind of cops were only in London.

"Okay." Ernie was busy sheepishly conceding Jack's point. "So a lot of folks are thinkin' the same thing, I'll give you that."

"Thaaaaanks, Ern," Jack stretched the word out, probably to make sure he didn't lose any of the intended sarcasm. He glanced up at the clock itself, and Henry caught himself doing the same.

It was 7:40 p.m. *Already startin' to get dark. And Skavenger's riddle said we only have till midnight.*

Jack let out a deep breath and walked over to Henry. "What do you think, Babbitt?" he asked. "Got any ideas?"

"You mean like somethin' besides the clock?"

"Yeah I mean somethin' besides the clock!" Jack rolled his eyes at him now. "If you think the clock's right, speak up. If you think it's somethin' else, we wanna hear that too. We'll try and figure out where else it might be."

The gas lamps closest to the Depot were now flickering, ready for the night ahead. For the shortest of seconds, Henry caught himself thinking of the candles back in Chief's study— the dozen or so he always kept there, lighting each of them the second the sun dipped out of view through the window. In Henry's mind, those candles were the centerpiece of a room that had plenty of contenders for that title.

"Babbitt?" Jack dropped his head a bit so he could look Henry straight in the eye. It didn't even register.

The flames. In the old man's study.

Something was once again nagging at Henry. It was a feeling that had been bothering him ever since Ernie first read the clue back in the Kitchen. The reason he hadn't said anything then was because he didn't know what the "something" was.

But . . .

The flickering streetlights across the way.

Chief's study.

'Kay.

Candles.

All right, sooooo?

Back home.

"Babbitt." Jack snapped his fingers an inch away from Henry's eyes. "Ideas? Got any?"

Not yet, hang on. Okay, back up a second—what is it about the clue that you're sure about?

"The track to his own heart . . ." Henry blinked and quietly said, not sure where the thought might take him.

"What about the heart?" Ernie asked as he moved closer. Across the street, the cop was still rattling his baton inside the ladder rungs, only with more gusto this time.

"Yo, pally!" the beat cop yelled up at the ever-scaling hunter. "Down! Now! You wanna climb up to a big clock? Go to London!" The crowd around him broke into laughter.

See what I mean? London! I knew I was righ—

Jack moved between Henry and the circus across the street—probably to make sure nothing distracted him, as clearly it just had. His eyes went back to the streetlamps. Warm and . . .

The heart . . . the heart is where the home—no, no, it's not that. It's the other way around, right?

Henry scrunched his brow. "The home is where the . . ."

His voice fell silent. He barely heard the sudden cheers in front of the Depot, where the beat cop's words finally had convinced the clock-climber to start heading back down.

"Where the *what*, Henry?" Ernie quietly nudged him.

"The man who follows the track to . . . to . . . TO HIS OWN HEART!"

That's it!

"Home is where the HEART IS!" Henry's eyes grew bright. "IT'S VANDERBILT!" he shouted. "It's gotta be Vanderbilt. I think we've got game on here!"

Jack clamped his hand over Henry's mouth, angrily whispering to him, "Holy smokes, Babbitt! What are you, the town crier? And what the heck does 'game on' mean? You think that's what this whole thing is? A game?"

Jack looked around to make sure no one had overheard anything before turning back to quietly ask, "Now, what do you mean, it's Vanderbilt?"

Henry couldn't get the words out quickly enough. "The man who follows the track to his own heart. Ernie, you were right. I mean, not completely right, but close to right."

"Shhhh," Jack had to remind him.

But Henry was already plowing ahead. "The only reason the word 'track' is in there is to throw everyone off." He nodded toward the dozen hunters across the street and the British-bobby-looking New York cop. "That's what Skavenger wanted to do, but it's the rest of it that's the real clue!"

He stopped to catch his breath. "A man's heart is his home. Vanderbilt's home! Once there, we're supposed to seek out the greatest of these, right?"

Ernie had to admit, "Well, Vanderbilt's home is pretty great. It's one of the mansions on 5th Avenue. Bigger than most of the buildings in the whole city."

Henry nodded and picked up right where he'd left off. "There your journey shall be unlocked, but only by a second! And only before midnight!"

"Which," Ernie shook his head and admitted, "makes no sense to me. I get that we gotta solve it by midnight or we might be out of this whole thing, but . . . our journey's gonna be unlocked? And only by a second? What's that mean? One second before midnight?"

Henry's breathing had calmed down a little, but his excitement was still running high. He turned to Ernie. "You told me Vanderbilt died a few years ago. Who lives there now?"

"His grandson does," Jack said with what sounded like a fresh supply of impatience. "Do you even live in this city, Babbitt? Everybody knows that."

"Just . . . just . . . tell me his name," Henry demanded.

"Vanderbilt's grandson?" Even Ernie's tone of voice was now moving into Jack territory. "You mean the grandson who owns this Depot right here? Who owns every railroad in town? *That* grandson? Yeah, his name would be Cornelius Vanderbilt the Sec—"

Ernie's voice slammed to a stop. Frantically he dug his hand into his pocket for the journal, his fingers finding the clue quicker than he expected.

"There your journey shall be unlocked," he read, shaking his head at the words to follow. "But only by a *second*."

The three boys looked at each other, not wanting to jinx anything with a smile.

"You"—Jack looked toward Ernie—"keep your voice down. And you"—he turned to Henry—"you *really* keep your voice down."

TEN

The Mansions of 5th Avenue

HENRY GUESSED IT was a little after 9:30 p.m. by the time the boys reached Vanderbilt's neighborhood—a neighborhood where not one of them fit in, given the look of their shabby clothes and the gaudy structures all around them.

It was actually darker than Henry figured it might be. The towering streetlights sprayed tight, perfect circles of dim light onto the ground, but those circles were surrounded by even larger patches of sheer darkness.

This whole neighborhood should be dark, he thought to himself. *Every mansion here's so big, there's no way you could ever light up any one of 'em. Do all these guys own railroads?*

Saying the colossal mansions were "grand" was kind of like saying St. Patrick's Cathedral was a "nice little church." These houses were seriously spectacular—each designed and built to be slightly *more* spectacular than the next. And just as Ernie had suggested, the "grandest of these" was the one belonging to Cornelius Vanderbilt the Second.

The mansion took up an entire city block. It was four stories high with amazingly designed gables that reached even higher. Sturdy marble decking wrapped all around most of the second level, with porthole windows providing just enough light. Not too much, not too little. And the stonework was like nothing Henry had ever seen before. It put the so-called mansions from his own time to shame.

Henry, Jack, and Ernie had set up shop in the darkest patch of sidewalk they could find, which was helpful, because of the lone policeman walking the sidewalk a half block away.

At first glance, Henry thought he looked like a slightly better-dressed version of the cop at the Depot. He wore a rounded hat, a crisp dark coat with four buttons, and bright white gloves; very appropriate for the area he was patrolling.

Right now, though, the only thing Henry was thinking about was that the cop was walking toward them.

The policeman stopped mid-stride at a nearby corner, cocking his head toward the thirty-foot-tall oak tree the boys were hiding behind. The night air had fallen completely still.

"Nobody move," Ernie whispered an unnecessary warning as the officer strolled into the street that separated them, looking in one direction, then turning to look in another, before finally choosing to look straight in their direction.

For way, way too long.

If it hadn't been for the sound of someone else's footsteps a block away, Henry was pretty sure they would have been spotted. The policeman gave one more long look before slowly wandering off to see who was walking in the darkness behind him.

"Well?" Ernie asked after the cop had disappeared around the corner. "Is he gone?"

"I think so," Jack replied.

It was right then that a nearly imperceptible sound caught Henry's attention from up above. Jack and Ernie seemed to have noticed it as well, considering that they were both looking up into the tree. The only thing they could see up there, though, were branches and oak leaves. And all they could hear was the sound of the policeman's steady, but now fading, footsteps.

Must have been the wind. Had to be the wind. Or a squirrel, maybe. Sure. Could be a squirre—

Creeeaaaak.

Okay, so maybe a really big squirrel. Could be a cat. Cats go up trees all the time.

Creak . . . crrrrr . . .scruuufff . . .thhhhh . . .

With the quietest whisper in the history of quiet whispers, Henry meekly suggested to both Jack and Ernie, "Y'know, maybe we should just try and find a new tree to hide behind."

"Good idea. You want to go ask that cop for a recommendation?" Jack's voice was somehow even quieter.

Good point.

Whatever it was, Henry knew it was right up in the tree, only a few feet above them. Even though he couldn't see anything.

The moonlight, what little there was of it, wasn't much help. Had they been lucky enough to have a full moon, it probably would've helped that curious cop more than it was helping them right—

The something moved again.

Something large.

A light breeze blew and the leaves rustled enough to reveal a dark shape holding on to the biggest of the lower branches. Until . . .

Crack!

Henry's heart thumped loudly. At least he thought it was loud. So loud he didn't think he'd be able to hear anything else because of it. Jack shot him a look and silently mouthed, "What is wrong with you?"

Henry shook his head and pointed up to the shape above them.

Scuuuuffff . . .

Chuh . . . chuh . . .

Craaaaaaaaaaack . . .

Whatever-it-was-up-in-the-tree was now slipping and falling fast, frantically reaching for every branch on its quick trip to the ground.

Kuh-thumppppp!

The something landed right in front of the three boys. Even though it was dark, Henry could see the something was a "who," not a "what," and the who was wearing a cape. A cape draped over the shoulders of someone scrambling to his feet to run away.

Henry felt Jack shove him out of the way, catching just enough of the silhouette's heel to trip him up.

"Ummmmphhh!" The figure hit the ground again, and Jack was on him in a heartbeat.

"Oh no, no, no! You're not goin' anywhere, pal." Jack rolled the runaway onto his back and demanded, "Not until you tell us what—"

Jack whipped back the cape's hood, and all three looked into the frightened, wincing face of a young girl.

"I'm sorry! I'm sorry! I'm sorry!" she cried out, then held her breath, unsure of what might happen next.

A girl? Is that a girl?

"What the heck?" Jack sat back on his heels. "What . . . you . . . ? Up there in the tree? You were up there watchin' us the whole time?"

"I wasn't watching you," the girl answered defensively, getting up on her own and wiping the dirt off her black knee-length dress, covering a pair of equally dark pants. "I was waiting for you to leave." She pulled an oak leaf off her cape and flicked it to the ground to help make her point.

"Huh," Ernie said as he smiled and scratched his head. "Whatta ya know?"

"Hi," the girl said, having noticed Henry.

"Hi," he said back to her.

"You almost broke our necks just now. You know that, dontcha?" Jack still looked upset. "Whatta ya even doin' around here? All by yourself?"

"What are *you* doin' around here?"

"I asked you first," Jack countered.

"Same thing you are, I'm guessing." She shrugged. She looked to be thirteen or so, maybe the same height as Henry, with freckles that were framed by long, curly hair that was brownish but closing in on light red. A few strands, but not all of them, fell halfway down her back, suggesting she may have cut it herself. "Track to his own heart? Greatest of these?" she stated matter-of-factly. "You prob'ly have that much figured out if you're in this neighborhood. Not that you don't look like you might own one of these shacks."

Ernie broke into a smile.

"Ernie Samuels." He held out his hand. "This is Henry. That's Jack."

"Mattie," she replied, wiping off her right hand before taking each of theirs. "Mattie McGillin. Nice to meet *most* of you," she pointedly said to Jack.

"Yeah, you too." He nodded dismissively, before turning to Henry and Ernie. "All right, let's go."

"Wait, wait, wait," Mattie shook her head, then scratched the side of her button nose. "You really think I'm just gonna stand around until the three of you are done lookin'? I was here before you! And there's a midnight deadline, remember?"

Jack put his hands on his hips. "What? Ya think 'cause you're a girl ya get to go first?" he asked.

"No, I get to go first 'cause I was here first," Mattie said as she straightened the hood of her cape. "Even though all of us are looking for the same thing at the same time. If I go, you'll follow me. If you go, I'll follow you. That's what I get for falling out of a tree, I guess."

Even here in the darkness, Henry could tell the cape made Mattie look larger than she actually was and slightly more intimidating. Same with the black pants under the dress.

Might be what she's tryin' to do. Takin' on Skavenger's Hunt all by herself.

Casually, she leaned against the base of the oak tree, taking a second to glance at the back of her fingernails.

"Tell you what," she said to none of them in particular, "you three go ahead, and I'll just stay here and watch for a while. When our friend the cop comes along in about, oh, twelve minutes, I'll tell him to go over to the Vanderbilts' and see if he can help you out."

Mattie yawned and gestured for them to go ahead and get on with their business.

Smart. A little backbone there too. If I'd said that to Jack, he would have thrown me into that tree by now.

"Okay, all right," Jack said after only a few seconds of thinking, knowing he didn't have a choice. "We can do this one together. We'll figure it out later." He motioned for her to come over. "Where do you want to start?"

Mattie hopped over and turned her attention to Henry. "This one looks smart. What do you think?"

Me? Why does everyone keep pickin' me?

Caught off guard, he didn't say a word for a second. Mattie tried to get his attention.

"Hello? Hennnnnrrrry? I'm sorry, that was your name, wasn't it?" she prodded him with a smile. His flustered look must have looked a little too flustered, he guessed.

"Quiet. Hold on a minute." Mattie, suddenly serious, raised a hand as her eyes caught something from one of the neighboring estates.

Henry looked over and saw that a lamp in one of the adjacent mansion's windows had brightened. All four of them could see the silhouette of someone inside moving behind the newly lighted curtain. The Vanderbilt place, however, stayed eerily dark.

Mattie looked back at him, a hint of urgency in her eyes. "May not have a lot of time here," she said. "So, what was my question? Oh, right, what do you think?"

Henry looked up at the towering Vanderbilt estate. The very largest of the 5th Avenue mansions loomed high above them, its windows fixing the foursome with what looked like an unwelcome stare. Henry stared back, taking in as much of it as he could before turning to the trio not-so-patiently waiting on him.

"Whatever it is, it's gotta be inside," Henry finally said.

"I agree!" Mattie enthusiastically nodded. "Well done, Henry!"

"Inside where?" Ernie asked, incredulous, tipping his head toward the block-filling mansion. "Inside *there*?"

Henry nodded as he reminded them of the clue. "There your journey shall be unlocked . . ."

". . . but only by a second!" Mattie smiled in agreement. "Yes. Okay. Let's go."

Go? We can't all go in! I mean, yeah, the next clue's in there, but why don't we just send Jack in?

Mattie, though, had already begun walking toward the intimidating structure, Jack right alongside her. Until the two of them stopped, realizing they were the only ones doing any walking.

Mattie looked back over her shoulder at Henry and Ernie. "What's wrong?"

It was Henry who finally took a deep breath, the kind usually marking a brave announcement, only to say, "I don't think I can go in there."

"Whaaaat?!" Mattie said with a wincing look as she and Jack walked back to them. "What are you, yellow?"

Yellow? What's "yellow" mean? If that's 1885 for "scared," then yeah, I'm yellow. School bus yellow.

Ernie quickly agreed with Henry. "Are you kidding me? I'm with Henry. Do you know what'll happen if the four of us break into the Vanderbilt Mansion? We'll wish we only had to deal with one cop."

"Ernie, we are not gonna have to break in," Mattie assured him. "Henry knows that much, I can tell you that. All we gotta do is find the greatest of *these*. That means the biggest door in the place, of which it looks like there might be plenty."

Jack had been quiet for too long, which could either be a good thing or a very bad thing. Henry saw him look over his shoulder at the enormous door to the Vanderbilt home.

"Anybody else wondering why no one else is even here?" the big suspender snapper asked suspiciously.

Ernie shrugged and said, "Maybe we're just slow."

"Or maybe we're wrong," Jack threw out the possibility, looking at Mattie. "All of us."

"Nuh uh." She frowned as she shook her head. "Whatever the clue leads to, it's gotta be inside. Why's everyone goin' dotty on me?"

Dotty? What's . . . never mind.

Jack's expression backed her up 100 percent, proving that he now had a growing appreciation for Mattie's gumption. At least that's what Henry thought—even though he was still to-tally preoccupied with the question:

What's there to be dotty about? How many things you want? Look at this place. They've prob'ly got guard dogs, guard tigers, guard ninjas.

"All right," Jack started handing out orders. "Ernie, you check the door on the Sixth Avenue side. If ya ain't gonna go in with us, least you can do is find out if that door's bigger than this one right here." He switched to Henry. "Babbitt, you check the one on the other side. Also, the one around back. Two of us'll wait here in case anyone else shows up."

⌒

Henry had been gone barely two minutes when his fear of go-ing inside the mansion had started to ease just a little.

It wasn't just because of the amazing mansion itself, though that was a part of it. Even the towering wrought-iron gate he was walking next to was incredible. Small lanterns glowed on the main posts and dark green iron vines wrapped their way around the bars. If Gigi had seen it, she would have passed out.

No, Henry's fear had mostly eased because of some-thing else.

Mattie.

She's pretty cool, gotta admit. Kinda hard not to like those freckles, right? 'Specially when they scrunched up when she was standin' up to Jack.

The way she just wanted to walk up and knock on the front door? That was impressive.

Too bad you went ahead and embarrassed yourself, though, Ace. Hanging back like a wuss, feet planted in the ground while she's ready to march right inside. Maybe one of these days you'll actually get around to doing or saying the right thing when you're with a girl. 'Stead of goin' all dotty.

Henry walked toward the corner ahead, mentally kicking himself. He'd already passed one door that was big enough for a small truck to drive through, but it wasn't as large as the one on Jack and Mattie's side of the estate.

He was on the 5th Avenue side of the Vanderbilt house now. Fortunately the street around him was empty, but Henry still walked close to the brick wall in case the cop was anywhere nearby. It was somewhat darker there and he figured he'd be harder to spot.

Henry craned his head to find out if he could even see the top of the mansion: barely able to spot the towering brick chimneys next to the fifth-story gables. The whole thing looked like it went halfway up to the moon.

For the first time in a while, and even though he was alone and walking in the dark, he smiled.

"Henry," his father's voice tumbled back into his head again. *"When you get a little older, you and I are going to find an adventure. We'll sail somewhere. We'll fly. We'll climb the highest mountain we can find."*

Henry let his hand run along the bricks of the gated wall. *"And when we're done with that adventure?"* his father's voice promised, *"We'll move on to the next one. All right?"*

"All right," Henry whispered to himself, realizing he'd stumbled into an adventure even his father could never have imagined. For good and for bad.

Without thinking, he reached into his pocket for the ledger sheet and gave it a quick look.

Another destination line had magically been filled in.

THE VANDERBILT MANSION, NEW YORK

Great, he thought to himself. *Another ledger entry gone. Gone, gone, gone.*

That meant four spots were now filled, even though Henry was sure Grand Central Depot was a wrong guess. One by one, wrong or right, they were steadily being filled in.

He folded the ledger sheet up and tucked it away. It might be out of sight down in his pocket, but it still taunted him.

Still haunted him.

Henry gave one more glance up toward the Vanderbilt's darkened windows before turning the corner to the far side of the mansion, and suddenly found himself face-to-face with the one person in Chief's story he'd forgotten all about.

ELEVEN

Doubt and the Dark Men

HIRAM DOUBT'S HANDS were gently folded over the crown of his walking stick—the first thing Henry saw as he nearly walked straight into him.

"Looking for something?" Doubt inquired with a sparkling gleam in his otherwise bleak gray eyes. The old *New York Times* photograph in Chief's study had been frightening enough—and that was just an old, faded black-and-white image. Fuzzy on the edges.

Here the man was all too crystal clear. The eyes that had somehow managed to pierce through century-old newsprint now leveled icy daggers into Henry's rapidly blinking ones.

No! No, no, NO! Sorry, can't . . .

Henry started to back up as if to turn and run, but the idea was quickly squelched.

"Try to move?" Doubt advised with a clipped voice, raising a slender pointed finger, "You won't move for long. Call for your friends? It'll be the last call you make."

Henry's heart stopped as he glimpsed something moving in the shadows behind Doubt.

The Dark Men!

One by one, all four of them appeared, all wearing black top hats and long black coats that reached all the way to the ground. Henry decided the safest place to be, ironically, was standing right where he was, in front of the man with the pale-gray top hat and the bleak and dreary eyes.

"Allow me to introduce myself," the disconcerting man said. Without raising a hand, but with a slight tilt of his head, he gloomily uttered, "Hiram Doubt."

"I know," Henry replied, his voice cracking.

Doubt's lips curved into a wicked grin. "I'll take only a moment of your time," he said, "because at this moment, young man, you and your friends are impressively close to cracking Mr. Skavenger's next clue. A clue which, yes, I have already solved."

Despite being more frightened than he could remember, Henry couldn't help but take in the thin gray scar running the path of a teardrop down Doubt's left cheek. The snaggled and wisping gray edge of each eyebrow was hard to miss too. Everything about the slim man in the dark charcoal suit—his sixty or so years of age, his height of six feet and maybe another inch, seven feet with the hat—felt gray and threatening, though oddly cultured as well.

The sinister-looking man continued on, "While hundreds still aimlessly wander the grounds of the Dakota and others still climb the walls of the Grand Central Depot, the four of you have displayed a deductive intelligence far, far beyond your years. Worthy of commendation."

Doubt unfolded his malevolent hands and Henry saw that his cane was capped with a gold-plated head of a snarling wolf.

"Now, listen to me carefully, young searcher," Doubt's voice dropped low. "If I see you again—and I'm certain I will—it will be either because you have solved a clue I have also solved, or because you have solved one I've yet to decipher."

He raised his cane and the wolf's golden teeth drew close to Henry's nose. "And when I ask you for the answer to that riddle? The one you have solved, and I haven't?" Doubt let his words settle before finishing. "You. Will. Tell. Me."

The edge of his dark lips raised into a baleful smile. "Because if you don't," he ominously added, "I will go about eliminating your friends. One . . . by one . . . by one. Starting with the largest, moving to the smallest, and then finishing with you."

Henry heard the sound of footsteps approaching just behind him. A pair of polished black shoes stopped at his side, complemented by white gloves and a crisp dark coat with four buttons.

The cop! Yes . . . finally!

"Everything all right here, Mr. Doubt?" the New York policeman asked with a tone that suggested the two men had already talked, perhaps only minutes earlier.

Oh no.

"Everything is fine, good sir," Doubt assured him. "Just a young lad inquiring of directions. We'll make certain he's on the proper path."

The police officer nodded and walked away with a hard look at Henry. Skavenger's rival once again folded his hands over his walking stick.

"Now." Doubt bent slightly, almost politely. "You will say nothing of our meeting to anyone, most especially your fellow young hunters," he cautioned. "The four gentlemen accompanying me would be most disappointed should you choose to do so. So, young man . . . until our next conversation. Happy hunting."

Doubt smiled one last time, his way of bidding Henry farewell. He turned and walked away, without the slightest of limps despite having a cane. As Doubt faded into the darkness, Henry looked toward the shadowy quartet of Dark Men.

And immediately wished he hadn't.

He heard them as they turned to walk away. Not their footsteps, which were oddly, terrifyingly silent. It was another sound that accompanied each of them—a sound that didn't make sense. At first Henry thought it might be some kind of low and deep whistle.

It's different than that. It's . . .

Three of the four men had already followed Doubt into the darkness. The fourth, though, had stopped and turned around. He was moving straight toward Henry.

That's not whistling. It's a . . . a hissing.

The last of the Dark Men stopped right in front of him. He towered over the boy, easily six and a half feet tall. His face was shadowed by the brim of his hat, at least most of it, but his eyes were icier than any the twelve-year-old had seen in the worst of his nightmares. Eyes that glowed silvery blue through the darkness.

Grace.

Doubt's most trusted and dangerous bodyguard hissed just one single word that Henry was barely able to make out, but it made his blood go cold.

"Soooooooooon."

The word whispered through the fog as Grace turned and walked away, the echo cutting through the pounding of Henry's terrified heartbeats. A half second later, the entire moment was overpowered by another sound: that of the twelve-year-old boy's clumsy footsteps as he turned around and ran.

CO

Mattie had just nudged open the main wrought-iron gate as Henry ran up—completely out of breath, eyes still wide with fear.

"Hey, hey, calm down! Where have you been?" She looked at him with real concern. "Are you all right? You look like you just saw a ghost!"

What do I tell her? What can *I tell her? What can I tell any of 'em? Doubt said to keep quiet . . . to keep quiet, or else . . .*

"Cop," was all Henry could manage to squeeze out. "Just another cop. I think he's gone, though." He leaned down to catch his breath.

Ernie, who had already returned from his own scouting trip of the mansion, gave Henry a much-needed reprieve. "Uhhh, if we could not use the word 'ghost' around this place, I would really appreciate it."

"We almost gave up on ya, Babbitt," Jack said, more than ready to head toward the dimly lit front landing. "You find any doors bigger'n this one?"

Henry shook his head, still not able to even say a simple "no" through his panting breaths. Or move, for that matter.

No. No doors. Plenty of other things, though. Like Doubt and four guys I can't tell you about.

"All right then," Mattie said with a still-worried look aimed directly at Henry, "Jack and I are going in."

She shoved open the gate to the massive Vanderbilt Estate and walked a straight path to the mammoth front door. Jack grinned and ran after her—leaving Henry and Ernie to fend for themselves out by the front gate.

Hopefully it was just the two of them.

Great. Now I'm out here with Ernie—and Doubt—and everyone else.

Henry looked in every direction, remembering that the Dark Men, at first, had almost been invisible on the other side of the mansion.

Soooooooooon.

He heard the word echo in his mind as an eerie breeze brushed through the leaves of the oak tree from which Mattie had fallen. Meeting her seemed like days ago now.

Hopefully the hissing was just a breeze. Hopefully it wasn't something much worse. Something connected to Doubt's piercing eyes, his cane with the gold wolf head on top, or worst of all: Grace's hisssssssssing and strangely silent footsteps. For all Henry knew, the scariest of Doubt's men could be anywhere.

"I'm goin' with 'em," Henry said to Ernie before promptly heading for the door.

Ernie's shoulders sagged. "What? Why?" he asked.

Mattie was already standing a foot away from the front door when Henry walked up. Ernie was a step or two behind—apparently thinking twice about being out there by himself.

"Okay, Henry Babbitt and Ernie Samuels!" she whispered and winked with approval.

"Surprise, surprise," Jack said with a smile of his own. "I thought the two of you might be too pigeon-livered for this."

The four of them gave each other one last look for luck, before Mattie slowly reached her hand out for the two-foot-long bronze handle.

She let out a long and deep breath, strong enough to puff out her cheeks. Her fingers wrapped around the handle, her thumb eased softly onto the latch, and having already closed her eyes, she quietly said, "Your journey shall be . . . unlocked," and then Mattie McGillin gently squeezed.

Click.

Henry heard the hammer inside the lock fall with ease, along with Mattie taking in the shortest of breaths.

It's unlocked. She was right! The biggest freaking door on the most expensive house in New York. Totally unlocked!

Mattie sent Henry a quick grin of disbelief as she leaned all her weight against the door, quickly discovering it really wasn't necessary.

Despite its massive size, the door swung open without so much as a single squeak.

Slowly, the four of them peered inside. The small amount of moonlight coming through the ample windows still left the foyer dark—dark enough, Henry was sure, to hide any number of armed guards ready to shoot intruders. Not to mention the ninja tigers that had to be crouching low somewhere.

As their eyes adjusted, though, they saw that the large entry room appeared to be empty. It was also magnificent. A foyer larger than any Henry had ever seen, chiseled out of pure granite. Wrap-around stone staircases—not just one or two, but *six*—curled from the level they were on to the one just above, like the arms of an octopus.

It appeared as though there were no people anywhere around, but that was only a guess, given the darkness and complicated architecture.

"Okay, looks like nothing," Ernie's voice could hardly be heard. "Can we go now?"

"No." Mattie looked at him with friendly disdain. "We're in here. We might as well look around. Midnight's the deadline, remember? It's this or the hunt's over."

She looked to Jack and Henry. "Agreed?"

"This or nuthin'." Jack nodded with conviction.

"Yeah. I guess," Henry whispered.

Jack was the first to take a serious step into the foyer. And he didn't stop at just one step. It looked to Henry like Jack was heading in big-time.

Hang on, Jack! Not till we can check for . . .

Crack!

The sound echoed around the massive hall.

"Damn it," Jack whispered, even though the need for keeping his voice low was now somewhat irrelevant. He stooped down to run his hand over the floor, finding nothing for a long anxious moment or two, until his finger finally brushed over something.

He held it up for a look.

"What is it?" Henry asked.

All four of them crowded around as Jack held up whatever-it-was between his two fingers. "Feels like a clump of hard dirt or maybe a rock. I think there might be a lot of it right around here."

"Dirt? Rocks? In this place?" Ernie said with fresh concern. "No, no, no. Somebody else has gotta be in here."

Creeeaaak.

The sound was coming from just behind one of the half dozen stairwells.

"See? See? Come on, let's go," Ernie whispered a little too loudly.

"No," Mattie cut him off, her eyes suddenly fixed and locked on something in one of the side rooms. She looked almost hypnotized by what the three boys, almost as one, now turned their heads to see.

The etched-glass French doors to the room weren't closed, but instead were pulled wide and open. Welcoming.

For Henry, it was exactly as if he were looking straight into Chief's quirky study.

No one was in the Vanderbilt's side room, but around two dozen candles blazed on a center table, forming a half circle that softly illuminated one glittering item.

A clock.

And not just any clock, Henry knew as the four of them walked inside the room.

"The brass clock at Grand Central Station," he quietly said under his breath.

"The *what* clock at *where?*" Jack turned to him with a quizzical look.

"Never mind," Henry replied, not wanting to explain how he knew the future.

It is, though. The brass clock. A perfect, smaller version of it. Same color, same look, same everything.

For Mattie, who had now walked right up to it, it was something much, much different.

"The grandest . . . of *times*," she said, the glow from the candles illuminating her smile of pure wonder.

Fingers wide, she extended her hand toward the clock, which was all of maybe eighteen inches tall. Her eyes then dropped to the inscription etched into the sparkling gold plate at its base.

She leaned close to look at it.

"What's it say?" Jack put his hands on his knees to get a better look. Henry and Ernie moved closer as well.

With a proud yet once again disbelieving smile, Mattie read the words out loud for all of them to hear.

"Your adventure will soon leave Gotham, but only after a successful trip to . . . the Jennings Establishment." Her eyebrows scrunched in bewilderment. "There you must search for the origin of my *own* favorite adventure, the nine-year-old answer clearer than you might expect."

Before anyone else could say a word, all four of them heard a gracious and generous voice coming from the door behind them.

"Congratulations."

They spun around to see a slender tuxedo-clad gentleman stepping out of the darkness, wearing a smile so subtle it could turn into a frown with perfect ease. At this moment, though, his expression assured them without a word that they weren't in any danger.

Henry thought the man looked to be in his early forties, dark black hair combed straight back, long sideburns, and arching eyebrows that somehow gave the perfectly postured man a look of bemusement. The pocket square in his sharply tailored coat was exactly that: a tidy and precise square.

"Cornelius Vanderbilt," he introduced himself. "Cornelius Vanderbilt *the Second*." The gentleman gave those last two words the emphasis the hunt required. "A pleasure to meet you all."

"You too, sir," Mattie spoke for the group. "Sorry about . . . coming into your house. It's really nice, though."

Vanderbilt held up a hand to assure her all was fine. "Not to worry, miss. The four of you solved the puzzle. You now have the next clue." He nodded toward the brass clock. "With how much time until midnight? When my front door will lock tight again?"

Mattie glanced over at the clock, then turned back to Vanderbilt and smiled. "Less than two hours, sir."

"Again, well done." He nodded.

Henry's eyes strayed over Vanderbilt's shoulder to the enormous window behind him. The thought of Doubt and his shadowy men still out there prompted him to look back just as quickly.

"Everything all right, son?" the railroad tycoon asked him.

"What?" Henry looked up. "Oh . . . yes. Everything's fine, Mr. Vanderbilt, sir."

"You looked like you might have had a concern."

Well, yes . . . a few, actually. And a question too.

"Sir?" Henry asked. "Aren't you worried at all about leaving your front door unlocked? I mean, there's no way of knowing who might come in here."

Barely had Henry finished asking when two lines of men wearing polished black shoes, white gloves, and crisp dark coats with four buttons walked into the room. At least thirty of New York's finest. The only thing they weren't wearing was a smile.

"Not really, no," Vanderbilt the Second answered Henry's question with a confident smile, letting the officers' presence be felt.

His next words, though, signaled they had best keep the proceedings moving.

"I'm afraid the four of you have quite a bit of catching up to do. More than a few other hunters have already paid me a visit tonight." He then reached into his suit pocket and pulled out a light blue envelope, handing it to Mattie.

"The Jennings Establishment, Third Avenue at 55th Street. It's written down in there, along with the message on the clock, and enough money to help you through the next stage of the journey. Mr. Skavenger does place a premium on fairness."

Vanderbilt offered one last smile, which was accompanied by a word of caution.

"And do be careful," he said to them with a serious voice. "The four of you aren't exactly the proprietor's usual clientele."

TWELVE

Clearer than One Might Expect

THE JENNINGS ESTABLISHMENT—EST. 1884.

As the small brass nameplate informed Henry, the structure belonging to a certain Mr. Jennings had been open only a year. But judging from the shoulder-to-shoulder crowd inside, he was pretty confident it'd be open for a good many more.

The "Establishment" was a street-corner tavern; a fairly narrow one, if you were looking at the red brick two-story exterior that framed the smoke-stained front windows. It was more than made up for, though, by how deep the building stretched alongside the neighboring street.

From the size of the crowd, Henry guessed the establishment didn't have any rules concerning the exact number of people allowed inside. For that matter, it didn't appear to have any rules about smoking either, other than it seemed to be mandatory.

Despite the late hour, the place was packed with an odd assortment of customers. Men wearing bowler hats and suits, even though the business day was long over; exhausted, irritable Irish laborers; and a smattering of mostly quiet immigrant dockworkers. It looked to be an uneasy alliance that Henry could only assume was held together by a shared love for what was steadily pouring from the barrel taps.

Jack was busy peering inside through the window, trying to snag a view in between the nearest line of black suits—if he could even see anything through the hazy, thick smoke stains.

"All right," Jack whispered to the gang, "we go in and see what we can find. And remember, we're looking for *Skavenger's* favorite adventure, something nine years old."

"I don't think there's anything in there that's only nine years old," Ernie quietly chimed in. "Where'd this Mr. Jennings get all this junk?"

"I'm sorry, did I ask for smartass comments?" Jack shot back. Ernie wisely chose not to answer.

Henry was already scouting out the front door, trying to guess how long he'd be able to hold his breath once he got inside.

My first bar. Wouldn't have guessed this would be happening when I went to bed last night.

Jack overheard him let out a nervous breath. The big kid shook his head at Henry's edginess for about the hundredth time that day. He popped one of his suspenders as his eyes moved to Mattie.

"What?" she asked.

"Would you take that stupid thing off?" Jack nodded at her cape.

"How come?"

"I'll tell you how come. We're about to go into a place where we don't want to stand out. That's gonna be hard enough even if you're not wearing that."

Mattie frowned. "All right," she said, sounding annoyed. "I'll take it off. But I'm putting it back on when we come back out."

The main door whipped open and three businessmen stumbled out, trailed by a thick yellow cloud that quickly rose to the second-floor windows. Only one of the men bothered to look at the four kids, and just long enough to toss the last inch of warm beer from his glass at their feet.

"Get outta here, you ragamuffins," he growled before placing his empty glass on the bricks below the main window. The other two men laughed and put their empty glasses there as well.

This time it was Henry who grabbed Jack by the collar. "Don't," he warned him. "It's not worth it."

Henry held on tight, but not before Jack yelled as loudly as he could, "We're not ragamuffins! We're not garbage, okay?" The three men simply laughed and stumbled off to find their next round of drinks.

Mattie had finished removing her cape, her look telling Henry she was worried it might have been the reason for the ragamuffin comment. She shoved it in a chunk of the wall where four or five bricks were missing.

Jack whipped around and gathered up the three empty glasses.

"Forget it. Don't let 'em bother you," Ernie told him, not wanting to see the empties flying toward three heads.

"I'm not gonna do anything. Don't worry," Jack assured him, handing a dirty glass to each of them.

"Okay," he said, "we're not gonna have much time before they toss us out of this place. Anyone asks? We found empty glasses, and we wanted to see if they'd give us a penny or two for bringin' 'em back. They want ragamuffins, we'll give 'em ragamuffins."

A pair of Irish dockworkers burst through the door, much more stable than their singing suggested they should be.

"AND IT'S NO! NAY! NEVER! NO NAY NEVER NO MORE! WILL I PLAY THE WILD ROVER!" The two men laughed and staggered left, then right, before deciding left felt right in the first place.

Ernie caught the door before it could close. Jack moved to go in, but not before offering one last bit of advice.

"Stay behind people and don't let the bartenders see you," he said with an encouraging nod. "And look at *everything*. Let's find what we're supposed to find and get outta here."

cs

The smell of beer—a good share of which was on the floor— was the first thing to greet them. That, and the smoke from the cigars and what passed for cigarettes.

Once inside, Henry couldn't help but stare. There was no Yankees baseball game on TV, because, of course, neither the team nor the screen to broadcast a baseball game existed. Same applied for music. There wasn't any—besides the occasional spontaneous Irish vocalist.

The customers were here for the serious business of doing two things: drinking and smoking.

How did anybody live past thirty? Henry caught himself thinking. *Oh, right . . . a lot of 'em didn't.*

Without a sliver of hesitation, Jack was beginning to elbow his way through the drunken clientele, while the other kids—Henry included—quickly moved to study the walls, the old paintings, even the bar itself from a discreet and hopefully safe distance.

Henry was in the neighborhood of Mattie as she peered between two men whose ample bellies were squished tightly against the bar. She looked to be studying the chalk-written prices for beer and whiskey that surrounded the smoke-tainted prints of Abraham Lincoln.

"Ay! Little mot!" An elderly patron's hand fell hard on her shoulder. "Whatta ya doin' in here?" he demanded to know.

The deeply wrinkled man's bleary eyes weren't the most pleasant she'd seen, and for a second, Henry could tell Mattie may have forgotten what she was supposed to say if she ran into trouble. He tried to edge his way closer.

"Speak up now," the man grumbled at her as he took a pull from a hand-rolled cigarette, followed by a sip from a chipped glass that looked to be half-filled with equal parts beer and ash.

"Oh, I forgot!" she suddenly blurted out. "I'm returning empty glasses, they told us to bring 'em in."

"There ain't more of ya, are there?" The man looked ready to call for someone, but Mattie was able to convince him otherwise.

"I can take yours if you want?" she offered with an innocent look, just as Henry showed up.

"Agggh," the crusty old voice scratched out. "There *are* more of ya."

The man kept his smoky stare locked on Mattie, until he downed his beer and handed her the smoke-darkened empty. "Tell 'em I want another." He burped. "Then you two and however many else ya came with, get outta here."

"Yessir," Mattie assured him.

She turned to Henry. "I'm gonna go over and look at that side of the place." She nodded to a far corner and immediately headed in that direction.

Henry decided to work his way toward the opposite side of the crowded bar, trying his best to avoid suspicion.

Nothing on that wall, nothing up there on the shelves, a couple of photographs of . . . could be anyone. Man, does this place reek. Worse than Hell's Kitchen ever dreamed of reeking.

Henry spotted a map of the United States on a cluttered wall without windows. He wandered through the smoky haze for a look. Something about it looked odd.

Ernie shouldered his way past him. "Anything yet?" he asked, barely stopping.

"Nope," Henry replied. "How 'bout you?"

Ernie tapped the bag on his shoulder and said, "Enough food for a couple more days!"

Henry grinned, then turned back to study the map again, quickly shaking his head.

Would ya look at that. Dakota Territory, Utah Territory, Arizona Territory. They're not even states yet!

"You!" a voice called from across the room. A young man who looked to be of considerable means—by Henry's guess, at least—lifted a finger and motioned for the young map-gawker to come over.

Oh, c'mon. C'mon! Are you kidding? Not already. I've been in here, like, maybe five minutes. I'm not even close to finding anything!

Ignoring the man was out of the question—the look in his eyes already made that much clear. A tingle of fear rolled down Henry's back as the young man motioned to him a second time.

Okay, think smart here.

Henry let out a breath and wedged his way through the crowded room, easing his way between one swaying customer after another, until reaching the table and finding it home to not just *one* young man of considerable means, but *two*.

They were twin brothers; maybe twenty-five years old, both wearing ink-black suits, along with identical looks of curiosity. Each looked at least six feet tall with dark brown hair the color of a bay thoroughbred horse—an appropriate comparison given how athletic the young men looked.

"Evening, young sir," the one who'd been doing the motioning greeted Henry. "What brings you to such a fine and upstanding establishment tonight? Or should I say, this morning?"

"Oh . . . well . . . just . . ."

"Yes?" The other brother raised an eyebrow.

Henry looked between the two brothers, pretending to search for his friends, trying to hide his percolating panic.

"Excuse me, have either of you guys seen—"

"We have," the second brother interrupted, as they both stood up. "We've seen all four of you." The twin brother who'd just spoken switched his beer from one hand to the other so he could properly introduce himself.

"Clyde Colton. My brother Clifford."

"Henry Baaaaaaaab . . ." he started to reply, then winced as Clyde took his hand in a crushing grip.

Eeeeeesh, that is the strongest handshake I've ever felt in my life!

"Good to meet you, Henry Babb." Clyde thankfully let go. "It is a little late, though, isn't it? A young man of your age in a place like this? How old are you, Henry? Ten?"

"Twelve," he answered. "Thirteen next month."

"Ah, good for you," Clifford said before taking a quick sip.

The brothers really didn't appear to be all that interested in whether he was twelve, thirteen, or a hundred years old for that matter. Ever so calmly, Clifford set down his beer on the edge of the table.

"Let me ask you a question, Henry," his even—yet now somewhat cold—expression suggesting he wouldn't ask twice. "Why are you and your friends here? Looking at each and every thing inside the place?"

Clyde checked his pocket watch. "At half past twelve in the morning," he added. The snapping *click* as he closed the watch told Henry all he needed to know.

They're hunters! They've been everywhere we've been. Made the phone call. Saw Vanderbilt. Now they're here—but that means they haven't found it! They'd already be gone if they had!

Clifford broke into a thin smile under his slicked-back thoroughbred hair. "There's a lot of money at stake here, Henry." He was trying to sound casual, but failing. "Our father's rich, but even his money's a fraction of what Skavenger's offering. A fortune both enormous and incalculable, witnessed by New York's finest bankers. Remember?"

Both men moved an intimidating step closer to Henry. He was eye level at best with the second-lowest button on their suits.

"Now," Clifford calmly continued. "If you and your friends are smart enough to share what you're looking for here, I'm fairly sure we could reach some kind of agreement—an agreement that might help us both."

Clyde was in the process of finishing off his beer as well. He issued a gentlemanly belch, before saying with genuine appreciation, "It's remarkable you got this far, Henry. Skavenger always makes the first clues the most difficult. Gets the number of hunters down in a hurry."

A glass crashed to the floor in a far corner, and Henry waited to hear someone dragging a flailing Jack, or Ernie, or even Mattie toward the closest door. But there was barely a ripple in the steady buzz of mumbling drunkenness.

"What do you say, Henry? We have a deal?" Clifford asked.

A deal? A deal with you? Sorry, my deal's about getting back home. I've got enough to worry about with Hiram Doubt.

Even under the pressurized gaze of the Coltons, Henry had no trouble keeping Doubt's threat at the front of his mind.

A threat to eliminate his fellow hunters one by one by one, starting off with Jack—who, odds were now good, was his great-great-grandfather. And if Doubt eliminated Jack? Henry would never even be born.

"Well?" Clyde asked him.

A quartet of customers broke into a loose semblance of song a few tables away from them—something about a girl leaving someone somewhere. Not much chance it would help with the twin's dwindling level of patience, nor would what Henry had decided to say next.

"I'm sorry," Henry finally answered them. "I don't know anything about that."

Clifford shook his head and sighed.

"Foolish boy. Foolish, foolish boy, Henry," he quietly said to him, tapping his fingers and waiting another second before raising his voice above the din.

"BARTENDER!!" he bellowed. "You got a bunch of low-life kids running around this place!"

Henry had already counted four bartenders on duty—and one of them had hopped over the bar and was storming toward him. In a flash, the entire room was roaring with shouts and laughter, each drunken patron stepping back to create a corridor toward Henry and the others.

Knowing the bartender's not-so-tender hands were about to grab him, Henry looked up at Clyde and Clifford.

"Should have talked to us," Clifford said with a privileged shrug. "Good luck making it out of New York."

"Get the hell outta here, ya punk!" the bartender snarled as he dragged Henry across the sticky floor, the remnants of more than a few lukewarm beers finding their way onto the twelve-year-old's face. He would have probably been doused with more had he—and his three fellow minors—not been tossed straight through the door onto the sidewalk.

The door slammed behind them. Some, but not all, of the boisterous yelling from inside was muffled. Another dark billow of smoke curled out of the windows above them.

Jack was the first to sit up, resting his hands on his knees as he gave his soaked hair a good shake. "Well, fellow ragamuffins? Anything?" he asked the three of them, surprisingly calm.

"Nothing," Henry answered, upset with himself.

"Nothing? Nothing?" Ernie had to laugh. "You got us thrown out of our very first bar!"

"Speak for yourself there, pal," Jack said, shaking beer off his hands as well, unable to hold back a half laugh himself.

Henry noticed that Mattie, though, wasn't laughing. She was far too engaged in studying an empty beer glass she'd managed to hang on to during her short flight from interior to exterior—a beer glass that was quite a bit cleaner and clearer than the others he'd seen inside.

She gave it a scrub, held it up to the light, then closely looked at it again. Her eyes almost crossed for a second as she slowly spun it in her hand . . .

. . . before her mouth broke into a small, triumphant smile. She handed the glass over to Henry.

"Hold it up in the light, then relax your eyes," she said to him as she sat back. "Read what's down at the bottom. It's really hard to see."

Henry looked at it longer than she had, enough that she seemed to grow concerned. "You see it yet?" she asked.

See what? What am I supposed to—wait.

There it was. And yes, it was really, really, *really* hard to see. A message that wrapped all the way around the base of the glass. Two lines' worth.

"I do see it!" he finally said, and Mattie rolled onto her back, shooting her arms up into the air in pure exultation.

"YEEEEESSSSS!!!" she shouted to the sky.

"Hey, hey, hey, stop." Jack scooted over to block the window. "We don't want anyone else seeing . . . whatever it is you two see. Down there at the bottom."

"I wanna see what's down at the bottom," Ernie said, reaching for the glass. He gave a long look at the same spot Mattie and Henry had studied. And for the longest of moments, it was obvious he didn't see it.

Until he did.

"Well, whatta ya know," he said with a growing grin as he slowly spun the glass. "Wouldja look at that." Ernie tossed the glass over to Jack.

"Hey, hey, HEY! Be careful!" Mattie gasped, but Jack reeled it in with ease, looking a touch perturbed that he was the last to get to look.

But just like the rest of them, a short moment peering at the now-clear glass was all it took to produce one last smile. Jack read the words out loud.

"*The Adventures of Tom Sawyer*, written nine years ago. Now to a new adventure. Journey to the gateway banks of Tom's travels. Search there from noon till midnight on July fourteenth for your next key. Through the Natchez door and then two fathoms deep is where you'll find it."

"Tom Sawyer! Skavenger's favorite adventure!" Mattie laughed with delight as she stood up to retrieve her cape, still tucked in the wall. "Whatcha think about *that*, Jack?"

He twirled the glass around to make sure there wasn't anything they'd overlooked.

"I think it is now very clear," he told them all, "that our journey is about to leave Gotham."

THIRTEEN

Westward

IT WAS NIGHTTIME, or so Henry thought—quickly deciding it had been the sound of rain that had just nudged him awake.

He'd gotten used to the steady loud rumbling of the locomotive, the occasional screech of the steel train wheels, and the rhythmic tilt of the railcar from side to side—so it was definitely the tip-tap patter of rain that had pulled him out of his sleep.

Mmmkay. How many days now?

It was easy to lose track of time, which for Henry was both a huge and ironic understatement.

Every time he woke up—after ten hours of sleep the first night—the routine inside his head had been exactly the same. In the fogginess of fading slumber, he'd hear his mother knocking on his door, telling him Christmas breakfast was ready and, yes, that he'd need a heavier coat, and, no, he couldn't go with Abigail Kentworth to Central Park.

He let out a sad and deep breath.

Mom.

That was the other thing he did every time he woke up: kick himself for the tone he'd used Christmas Eve when she was busy handing down the rules.

"Yes, Mom."

"Got it, Mom."

"Great. Perfect."

He'd regretted it then. He regretted it even more now— being as there was nothing he could do to make things right.

She said she loved you. And the only thing you said was, "You too." Kinda dropped the most important word there, buddy. "Love."

A louder sheet of heavy rainfall convinced him he was awake for good. He pulled the ledger sheet from his pocket, holding it up to a crack in the boxcar—which was really more of a storage car, with forward and back doors—to steal some light.

They were all there. Every destination entry, including those now magically written in for each day of the rail trip out of New York.

JULY 10TH, 1885, CENTRAL PARK, NEW YORK

JULY 10TH, 1885 TELEPHONE EXCHANGE, HELL'S KITCHEN, NEW YORK

JULY 10TH, 1885 GRAND CENTRAL DEPOT, NEW YORK

JULY 10TH, 1885 THE VANDERBILT MANSION, NEW YORK

JULY 11TH, 1885 THE JENNINGS ESTABLISHMENT, NEW YORK

JULY 12TH, 1885 PENNSYLVANIA RAILROAD, IN TRANSIT

JULY 13ᴛʜ, 1885 PENNSYLVANIA RAILROAD,
          IN TRANSIT

JULY 14ᴛʜ, 1885 PENNSYLVANIA RAILROAD,
          IN TRANSIT

His eyes drifted to the upper right-hand corner. He'd picked up a pencil stub that Ernie had tossed away—privately writing down "Christmas Morning" along with the exact place he hoped Skavenger could help him find: "142 Central Park West, New York."

"Chief's and Gigi's home," Henry quietly whispered to himself.

He still had time, he knew, or at least he was still trying to convince himself; but he also knew he didn't have forever until that last box would be filled.

That's when it'll turn into forever right here in good ol' 1885. Why'd I even get up and go into Chief's study that night?

Henry folded up the sheet and put it back, yawning and blinking his eyes. He'd slept next to a large storage box bearing the address of a Mrs. Mildred Parsons of St. Louis, Missouri. All of the address labels left were either from that city or somewhere nearby. Anyone with a trunk destined for a spot east of that had gotten off the train long ago.

"You hungry?" he heard Mattie ask. She was sitting on a box belonging to a Mr. Robert Jeremy, and she was holding up a plate of whatever she'd bought for breakfast.

Henry sat up. "Nope, not really," he said as he stretched, not as stiff as the night before. "What time is it?" he asked.

"Still nighttime. Closer to morning, I think," she answered. "I couldn't sleep. Kind of a big day. I think we're only an hour away."

Mattie had slept through Pennsylvania, but she'd been awake through the short sliver of West Virginia, a good portion of Kentucky, and a fair share of Indiana. She nodded her head toward the pair of wooden trunks behind her, the train squeaking again as it leaned into a turn.

"Jack and Ern have been out for hours," she said, quietly laughing. "We could run off the tracks and they'd sleep right through it."

"Let's not find out," Henry said through a yawn that drew a smile out of her. "Like you said, big day ahead of us."

He reached in his other pocket to make sure the money Vanderbilt had given them was still there—which it was— always a relief. Didn't need to be losing a dollar of that. The last thing the rail tycoon had told them that night was that every hunter who walked through his gargantuan door had received the same amount, which meant their team had received a total of four shares.

The amount of cash Mr. The Second had given them also supported the first decision they'd made about the riddle— being as it was totally consistent with the cost of rail tickets to Missouri.

Jack, though, had tossed out the smart suggestion that they save money not just by buying cheap tickets, but by not buying any tickets at all. Better to sneak onto one of the storage cars and save almost all their money for something more important down the road.

Just in case they were wrong about the riddle.

All four had quickly agreed "gateway" meant St. Louis, giving Ernie the chance to regale them with his Central Park knowledge of the Lewis and Clark Expedition. Mattie, being a big fan of Tom Sawyer, had figured out that "Natchez" was the name of a riverboat, so it was a good start on both of those fronts.

It was the last few words, however, that still had all of them stumped.

The part about the door and the key being two fathoms deep.

They all knew that "fathoms" meant water, specifically the depth of water, which, to be honest, didn't sound too great to any of them. Was Skavenger's next clue buried underwater? Underwater in the Mississippi River? Even worse, maybe "Natchez" wasn't what Mattie thought it was, and instead was the town of Natchez, Mississippi.

Three long days of railroad travel to St. Louis, and they still weren't sure.

The one stroke of good luck was that Mattie had befriended a rail porter named George, whose job was to manage not only the passenger cars in the middle of the train, but also to keep an eye on the half dozen storage cars at the back. This included the one they'd been hiding in the past few days. It was nice knowing there was someone, especially in an official capacity, who was watching out for them.

Mattie scooted a newspaper across the floor to him: the *Vevay Reveille* of Switzerland County, Indiana.

"Not much news about the hunt," she said matter-of-factly, then added, "Course it is an Indiana newspaper."

Mattie rarely sounded too overwhelmed—and certainly never worried—by where they were in the hunt. She was different from Henry in that regard.

"They did have a short article in the back about the groundskeepers at the Dakota being upset," she chuckled. "I guess they've still got a few people digging around, thinking that's where the first clue is."

Henry pulled the paper closer.

He admired the fact that Mattie seemed unshakeable—even after he'd brought everyone up to speed about Clyde and Clifford Colton and their threatening words back at the bar. Henry had even delicately mentioned, without actually revealing Doubt's name, the encounter behind the Vanderbilt

Mansion, all with the intent of keeping the four of them on guard.

Mattie had asked George to keep an eye out for twin brothers, or anyone else who looked like they might be trouble. She'd told him to let her know if he saw anyone suspicious, no matter what time of day or night it might be. Midnight, 3:00 a.m., 5:00 a.m. Didn't matter.

That was the other thing bothering Henry.

How is it I go back more than a hundred years in one second, but once I get here everything feels the same? Days and nights feel like they're exactly twenty-four hours. It's crazy.

The forward door of the storage car opened and the clanking noise of the train, along with a fresh swirl of rain, accompanied George the porter as he moved inside. He shook off the mist still clinging to him—and there was plenty of him to cling to—before wandering over to his young stowaways.

George had told them the first hour they'd met, long after he'd decided not to kick them off, that he'd been born and raised in Pittsburgh. Now in his late twenties, he was carrying on the family railroad porter tradition started by his father, who right now was working on the same train way up ahead in the luxury cars. A couple of decades earlier, he'd actually served in the 6th US Colored Infantry Regiment of the Union Army, having seen battle in Virginia and North Carolina. George had beamed with pride telling that story.

"Mornin', you two," the young porter cheerfully said, holding some food wrapped in a small towel. "I found some cheese up in the Parlor Car. Don't worry, they'll never miss it."

"Thanks, George," both of them said.

He waved 'em off and said, "Aw, it's just a special treat for you kids finally gettin' to where you're goin' this morning. Less than an hour now. Hopefully the sun'll be shining by then."

He glanced around the car. "Other young gents still sleeping?"

"They're over there," Mattie nodded to the other side, her eyes sticking tight to what was inside the towel. "This looks delicious. I'll give you some money for it."

"Noooo, it's my pleasure, little one," he kindly assured her. "They would have thrown it away anyway. It's not like anyone's stealing it."

"It is, though, George." Her steady smile slipped a bit. "You're a good man for helping us out so much."

"Won't be the last time." The porter winked at her and smiled.

Henry knew that Mattie had captured a big part of George's heart. It seemed to be that way with anyone who spent time with her. It was how he felt about her too, that's for sure.

George meandered back toward the front door, which had somehow strayed back open. He closed it with a firm shove, tight as he could, and the collection of rolling and lumbering sounds faded as he shuffled back to the passenger car ahead of them.

"I do hate thinking that," Mattie admitted to Henry. "That we're kinda stealing something."

Henry folded the newspaper and set it aside. "Come on, Mattie, it's nothing. You heard what George said."

"It isn't nothing," she shook her head. "It's what my father did. That's why he's in prison right now."

It was the first time Mattie had mentioned anything to Henry about why she was here and not somewhere else. Ernie's parents had died, he knew that much, and Jack had mentioned losing his own father.

He knew nothing about Mattie's family, though. Until now.

"There are nine of us," Mattie revealed. "Nine kids. And I'm the youngest. I'm the one who forced him to steal, so he could provide for all of us."

She looked down, ashamed.

"That's not true, you can't think that."

"Don't tell me what I can and can't think, Henry Babbitt," she said with an edge in her voice. "Mother did what she could, but . . . I think she started getting tired of being around us all the time. My older brothers and sisters . . . most of them left too. It's hard to blame anyone, 'cept for me."

The two of them sat in silence, the wobbling and screeching steel not accompanied by any words for a good long while.

"I figure if we can win Skavenger's prize," she finally spoke up again, "maybe I'll take my share and go back." Her eyes drifted back to Henry. "And if that doesn't make anything better, if it's all still a mess like it is now? I'll find someplace else to go."

Mattie sighed with a tone that told Henry she'd said more than she wanted. She reached for the newspaper she'd already read.

"So," she tried putting a spark back in her voice, "what's your big secret? You gotta have some good reason you're doing this."

Well, Mattie McGillin. I'd say there's a pretty good reason I do.

But he merely looked down and smiled.

"What?" She leaned forward, suddenly curious.

"Nothing. You . . . you wouldn't believe me."

"I already know about your father, Henry," she said gently. "Tell me about the rest of your family."

The train wobbled just enough to pop the door back open a couple of inches again—an annoyance more than anything.

"Henry?" Mattie asked once more.

Instead of answering, he pushed himself up to give the door a shove that might catch. Once. Twice. But the latch stubbornly refused to hold.

"Think maybe I'll get some fresh air," Henry said to her, wanting to skirt the topic. "Big day ahead of us, remember?"

Mattie gave him a small smile and nodded as he walked out to the narrow open-air landing that separated the cars. After that very first day on board, it had become his favorite place on the train. He could think out here. He could remember.

There was a thin metal bar that may or may not have been able to keep someone from falling off if they really leaned up hard against it. Henry, of course, didn't push his luck, or even come close; he always kept a more-than-safe distance.

Instead of holding the metal bar, he clasped on to the stout hook that allowed him to lean out enough so his face could feel the wind and he could watch the night-darkened landscape whip by.

It wasn't quite the same as flying—not in the way Henry imagined it felt for Superman—but it sure did feel good.

Really good.

The dark black of Missouri's dying night was now resting on a rising line of light blue behind them. Sunrise was coming fast, he could tell. The heavy rain that had awakened him was also starting its retreat.

It was out here—over the last three days—that Henry allowed himself, in the spare few moments when he wasn't thinking of his family, to think about the hunt.

And there was plenty to think about.

If only you could be here, Chief. All those riddles you and Dad looked for? I've been solvin' 'em! Wait'll you see that ledger sheet of yours.

He smiled as he leaned a bit farther out and looked back toward the horizon's oncoming morning.

*Also, I'm pretty sure I've been hanging with your grandfather.
Jack. We went to Grand Central. Nope, not the station—Grand
Central Depot! They had railroad tracks running right down the
middle of Park Avenue!*

*Oh, and how 'bout this? I got to meet Cornelius Vanderbilt the
Second—in his mansion! The one on 5th Avenue. How great is that?*

Henry smiled and sighed.

*Maybe someday I'll get to tell you about it. About everything.
If I actually make it back.*

Henry looked off to his right to see the distant locomotive,
dozens of cars ahead of him, crawling into view. Its tail of steam
churned high and flat as the train curved into the last stretch
before St. Louis.

Almost there.

Just a few more minut—

And that's when he saw one of them.

Up ahead . . . impossibly . . . on the train . . . outside of it.

No. No, no, no, no, it can't . . .

Henry blinked to make sure. Then blinked again. It took a
few seconds as his eyes adjusted before he was totally convinced.

Oh no.

Standing between two of the passenger cars . . . far, far
ahead of Henry, on the same type of landing on which he
stood, loomed one of Hiram Doubt's Dark Men.

The man, wearing his familiar top hat and longcoat, stood
on the metal deck over the coupling. A surge of panic rushed
into Henry's head as he watched.

Watched the Dark Man—who was watching *him.*

No. They can't be here, they can't be.

Henry realized he wasn't breathing and forced himself to
inhale. That was followed by what seemed like a hundred more
shallow breaths—all coming too close to each other.

The powerful locomotive rumbled forward, and with each churn of gray and white steam, another passenger car would slowly come into view as the lazy, long turn continued toward St. Louis.

Please let him be the only one. Don't let the others be here. Please don't let Doubt be here.

Henry couldn't help but look and wait for the next railcar to appear, already knowing deep in the pit of his stomach that the one man might not be the only—

He saw the next one.

There.

No. No, no. He sees me too.

The second Dark Man was closer and just as ominous as he stood between another pair of the forward passenger railcars. Henry leaned back, but not enough to avoid seeing the third of Doubt's men—and then, closest and worst of all, the fourth:

Grace.

The one who had drawn close to him, like a specter, at the Vanderbilt Estate.

The four men remained nothing more than dark silhouettes, but there was no doubt in Henry's mind as to who they were and why they were on the train.

The only doubt he felt was Doubt himself, because the presence of the Dark Men meant . . .

Doubt's probably here. Right here on the train.

A shudder trickled down Henry's back. If Hiram Doubt knew that he was on the train as well, he also knew they were closing in on the next of Skavenger's clues.

He'll want to know what I know.

Henry remembered Doubt's words as clearly as the night he'd heard them spoken:

When I ask you for the answer to that riddle?
You. Will. Tell. Me.

The top of the sun broke above the horizon far, far behind the train, and it was almost as if in that single second, the light itself grew much brighter—enough to illuminate the image that Henry knew would be visiting his nightmares.

One by one, with the most distant Dark Man making his move first, Doubt's men disappeared back into the train, with what could be only one destination in mind.

They're coming for me.

Henry leaned out to take another look, still holding the stout hook tightly. Three of Doubt's men were already gone— out of sight, now on board the train.

But Grace still stood outside the railcar on the landing. Only a half dozen cars away from him.

And as sure as Henry was of anything he'd ever seen in his life, he watched as Doubt's elegant henchman looked straight into his soul, silently mouthing that one single word:

"Soooooooooooon."

Henry stumbled backward and then turned toward the door of the storage car, which was—

Still open! They're gonna walk right in!

He dashed through the opening. Jack and Ernie were now awake as Henry tripped and crashed onto the floor right in front of them. He scrambled to his feet and quickly tried to close the sliding door.

Click clunk click clunk click clunk.

The door wouldn't catch. Not a single time. Sliding back not just open—but *wide* open.

"Henry?" Mattie pushed herself off Mr. Jeremy's wardrobe box. She took a step toward Henry, a worried look on her face.

"Holy smokes, Babbitt, what are ya tryin' to do?" Jack laughed, until he saw the look of overwhelming terror that Henry knew had to be in his eyes.

The young hunter had been able to somewhat hide that expression after his first run-in with Doubt's men, but he wasn't able to conceal it now.

Door! Door!

"Cripes, pal," Ernie said with growing concern. "You almost fall off the train?"

"No," Henry answered with a wavering voice, anxiously looking all around. He spotted a nearby storage trunk.

"Help me push this. We gotta block the door, c'mon!" He whipped over to the padlocked wooden box and leaned into it hard.

"Why? What the heck for?" Jack held his hands out wide, looking more and more confused by the second.

"They're coming!" Henry answered him, giving Jack a look that assured him this wasn't a false alarm. "I said NOW!" he yelled for good measure.

"Come on, Ern!" a more-than-convinced Jack shouted to Ernie. The two of them rushed over to help, while Mattie stayed put, looking more and more unsettled by the second. All three boys leaned their shoulders against the trunk and gave it a strong push. It began to move, but only by a foot or two.

"How many hundreds of dresses are in this thing?" Jack wondered out loud.

Henry knew they had to be getting close to St. Louis—close enough there wouldn't be any more passenger stops before they reached that final station. Very, very . . .

Soooooooooooooooooon.

He closed his eyes, shoving with all his strength against the enormous trunk, the one he knew from that first day on the train held the wardrobe of a woman named Meredith Winningham.

The train's steam engine started to throttle down; still loud, but not loud enough to muffle Mattie's next words. Words of sickening realization that chilled Henry to his very core.

"It's them, isn't it?" she said.

The three boys turned as one. For the first time since Henry had met her, he could tell she was terrified.

"They're on the train with us, aren't they?" Mattie asked with a trembling voice. "All of them."

Jack pushed himself away from the trunk. "Who's on the train with us?"

"Hiram Doubt," she answered, her eyes moving to the open and now banging door. "Doubt and the others. I saw 'em at the Vanderbilts' before you got there that night."

She looked back at Henry with fearful eyes. "That's who you were warning us about, wasn't it? The ones you said you saw."

Jack spun around to Henry. "Hiram Doubt's on this train?! Right now?!"

Henry swallowed and nodded. "Yeah. They all are."

Now it was Ernie's turn to panic. "Oh, no, no, no, no. You don't think he knows what we're doin', do you? He couldn't know that, could he?"

Henry wasn't sure what he should say. He really didn't need to say anything—his own silence more than answering Ernie's question. The only sound they could hear at that moment was coming from the railcar door, which was still thumping open and shut.

Open . . . and shut. Open . . .

"We gotta get off this train." Jack was already looking around for a way to do just that.

"We can't get off this train, Jack!" Ernie somehow had the sense to know. "We're going too fast!"

The locomotive's breathing was beginning to slow, but its steel wheels were still sprinting. Ernie was right. They were going too fast. St. Louis was close, but the Dark Men would get to them before they got there.

"How many storage cars behind us?" Jack quickly asked anyone who might know.

"Eight," Mattie answered him.

"How many cars ahead you think these goons are?" He looked at Henry now.

"Three, maybe four."

Jack shook his head. "Okay," he told them all. "Let's head to the back of this thing."

ↄ

The most immediate problem they discovered with the storage car just behind them was that it no longer stored anything. It was empty. Dead and completely empty. The big trunks and various wooden shipping containers that had been there just a day before were now gone.

The only thing left was fifty-five feet of open and uninviting space without a single spot for the four of them to hide.

"Keep going! Keep going!" Mattie yelled out as she ran through the middle of empty nothingness, the rest of them running right alongside of her.

Except for Henry, who had just stopped and turned.

"Wait, hold on." He rushed back to the sliding forward door to see if it might lock, unlike the broken one on the car they'd just abandoned.

Henry leaned into it.

Click. Click. Click.

No grab, no lock. He gave a quick glance through the stubborn door, still open, not wanting to see an approaching black hat. For the moment, there was nothing up there—just the familiar lazy motion of the broken door on that car opening and closing.

Which was better than the one Henry was currently struggling with. It was refusing to latch at all.

"Henry! COME ON!" Ernie yelled for him to leave it. Better to run. He turned and did just that, following them through the open door into the next storage car—finding that it too was empty.

The rhythmic sound of the steam engine now seemed to match the blistering pace of Henry's heart.

Chikuh chikuh chikuh chikuh chikuh chikuh—

He stopped to give the door on the next car a quick try too. Jack doubled back to help, pulling on it from one side while Henry pushed.

Thump. Thump. Thump. The door hinted that it was almost ready to latch, almost ready to give them at least a small measure of protection. But—

Nothing. Whatta ya gotta do to close these things?

Mattie ran back to them, panicked urgency in her voice as she yelled, "Henry! Jack! HURRY! We gotta keep moving!"

Thump. Thump. The door still wouldn't grab.

Chikuh chikuh chikuh chikuh.

Ernie ran back to the door, even though there wasn't much he could do—nothing except steal a look through the opening.

"Henry . . ." he said with a shallow and failing voice.

The way he said it put an end to both Henry's and Jack's efforts to get the door, to get *any* door, to latch and to lock. Instead, they looked at Ernie as he nodded toward what he'd just seen.

"Look."

All four of them did.

There, just beyond the first of the open doors two cars behind them, on the landing over the coupling, stood Grace.

Though it was still lightly raining, a menacing smile began to grow on his spiteful face, made worse by his cold blue eyes and chilling black longcoat.

"Oh no," Ernie said in a voice that could barely be heard. "No, no, no, no."

With a smooth motion that gave credence to his name, Grace slowly eased the door open and began to walk toward them . . . right in the very same moment that the door the four of them had been pinning their hopes on finally closed and latched.

Click.

"YES! Let's go! Let's go!" Henry yelled, and the three boys spun around to run to the next car. Mattie, though, couldn't take her eyes off the gloomy, threatening man now headed her way. Couldn't move . . . until Henry hurried back for her.

"Mattie! Now!" He reached for her arm and pulled, enough to get her to turn and run again.

Chikuh chikuh chikuh chikuh.

The four of them raced into the next car, seeing right away that it was half-filled with wardrobe trunks and other boxes. Better, Henry knew, but not enough to hide all of them.

And what do we even do if there is enough?

The foursome of frantic hunters burst into yet another storage car, finally discovering dozens and dozens of massive trunks and upright boxes. All were positioned in a haphazard manner, which meant there should be nooks and pockets and lots of areas where they could hide.

But if the lock back there doesn't hold, Grace is still gonna have all the time he needs to find us. George . . . c'mon . . . where are you? We could use some help down here.

"Wait!" Jack shouted before turning back, retreating to the car that was half-full of boxes.

"WHATTA YA DOIN'??!!" Ernie reached for him, but he was too late. Jack was already back in the car—the car *closer* to the Dark Man.

He had something in mind, Henry could tell. He even rushed back himself to find out. Without a second of hesitation, Jack hurried over to the large side door of the car, the one the porters and luggage crews used to offload the boxes at any given stop. He unlatched the door and pulled it open with ease.

Blurring landscape whipped by outside the train.

"Jack!!! NO!" Mattie yelled out.

"Don't worry!" he called back as he wedged the door open with a stray piece of wood from the floor. "We're gonna jump off without jumping off!"

And with that, at about four minutes after sunrise, Jack had just tossed in the opening bet on the only hand of cards they had left to play. Bluffed it, really. He turned and ran back into the railcar that offered them the nooks and pockets and the areas to hide with his three fellow hunters dashing in just behind him.

ఌ

Chikuh chikuh chikuh chikuh chikuh chikuh chikuh . . .

Nine minutes after sunrise.

Chiikuuh chiikuh chiikuh chiikuh chiikuh . . .

Fourteen minutes after sunrise.

Chiiiikuuuuh chiiiikuuuuh chiiiikuuuuh chiiiikuuuuh . . .

Twenty minutes after sunrise, the train had clearly begun to slow. It felt like two hours had gone by, but the four of them knew it had been only minutes.

Twenty unbearably long and nerve-racking minutes.

Henry's best guess, and it was only a guess, based strictly on the sluggish swaying of the train and the slowing steam belch from the locomotive, was that they were covering the final mile or two before their last stop on the east side of the Mississippi River.

East of St. Louis. Gateway to the West.

And in between the slowing chug of the coal-driven engine, and the whoosh of steam billowing into the air, the only other sound had been . . .

Nothing.

Nothing at all.

Which was more than unsettling in itself.

It had already been at least a few minutes since they'd found the perfect cavern deep within the haphazardly stacked boxes in the storage car. All four of them had quickly wriggled their way in, knowing they'd completely disappeared from view, trying their best to stay quiet.

Which wasn't easy.

All they could do was look at each other with eyes trying to say what they were thinking. Henry and Mattie had already shared about a hundred glances.

It was the waiting, of course. The wondering where the Dark Men were and why they were even there.

"When's George gonna get here?" Mattie finally asked with a faint voice lower than a whisper. "He has to know we're not up there, doesn't he?"

"You think George is gonna be able to do anything?" Ernie raised his eyebrows as he whispered back. The look she returned didn't exactly scream confidence.

Jack stayed quiet, content just to shake his head and let out a deep breath. Just seeing him slightly uncertain was enough to concern Henry.

"What are we gonna do when the train stops?" Henry asked him. "They're gonna be out there waiting for us."

Jack still didn't say anything, nor did anyone else. Silence, it seemed, was the only plan any of them had right now—though Henry knew they'd have to come up with a better one soon.

"Maybe they couldn't get through the door?" Mattie asked hopefully. "You did get it locked."

"Fat chance of that," Jack finally whispered.

Chiiiiiiiikuuuuuuuuh . . . Chiiiiiiiikuuuuuuuuh . . .

The steel wheels were beginning to screech a bit more loudly, signaling that a full stop was fairly imminent.

"Jack?" Henry asked, but got nothing in return. "Jack, c'mon!" he tried whispering a little louder. "What do we do?"

"The four of you leave very soooooooooooooooooon . . . that'sss what you do."

A cold and icy voice answered Henry from the other side of the storage boxes behind which they were hiding. They all gasped in unison. None of them had heard a sound since they'd hidden in the small mountain of large boxes, yet here the man was, unseen but right there in the same car as them.

He'd known precisely where they were. Had gotten through the locked door, past Jack's open-door diversion, without making even a hint of noise. From the closeness of his voice, Henry guessed, the Dark Man was no more than three feet away from him.

"Pleassse, please," Grace's scratchy voice continued. "None of you have anything to fear . . . at leassst not for now."

Ernie and Mattie squeezed their eyes closed, much like Henry had tried to do so many times during the worst of his nightmares.

"You sssssssee," Grace hissed almost softly, his face unseen. "Mr. Doubt right now is already ahead of you, on his way at this moment to ssseize Skavenger's next clue."

Henry hadn't moved in minutes, but he was still breathing too quickly. He shared a quick glance with Jack, waiting for whatever they might hear next.

"And . . . in the extreme unlikelihood," the voice continued, "that his guesssss turns out to be incorrect, the four of usssss will be following . . . the four of you. In case your assumption proves more accurate."

Mattie's eyes lifted toward Henry and she silently mouthed the words, "They're all there? Right now?"

From the other side of their hiding spot, Grace answered her as if she'd stood up and shouted the question.

"Yessss, dear," his words slid through the creases of the wardrobe trunks. "We are."

A second later, they heard the sound of four quiet but very distinct taps on four boxes—enough distance separating them that they could only have come from four men.

Knock. Knock. Knock. Knock.

Now it was Henry's turn to close his eyes, not knowing if any of the rest of them were doing the same. Not caring. Just wanting Grace to finish whatever he needed to say—wanting to avoid the nightmare of seeing him.

"Sssstill there?" Grace asked. "Because that's what the four of us are about to be for the rest of your journey. Sssstill here. Not gone. Never gone."

Henry opened his eyes just in time to see Jack look his way, shaking his head at the Dark Man's words.

"Good luck, young hunters," the scratching and hissing voice went on. "Don't bother trying to look for ussss. Just be content to know that we will be watching you. Every minute of however many days you might have left."

C h i i i i i i i i i i k u u u u u u u u u u h chiiiiiiiii—whooooooooooooooosh—

WHUMP.

The train stopped, but not before Henry finally heard the sound of the quartet of Dark Men slowly walking away. Wanting to be heard, it seemed. Before they were gone, though, Grace offered them all one last message:

"Welcome to Sssssssaint Louisssss."

FOURTEEN

The Door and the Pair of Fathoms

IT WAS STILL barely dawn, and yet it felt like they'd been up a full day. The bone-chilling twenty minutes they'd all just experienced together had made sure of that.

Exactly when the four of them should get off the train had turned out to be a tricky decision of its own, especially after Grace's warning.

But while the thought of emerging from the big cavern of boxes wasn't appealing at all, the kids also knew they couldn't just stay on the train. Eventually they crawled out, thinking it smart to get outside while a good many disembarking travelers were still there to provide cover. Grace had promised it would be a waste of time for the youngsters to look for the Dark Men; and sure enough, they didn't see any of them.

They did, however, find George the porter, absent for the past terrifying twenty minutes, frantically searching for them in the crowd of busy passengers and piles of steamer trunks.

Mattie didn't want George worrying too much, so even though they were still shaken by the morning's events, she'd simply told him that they'd gone back to explore the caboose for a while.

The four of them then thanked George for all his help and said their good-byes. They repeated the same story they'd told him a few days earlier: that they were meeting relatives in St. Louis and he needn't worry about them further.

It was a fairly short excursion from the train station to the levees of the booming Missouri port city, filled within the last few years with wide-rutted dirt roads and squatty, quickly built structures.

It was in St. Louis that they hoped Skavenger had planted his next riddle, even though they all knew the stop stood a very good chance of being their most dangerous one yet. The checklist of things they had to keep in mind was getting longer by the minute. The Dark Men were following their every move, they'd been threatened in New York by twin adult men, and their next clue might be two fathoms underwater.

Ernie, whose head spun around like an owl all morning in search of Grace, said they needed to at least have a talk about whether they really, really, really wanted to walk right up to the not-exactly-discreet location awaiting them.

But Jack put an end to that conversation before it even got started. To heck with Doubt and his crazy Dark Men, he'd said. They'd come halfway across the country and they weren't about to turn back now. Once they solved the next clue, they'd just do a better job of hiding from them. Mattie agreed in an instant.

Henry had been struck by her response.

He remembered how calm she'd seemed that night at the Vanderbilt Estate, even though—he knew now—she'd just encountered the Dark Men. *Out of sight, out of mind* was how Mattie seemed to deal with problems.

With Jack and Mattie so firm in their conviction, there was nothing to do but keep to the plan. And so, they'd continued to stride right along the grassy banks of the Mississippi, the steady murmur of the majestic chestnut-colored river helping to soothe their nerves. Until, that is, they caught sight of their destination: a series of huge docks and boat landings where dozens and dozens of massive steam-driven riverboats awaited their next paddle journeys.

One in particular stood out. Simply because it was easily the very largest of the bunch.

Getting on board that steamboat, though, presented a bit of a challenge. Henry knew the four of them looked ratty enough when they'd left New York, and three days in a dusty railcar hadn't done much to improve their appearance. Or their scent, for that matter.

Jack, however, declared that if sneaking onto a train in New York had worked, the same would probably hold true on a Mississippi riverboat.

It was good thinking, Henry had to admit—right up until they came face-to-face with the loading supervisor and discovered he wasn't exactly cut from the same cloth as George the porter. Even the sight of Mattie's winsome grin had failed to sway him.

So, with Plan B now in effect, they waited forty-five minutes until the loading crew began delivering luggage to the passenger rooms, and then scurried up a catwalk that put them in the boiler room.

There they found Joey and two other boiler room workers, each of whom perked up at the sight of a small offering of money out of Henry's pocket. Not only did they agree to let them stay, but Joey offered to let them use the workers' bathroom for a cleanup session.

It didn't take long for the foursome to realize that the safety of the boiler room was a really, really good thing. Even though Skavenger's clue had said they could only search from noon until midnight, they agreed their best move was to stay right where they were until nightfall, when exploring the ship would hopefully be safer.

Joey, as it turned out, was the friendliest of the three boiler room workers. During his lunch, which featured some kind of overly smelly fish, he'd given them an impressive history lesson on the great Mississippi steamboat on which they were hiding.

Coated in sweat that looked like it would never dry, he'd said she was the biggest and the best of the boats exploring the Muddy Miss. The riverboat was three hundred feet from the bow to the back paddle. Henry could tell Joey took a lot of pride in it.

The forty-seven first-class staterooms were also the best around, Joey had gone on to tell them. Lots and lots of stained glass and fine paintings of the surrounding countryside.

Apparently, the first of these riverboats actually had been built in New York decades earlier, but it had been lost to fire.

So they built another, and then another after that, each one larger and more impressive than the one before it. This one was number eight.

The only thing that had stayed the same with each of the eight legendary Mississippi steamboats had been the name.

Natchez.

The name that had been on the bottom of the clear beer glass at the Jennings Establishment. The name that Mattie had gambled was meant to point them to a boat and not a town.

It was those instincts and smarts that had gotten them this far in the hunt, so none of them questioned her suggestion. She'd been right before, and they trusted her to be right this time too. Besides, it made sense.

Still, though, it was the clue's use of the word "fathoms" that had them extremely worried about the prospect of an underwater search, which would now have to wait until the dark of night.

Mattie asked Joey what the depth of the river was right around the *Natchez*—both right there where it was docked and later that evening when it was scheduled for a dinner cruise.

Without blinking as he munched down the last of his odorous lunch, Joey replied matter-of-factly, "'Bout a Mark Twain here, prob'ly not much more'n that out there in the middle."

The four of them had swapped a befuddled look.

"Mark Twain?" Henry asked, just as confused as the rest of them. "What's he got to do with it?"

Joey smiled. "Not him." He looked at the four New York kids. "A 'Mark Twain' is a river term. It means two fathoms . . . twelve feet. 'Mark' is the measurement, 'Twain' means two. That's why ol' Sam Clemens chose it for his writin' name. 'Cuz of how much he loved this here river."

He looked both ways as if someone might overhear him, adding, "Rumor has it they wouldn't let anyone have his usual stateroom today, the one he stays in from time to time. Number 36. Got it locked up tight. Nobody knows why."

Joey winked at the four poker faces looking back at him. Stunned poker faces, but pretty good ones nonetheless.

ↄ

Three hours later, with the sun having gone down and the music wafting from the top deck, the four hunters found themselves standing in front of Stateroom 36. The door was whitewashed the same color Tom Sawyer had convinced his friends to paint a fence with, and the similarity seemed like a good omen to Henry.

Mattie reached into a pocket under her cape and slowly removed the cloth-covered empty glass once owned by Mr. Jennings of New York, but no longer. She held it up to a corridor lantern.

"Through the Natchez door and then two fathoms deep is where you'll find it," Mattie read the last part of the clue with a growing smile. "Door . . . 36. Two fathoms deep . . . Mark Twain."

She let out a deep breath, just as she had during the previous moment of truth at Vanderbilt's front door.

"Well, I think we're right where we're supposed to be." Mattie reached up and rapped on the door a little too forcefully for Ernie's liking.

"Cripes, Mattie! You wanna borrow a hammer?" he said, looking both ways down the hall, his head still on a swivel as it had been the entire day.

"I barely touched it!" she insisted, probably too loudly as well.

"Shhhh," Jack hushed them both.

Thankfully, the hallway was both empty and dimly lit, though not as dim as Henry would have liked. He'd been giving his own neck a steady workout, looking this way and that for any sign of Doubt or his shadowy accomplices.

There was no answer at the door.

No sound of footsteps approaching from inside. Only the muffled churn of the boat paddles and the calming sound of a banjo quartet from up above.

"You knock this time," Mattie instructed Henry.

"Me?"

"YES, YOU!"

Okay, okay! Don't forget, we prob'ly got a person or two we don't want to see while we're down here. Even though there's a pretty good chance they're seeing us right now.

Henry tapped on the door so softly the four of them had trouble hearing it.

"Oh, for gosh sakes," Mattie muttered and then knocked twice as loudly as she had a few seconds ago.

Again there was no answer.

Footsteps rose from the far stairwell and the four of them froze, waiting to hear if the sound grew louder or softer.

Luckily, the rhythmic pattern began to fade and was pretty much gone with the sound of a topside door opening. The banjos seemed to be picking things up a little, the door slowly muffling the growing celebration as it closed tight behind whomever had walked through.

"Maybe we should come back in a few minutes," Henry suggested, able to breathe again, right as Jack reached for the knob and gave it a turn.

No, no . . . Joey said the room was locked ti—

Same as with the humble, small home of Cornelius Vanderbilt the Second, the door easily opened with a light whooshing sound, revealing the room's dimly lit interior.

Ernie shook his head. "Huh, an open door. Guess Mr. Smelly-Fish-for-Lunch doesn't know the ways of the great Hunter S. Skavenger, does he?"

Jack pushed open the door the rest of the way, allowing some of the hallway light to spill inside. It was difficult to see too much—except for one thing positioned against the far wall of the room, just under an open window. It was a not-so-large desk, maybe five feet wide and three feet deep, illuminated by a pair of cream-colored wall lamps.

Henry could hear the soft pulsing sound of the rear paddle slapping the river through the open window.

Course, that could just be your heart thumpin' a mile a minute. Calm down, okay?

Jack held a hand out behind him, signaling for the rest of them to wait until he was certain no one was inside. He then lowered it, and they all quietly walked in.

The contents of the room were fairly spare—as if the guest, or guests, preferred few distractions or temptations. The latter quickly proved to be unlikely, once they discovered an over-flowing ashtray filled with half-smoked cigars.

"Henry!" Mattie whispered to him, dipping her forehead toward the desk. Before he could move any closer, though, the sound of another round of footsteps began to rise from outside in the hallway, and these were undoubtedly moving toward them.

Ernie closed the door, the latch softly clicking just as the *thump, thump, thumping* passed by. His cheeks puffed with re-lief. "Whew, close," he muttered to Jack as they headed over to the desk.

Henry and Mattie were already there, their eyes growing wide at the expected, yet unexpected, discovery perfectly cen-tered on the chestnut-leather writing pad below them.

It was a book.

Just not the book they'd expected.

The book Henry thought they'd find—and Mattie as well—was a nine-year-old edition of *The Adventures of Tom Sawyer.*

That book title had made perfect sense to Henry from the minute they'd left New York. *It had to be Skavenger's favorite adventure! But this . . . this is not that.*

"Henry, I don't understand." Mattie looked at him out of the corner of her eye. "I'd heard that he'd written a new book, but . . ."

Henry couldn't say a word yet—the title of the book made sure of that.

A wise-beyond-his-years young boy grinned up at them from the light green binding. Two trees and a pair of fence posts formed the first letter of the boy's name and the announcement of a new adventure.

Adventures of Huckleberry Finn
(Tom Sawyer's Comrade)
By Mark Twain
Illustrated.

It was in that moment that Henry heard the stateroom's door latch fall. And before any of them could react, the bright light from the hallway spilled in and created an unmistakable outline around the gentleman standing there in the door's narrow frame.

"Well now," Mark Twain exclaimed to the four of them as he switched on the room's lights. "Looks like I've got myself a passel of young guests on my hands."

FIFTEEN

Sam

THE GREAT AUTHOR'S hair still had a touch of color, though by now most of his tangled mane was light gray and well on its way to white. The strands that still held the deep red of his youth were made lighter by the swirl of his cigar smoke. His eyes twinkled beneath the stray, meandering edges of his extremely bushy eyebrows.

"We're not gonna have any problems here, are we?" Twain asked as he casually wiggled what little was left of the cigar in his hand. "'Cause if we are," he added with zero concern, "I might just have to light myself up another one or two of these little devils. All things in moderation, of course . . . including moderation."

"No, sir," Jack said to him. "No problem at—"

Mattie cut in to try and help. "Yes, Mr. Twain," she assured him before quickly making a mess of things. "I mean, no, I mean . . . yes, there won't be any problem. We were only trying to . . . well . . . it's kind of a really long story."

Jack shot her a quick look.

"I'm very familiar with those, young lady." Twain puffed on his still-smoldering stub. "Though I tend to prefer short stories that lead to long conversations. Preferably with total strangers, which, correct me if I'm wrong, the four of you are. That's an ill we can easily remedy, I suspect."

He extended his hand to Jack, seemingly unconcerned that four such total strangers were standing in his private stateroom.

"Mark Twain," he introduced himself.

"Jack Babbitt, Mr. Twain, sir."

The two of them shook hands.

The smoke from Twain's cigar found its way into Ernie's nose. "Ernie . . ." he coughed and struggled as he and the great author shook hands as well. "Ernie Samuels, sir. It's an honor to meet you."

"Under the circumstances, I'm sure." Twain smiled as he turned to Mattie.

"Matilda McGillin, Mr. Twain, sir," she gave her name and then commenced with an out-of-the-blue, more-than-polite curtsy. "I've read everything you've written. *The Adventures of Tom Sawyer*, which, we kinda thought . . . well, never mind. *The Prince and the Pauper*. Oh, and there's the one about that frog in that one county. The . . . the . . ."

Mattie winced as she lost her train of thought. Until the great author kindly bailed her out.

"I think you might be referencing 'The Celebrated Jumping Frog of Calaveras County.' Not to worry, miss, you got further than most by just having read it." Twain chomped on his cigar before turning his attention to the last of the intruders. "And whom have we here?" he asked.

Chief? Dad? Mom? Gigi? Guess whose hand I'm about to shake?

None of these words came out, thankfully. Instead, Henry introduced himself with a reserved "Henry Babbitt, Mr. Twain."

The great writer didn't offer his hand right away, eyeing Henry closer than the rest. He tilted his head toward Jack and sent a glance his way. "You two brothers?" he asked.

"Oh, no, sir," Jack replied. "Just a coincidence."

"Ah," Twain said as he finally turned to shake hands with Henry. "Seems we have a healthy supply of those right now. Along with an unnecessary propensity to address me by the word 'sir.'"

He lowered the cigar into the brimming ashtray before adding, "The largest of these coincidences being the fact that apparently we've all been booked into this very same particular stateroom."

Twain pulled out a new cigar from his inner vest pocket and bit off the end.

"That is quite a coincidence, don't you agree?" he inquired of the room. "Unless, of course, there may be another story as to why the four of you are here?"

He spit out the tobacco stub, more than content to wait, but not without a dash of humor first. "Might as well tell the truth," he said with a wink. "I've long said that if you do that, you'll never have to remember anything."

Henry cleared his throat. "We, uh . . . well, we all came here from New York, Mr. Twain, sir," he said before remembering the legendary author's instructions. "I mean just . . . Mr. Twain."

"Much better." Twain nodded with approval, striking a match and lighting his next smoke. "Even though the proper stating of my name really represents just a start to whatever it is you're plannin' on sayin' to me. Oh, and please don't take offense to this, but how did a quartet of miscreants get all the way to Missouri from New York?" He took his first pull from the new cigar.

Mattie politely jumped in. "Well, Mr. Twain, we aren't really miscreants. We actually did kinda pay the boiler room workers once we got on board and, well, your door wasn't locked," she jabbered, "and we weren't planning to take anything anyway, as I'm sure you can tell, because we already would have, and then we heard footsteps, so . . . I guess that's maybe a long way of saying 'miscreants' might not be the best choice of words."

Ernie jabbed her in the side, but Twain had already allowed himself a hint of a wry grin.

"Miss McGillin, I do stand corrected," he said, cocking an appreciative eyebrow in her direction. "Even though I do pride myself on being a fairly adequate wordsmith." He paused again. "Still didn't answer my question, though. It'd be a shame if that turned into a habit."

The banjos on the main deck broke into a new song, the skilled players behind the quick-pickin' tune showing why they'd been invited as tonight's prime entertainment.

Down here, though, not surprisingly, it looked as if Mattie had barely noticed. "Have you ever heard of Mr. Skavenger's Hunt, Mr. Twain?" she asked him.

"Mr. Hunter S. Skavenger?" Twain inquired with a curious look. "Is that the Skavenger whom you're referencing, miss?"

"It is." She nodded. "We found a clue in New York a few days ago . . . and, well, it said the next clue might be here. Here on the *Natchez* riverboat."

For the first time since he'd walked into his room, Mark Twain looked speechless—something history books had taught Henry was a rare occurrence.

"One of Mr. Skavenger's clues? To his latest great hunt?" Twain said with an incredulous look. "In this room? My room? Ha! Ha, HAAA!" he laughed with disbelief.

Henry could see Mattie's lower lip quiver just a bit. He could tell the manner in which Twain laughed had made it all sound ridiculous, even though he probably didn't mean it that way.

Noticing Mattie's expression as well, the author shifted his tone in a hurry. "Ohhh, no, no, no. Okay, okay now." Twain raised his hands in apology. "Tell you what, darlin', you go right ahead and take a look at whatever you want in here. In fact, all four of you can. I'm as much a sucker for a great adventure as anyone."

He gave her a supportive, hopeful look, which seemed to settle her down a little. Jack and Ernie promptly began looking around the stateroom, while Henry turned back to the desk.

It's gotta be this. I mean, look at it. A first edition of Huck Finn? *Feels totally Skavenger-esque.*

Instead of immediately joining the search, Mattie showed Mr. Twain the beer glass from New York.

"This is why we came here, sir," she told him with gathering composure. "The clue we found. It's on the bottom. Go ahead, take a look."

Twain put on his reading glasses and held the empty glass aloft, studying it with a scrunched nose under an equally scrunched brow. It took all of maybe five seconds before his expression suddenly relaxed and he leaned back with a belly laugh.

"Natchez? Two fathoms deep? Ha HAAAAA! Well, I'll be." He shook his head and peered over his glasses toward her. "And trust me, this is good laughter, Miss McGillin. Maybe I should take a gander around this stateroom too!"

Mattie returned the smile and the two of them headed over to join Henry, who was still closely studying the unspoiled, new edition of *Huck Finn*.

Twain put an encouraging hand on the young hunter's shoulder and whispered right in his ear, "I think this is where I would've started too, had I not broken into—oh, wait, scratch that—I mean, had I not simply entered an unlocked room."

Twain made sure Mattie saw the wink he'd just sent her way as Henry quickly flipped to page thirty-six.

"Ohh, I like your thinkin' here, son." The great author seemed to understand what he had in mind. "I do, however, have a fairly strong working knowledge of this particular page, having pondered and scratched on it for more hours than I care to remember. Not sure where any of it might fit into Mr. Skavenger's latest quest."

Henry gave the page a look anyway.

Yeah, guess I do see your point.

There was no illustration on the page, only words that started with: "Well, I got a good going-over in the morning from old Miss Watson, on account of my clothes . . ."

Henry kept on reading until he reached the very last sentence on page thirty-six. Then he looked up with a sigh and without a turn of the page.

"Nothing," he declared with disappointment, fanning through the rest of the pages as Jack and Ernie joined them at the side of the desk.

"How 'bout you? Anything?" Mattie asked the two of them. Both shook their heads.

Twain put his remaining free hand on Mattie's shoulder, his teeth more than up to the task of holding the cigar.

"Tell you what," he told all four of them. "You've still got yourselves a good bit of time before we get back to dock. Riddle says you've got till midnight, so I'd keep on lookin', that's what I'd do. See if there might be another thirty-six somewhere else on board. Might want to be discreet, however, on the off chance you actually don't have passenger tickets."

"Nah, we don't," Jack admitted. "They let us hide out for a few hours in the boiler room and get cleaned up a little."

"Well, not to diminish their offer, but it mighta been even more neighborly if they'd let you clean up a little more," Twain replied as only Twain could. His nose crinkled, but his twinkling eyes told them he wasn't the least bit serious. He walked them to the door of the stateroom, his head wreathed in cigar smoke.

"If I think of anything, I'll head down to the boiler to find you," he promised. "And, if you'd like to just bandy an idea back and forth, I'll be right here. All right?"

"Thank you, Mr. Twain." Mattie was disappointed, but she held out her hand. "It was an honor for all of us to meet you."

"You as well, young miss," he replied, more than happy to take it. Each of the boys followed suit, before he closed the door with one last nod and a pleasant smile.

The foursome stood there and stared at the bronze 36 on the door. A wisp of white cigar smoke slowly rose to the corridor ceiling as a feeling of dejection began to settle over them.

"If we don't find anything before the night's over . . ." Ernie quietly said under his breath, not needing to finish the thought.

Henry could tell right away, though, he would have been better off not even starting the thought—with one person at least.

"Yeah, Ern, we know what happens if we don't find anything!" Jack shot back with a frustrated voice. "Thanks for reminding us."

"He didn't mean anything, Jack!" Mattie spoke up. "We're still gonna find it. It's on this boat somewhere, I know it is."

Jack now turned his anger squarely on her. "Before midnight? We're gonna find whatever it is we need to find before midnight?" He nearly spit out the words. "All right, let's do that, Mattie. Let's find the answer to this clue we traveled across how many states to find? Was it five? Six? Before midnight, remember. 'Cause y'know somethin'? What else do we have to do? What else do you, or any of the rest of us, have to do? 'Cept go back home and let everyone keep telling us we'll never amount to nuthin' more than a hill of beans."

Mattie didn't say anything for a second. Her lip quivered again, only this time it looked to be with boiling rage.

"Why would you say that, Jack?!" she started in. "Why would you say that about me, about you, about all of us?!"

"She's right, pal," Ernie said flatly. "You've got no . . ."

Mattie shoved Jack right in the chest. Hard.

"You think I don't know all that?" She went ahead and gave him a second rough push. "You think I don't know what happens if midnight comes and we end up finding nothing! Lemme tell you somethin', I know exactly what happens." Another shove, and then another, Jack patiently holding up his hands as he weathered the storm.

"We go BACK to BEING NOTHING, that's what! Nothing!" Mattie's voice broke as her eyes welled with tears of anger and failure. "We'll always be NOTHING!"

The last shove pushed Jack right into Henry, who barely budged because he'd yet to let his eyes stray from the front of Twain's stateroom door.

From the number thirty-six.

He'd overheard every word of Mattie's high tide of rage, but he hadn't responded because he was too busy figuring out what was bothering him.

Without even a word to any of them, he reached up and knocked.

It's in there. It can't be anywhere else.

"Henry?" Mattie asked as she brushed away an angry tear and fixed Jack with a brutally hard glare.

Henry knocked again, ignoring her for the moment.

Ernie spoke up from behind him. "What is it, pal? You forget somethin'?"

Before Henry could answer, the great author opened the stateroom door. A tumbler of whiskey had taken up residence in his hand next to the latest cigar.

"Back so soon, Mr. Babbitt?" Twain inquired.

Henry nodded and politely asked, "Mr. Twain. Sir. Would it be okay if I looked in your book again?"

Before the question was even finished, the sound of a fresh set of footsteps echoed from the closest set of stairs. Mattie, Jack, and Ernie snapped their heads around to look, but Henry's eyes remained fixed on the man standing in the doorway in front of him.

"I just need one minute, that's all. I promise," Henry said as the footsteps grew louder, somehow sounding more ominous than the banjo-seeking steps from earlier.

This time someone really was coming. Maybe Grace. Maybe Grace and the Dark Men. Whoever it was would be turning the far corner any second.

I don't care. I'm not leaving till I check one more time.

The footsteps stopped before making the turn. Whoever was there had decided to stay out of sight, and even Twain— standing just inside his room—could hear a match being scratched to life. He pulled the door open, quickly ushering all of them inside.

By the time he'd closed it, Henry was already over at the desk again. Twain had to hold back a chuckle as he and the others all surrounded him.

"Well, son," Mr. Twain said, resting both palms on the desk as Henry whipped through the pages again. "I respect a dramatic moment as much as the next man, but good Lord in Heaven, what should I be lookin' for here?"

Something, something, something. Here on thirty—

Henry stopped on the thirty-sixth page, just as he had minutes earlier. And just as he'd seen the first time around, the
thirty-sixth page was the very first page of chapter three.

Okay, start over again. Take your time.

"'Well,'" Henry read aloud to everyone. "'I got a good
going-over in the morning from Old Miss Watson.'"

His voice fell silent as he stopped, his eyes darting back and
forth, searching through each sentence. "It's here, I saw it, I
know I did," he said out loud, shaking his head.

"Saw what?" Mattie asked him.

Henry didn't answer. Instead he was reading each
word his finger was now tracking. Left-to-right-and-down.
Left-to-right-and-down.

*Okay, Chief, little help here. What should I be looking for?
What would you be looking for?*

His eyes went back to Twain's words again.

"Good going-over. Miss Watson." *Nope, not it. Not there.*
"'Then Miss Watson she took me in the closet and prayed, but
nothing come of it.'" *Okay, that's prob'ly nothing. It was right
around this spot, though. Come on, keep going.* "'She told me
to pray every day and whatever I asked for . . .'" *Wait. Wait,
hold on.* "'Whatever I asked for . . . I would get it,'" Henry
whispered under his breath, his eyes sparking as he repeated
the words again—though not as quietly this time. "'Whatever
I asked for . . . I would . . . get it.'"

Henry turned his head and saw a twinkle in the great author's eyes, matched only by the spark in Mattie's as she stood
next to him.

"It can't be that easy," he said to her, then glanced up at the
man who wrote the words. "Can it?"

"Go ahead, Henry! Go on!" Mattie nodded. Ernie and Jack
did the same right behind her. He looked back at the book,

double-checking to be completely certain before clearing his throat.

"Mr. Twain," he asked, hoping his wording was correct. "Do you have the next clue in Mr. Skavenger's Hunt? And if you do, may we please have it?"

Respecting a dramatic moment as much as the next man, Mark Twain slowly put down his cigar, paused for a good many seconds, then reached into his pocket . . .

. . . and pulled out a brilliant yellow envelope. Which he then handed to Henry.

"I do. And you may," the great author replied with a proud smile.

The four young searchers gazed at the envelope. Twain used the moment to retrieve his still-smoldering cigar.

"I was getting a tad concerned you'd overlooked the words that were right there in front of you." He chuckled. "Words I had written specifically to help my good friend, Mr. Hunter S. Skavenger."

The quartet of hunters stood there in front of him, stunned into momentary silence. Well, most of them anyway.

"You know Skavenger?" Henry asked.

"For as many years as I've tried to quit smokin'," he replied, "which is more than a few now. When I gave him my first manuscript of this here book, he asked if I'd be open to the possibility of conspiring on his upcoming quest. As you might imagine, I was more than happy to say yes."

Henry looked at the envelope. He dipped his finger into the upper fold to open it—

"No, no, no! Not yet!" Twain stopped him. "That's for you and the four other owners of these envelopes to do on your own. I'm not supposed to watch anyone open it either. Rules being rules. I usually say life's short, break the rules, but I did make a promise to ol' Hunter boy."

The declaration that *four* other yellow envelopes had already been given out caught Henry's attention, along with one other person in the room.

"What do you mean? Four other owners?" Jack wanted to know.

Skavenger's good friend smiled. "You don't understand, do you?" he asked. Nor would they, apparently, until such time as he was done relighting his struggling cigar. Once he was apparently satisfied in that regard, he nodded toward the envelope.

"There are five of those," Twain carefully intoned. "Five and only five. Which means there are *only* five of you who now have the chance to do what no one's been able to do these past two years."

He paused to spit out a stray speck of tobacco, before uttering the astounding words: "To solve Skavenger's great mystery."

Henry couldn't speak. None of them could. Aside from Jack once again.

"And this is the last one? The last one to be claimed?" He peeled his eyes from the yellow, almost-glowing, envelope— obviously thinking about what Grace had mentioned just that morning. That Doubt was already heading toward where he knew the next clue would be found.

Twain looked as if he knew the question would be coming.

With a half nod and a slow blink, he answered, "Yes, son, and that's all I can say. Though I am also instructed to give you this, which I urge you to handle with exceptional care."

Twain handed Jack a much different envelope. "Enough money for the four of you to go wherever you decide to go, which the other four envelope holders have received as well." Jack inspected the envelope reverently. "Do choose carefully, though. Hunter tells me if you make a mistake on this particular riddle, good chance it'll spell the end of the road."

The great author then looked at Mattie once more. "Oh, and Miss McGillin?" he added. "Congratulations on finding one of only ten clean glasses at the Jennings Establishment, placed there by Mr. Skavenger himself that night. Hence the lack of traffic here on the *Natchez*."

Twain now found himself looking at four equally stunned faces as he reached for a pen and flipped the pages of his novel back to the very front. He scribbled a message, then placed his pen in a nearby inkwell and gently slid the book to Henry. The twelve-year-old looked down at the inscription in awe:

To Henry—Good luck as your adventures continue! Your friend, Mark Twain

"Hope you like it." Twain shrugged, before adding with a note of sadness, "The critics have been vicious with this one, but I always feel the public's the only critic whose opinion's worth anything."

"The public will love it," Henry tried reassuring him. "Readers'll be reading it forever."

"From your lips to God's ears, son," Twain replied with a smile. "We need more readers out there. That's the other thing I sometimes say: the man who doesn't read has no advantage over the man who can't."

Bearing the gruff, curmudgeonly look Henry had seen in countless history books, Twain ushered them out for a second time, earnestly wishing the young hunters the very best of luck.

The door had barely closed before Henry began to open the envelope, only to be stopped by Jack's hand thumping hard onto his shoulder. This time, though, it wasn't to grab him by the collar. No, this time it was for something much different.

"You did good, Babbitt." Jack smiled at him. "The smarter Babbitt of the two, I mean."

It was as deep as he'd ever dipped into what Henry knew was a shallow well of compliments. Jack then followed with a burst of startlingly loud laughter.

"Did you hear what he said in there?! Did you?!" He leaned his head back and yelled at the ceiling, "Five envelopes! ONLY FIVE! WooooooHOOOO! We could win this entire hu—"

"Jack, Jack, Jack, no, no, no," Ernie tried to calm him, even though he looked just as excited himself. "We don't need anybody hearin' usssssss, like our friend Grace. We gotta get outta here!"

"Ernie's right," Mattie said, trying to subdue her joyful laugh as well. "I think we should open it in the boiler room. Better yet, when we get off at the dock. But for now . . ."

She suddenly wrapped her arms around Henry in a bear hug.

"Henry, you did it!" Mattie yelled with delight as she squeezed him tightly—long enough, thankfully, that she didn't see him blush.

"Yeah, yeah, beautiful." Ernie exhaled, clearly worried he'd never be able to herd them downstairs. "Can we get outta here before the Dark Men start collecting yellow envelopes? In case they already don't have one of their own?"

"Yes, good idea." Mattie broke away from Henry, just as they heard the lead banjo player up top announce:

"ON BEHALF OF THE FINE CREW OF THE RIV-ERBOAT *NATCHEZ*, THANK YOU ALL! AND MAY YOU CONTINUE TO HAVE AN EXCEPTIONAL NIGHT!"

The steady slap of the giant rear paddles slowed, signaling their imminent arrival dockside. The riverboat's steam horn gave a piercing blast, which may as well have been heralding the foursome's triumphant discovery to one and all.

Jack, Ernie, and Mattie broke into a run down the hallway. But Henry stayed behind, still marveling at what he held between his two hands.

"And sometimes . . ." a familiar voice suddenly echoed in his head.

"Henry?" Mattie turned and walked back to him. Ernie and Jack followed. "Henry, come on, we need to get off the boat," she reminded him with an urgent tone in her voice.

But Henry was too busy listening to his father again— hearing the words that had come back to him on more than one occasion during the hunt.

"And sometimes," the voice continued, *"if we don't act upon it right now, in this very minute, it'll be too late. Always remember that, son . . . all right? Never let an extraordinary moment wait."*

Henry slipped a finger beneath the envelope's flap. "I'm gonna open it now," he said with a tone that told them not to argue.

"You sure?" Jack looked over his shoulder, making certain no one was coming. Hearing the envelope getting torn open made him turn right back around. Four sets of anxious eyes watched as Henry gently removed a delicate, small slip of paper. The feather-light parchment was almost gold on the edges, with graceful black lettering.

The nature of the lettering, however, instantly drew a sigh of disappointment from Mattie.

"Oh no," she said, scratching her forehead. "This'll slow us down a little."

Ernie had taken out his notepad, but didn't even bother taking notes after seeing the first few words:

Une vision très haute à l'œil, complètement et impressionnant en tant que tout continent ou toute mer.

Trouvez-moi sur un voyage de neuf jours. Paris. New York. Le visionnaire et la vision.

"Anybody know anyone who can speak French?" Jack asked them.

"Oui." Henry beamed. "I know a little. Actually, more than a little."

Actually, more like a lot. You want Français? *I can give you* beaucoup de Français*!*

The time he'd spent inside the school library while the rest of his classmates were at recess had been devoted to the language. His mother had insisted. No recess—for safety reasons, of course—and plenty of French. While Henry had grumbled to his mom about the extra classes then, right now he was glad he'd taken them.

"What does it say?!" the three other kids asked him in anxious harmony.

Henry frowned slightly, recognizing this wasn't basic French. He'd always had better luck, though, when he slowed down and read the words deliberately; something that wouldn't be easy to do at this moment, with his three friends watching. Anticipation and all.

"A towering vision . . . to the eye," he haltingly translated. "Full and . . . full and . . ."

He let out a frustrated breath and stopped, unsure, seeing that Ernie was now writing down each of his words. He tried again.

"Full and . . . IMPRESSIVE, that's it. I mean, that's the word in the clue, not the clue itself. Ernie, got it?"

"Got it."

Henry dug back in. "Full and impressive as any . . . as any . . . as any continent or sea! Now we're talkin'!"

"Well, you are," Jack noted. "The three of us are just listening. Oh, and can we get outta this hallway? Somebody's bound to turn one of these corners any minute now."

They ducked into an alcove where they wouldn't be seen, Henry studying the clue as the others dragged him in.

The rest of the passage proved easier. "Find me on a nine-day journey. Paris. New York," Henry said and then looked up. "The visionary and the vision."

A trio of blank faces looked back at him.

"Find who?" Mattie scrunched her forehead again as she asked. "The vision? Or the visionary? I don't understand. Are we supposed to go back to New York or go to Paris?"

"Oh. Paris. That'll be easy," Ernie scoffed. "That'll be a cinch for four ragamuffins like us. How are we supposed to do that?"

"I think he wants us to find both," Henry ventured. "Not both New York and Paris, but both the vision *and* the visionary."

"Yeah, well, if it's Paris, how long does that trip even take?" Jack already sounded worried.

"A few years ago it took months," Mattie told him. "Now it's only a week, maybe a little longer, but not much."

"Twain's right. If we go to Paris, we better be really right," Jack shot back. "If we're wrong, we lose."

Henry went back to the start of the message again, just as the steam whistle on the *Natchez* sounded with three short pops. A deep-voiced porter shouted out instructions for disembarkment, even though a good number of passengers would be staying on board—not to mention coming downstairs to their staterooms.

Henry shook his head, eyes moving from left to right over the now familiar French text.

This one might not be easy.

"It's a towering vision," he decided to move ahead a few words. "They've got towering things in both New York and Paris, with visionaries who made 'em happen."

"Okay, so?" Jack was now pacing in the dimly lit alcove—or rather, *still* pacing.

"What's the tallest building in New York right now?" Henry asked. "It's prob'ly the Empire State Building, right?"

"The Empire *what?*" Mattie responded, just as the whistle sounded again up top, long and steady this time.

Great. The Empire State Building doesn't even exist yet.

"I know Mr. Pulitzer's been writin' in all his papers about building something," Ernie tried to help. "Says it'll be the highest building in the whole city once it's done. Twenty stories!"

It can't be New York, Henry decided—though he was just as puzzled as the rest of them.

It's gotta be France. Has to be. A vision that's full and impressive.

"Hold on a minute." He held up a hand, his eyes darting back to the first words of the clue.

A towering vision. A towering vision to the eye. Full and . . .

His pendulum-swinging eyes slammed to a stop.

"A towering vision to the eye, full . . ." He spoke the words out loud, but so softly that they hadn't heard any of it.

"What did you say, Henry?" Mattie asked.

"Tower," he repeated, now with a steadily growing smile. "Eye. Full."

One of the big E's! Riggins would love this. Einstein, Edison, and . . .

The rest of the clue—everything—tumbled into place. The vision *and* the visionary.

The vision had been constructed long before the Empire State Building or even Mr. Pulitzer's future twenty-story behemoth back in New York.

And the visionary was now a complete no-brainer.

He smiled and looked up.

"We're going to Paris," Henry told them with confidence. "Let's get off this boat, we've got a bigger one to catch."

SIXTEEN

A Journey to Le Havre

AH-AHHH . . . CHOOO!

Henry sniffled and wiped his nose—again. He lay back onto his cot, having picked up a more-than-determined cold during their nine-day cross-Atlantic journey to France. He even went ahead and pinched the top of his nose to make sure the next sneeze in line didn't get any ideas.

Fortunately, it was already the evening of day eight, and Henry was appreciating the fact that the rain had finally subsided.

Most of the trip on the SS *Persévérance* had been miserable. Besides Henry's cold, the quarters were cramped, Ernie had been struggling with seasickness, and the near-constant rain made everything feel damp. The only thing all of them kept very much in mind was that there was just one more day to Le Havre. The front door to Paris.

The tickets they'd bought a week and a half ago were for down in the very cheapest part of the ship, where satin sheets

definitely were not included. What they each got was a saggy
cot and a thin, holey blanket.

What they also got was an uncle.

Uncle Seymour, to be exact.

Even in 1885, Henry had learned, four young ragamuffins
couldn't exactly just cross the Atlantic together. That was the
bad news. The *good* news was that they didn't need passports
or anything else that might have slowed things down. All they
needed was a tidy little sum of money and a willing traveler
from Pennsylvania named Seymour Simonton to help get them
on board.

They'd found Uncle Seymour on the dock, waiting to take
the trip to France himself. Once the friendly transaction was
finished, he'd told the ship purser that the five of them were
family, and just like that, they were on board, heading down to
"entrepont," never to see their beloved uncle again.

"Entrepont" was what the French passengers called the
"lowest of the low quarters," which was where Henry had been
for the past hour, hoping to speed up the remainder of the trip
by getting some sleep.

He wasn't having much luck, though.

Ever since that late Christmas Eve or early Christmas Day,
just the thought of "time" had typically prompted him to reach
into his pocket for the old piece of ledger paper. He pulled it
out just now without thinking twice about it.

Skavenger's written words were still inscribed right there up
top, just as they had been from the first day.

TO WHOEVER HAS FOUND THIS PAGE FROM MY
LEDGER: FIND ME. THERE IS A WAY BACK. OR
FORWARD. BUT KNOW THIS TOO—WHEN THE FINAL
EMPTY BOX OF THIS SHEET IS FULL, SO ENDS
YOUR ADVENTURE. WHATEVER THE DATE AND

LOCATION, THERE YOU WILL STAY. FOREVER.
SINCERELY, HUNTER S. SKAVENGER.

Henry turned over the front side of the ledger page, only to find there were just nine empty boxes left on the back.

Nine. That was it.

Now a keen student of what might persuade the ghostly lettering to steal another ledger box away from him, Henry was certain of one thing.

They had to win the hunt in Paris. If they didn't, he would never get back home.

Henry figured they had, at most, one week left. One week to meet Skavenger face-to-face before the ledger page would be full and he'd be stuck in 1885 forever, haunted by the unthinkable pain his disappearance had brought to those he loved most.

"You awake, Babbitt?" he heard from the bunk across from him.

Jack had his hands folded behind his head as he stared at the bottom of the bunk just above him. That's where Ernie was, apparently able to sleep from the sound of his snoring.

Mattie was probably outside, Henry guessed. She'd been hesitant to wander the ship at first, informing all of them that she'd never really learned how to swim, but after that many days breathing the stale air in *entrepont*, she'd decided a stroll on the deck was worth the risk.

"Babbitt?"

"Yep, I'm awake," Henry finally answered.

"You weren't sleeping, were you?"

"Nah, I don't think so. Maybe a little."

"Me too," Jack said, then waited a few more seconds before continuing. "So I've been thinkin' about things a little bit. What do you think happens if we get over there and we solve this next clue? We're one of only five, Babbitt. Five envelopes. What happens if we win this?"

Henry folded the ledger page and tucked it back in his pocket. "I don't know," he replied. "What about you? What do you think happens?"

"I don't know either," Jack answered, still keeping lazy watch on the low-hanging bunk springs above him.

Neither said anything for a while. Henry was content to listen to the sloshing sound against the dank green walls that separated him from a bazillion gallons of seawater.

It was strangely calming, actually. On the rare occasions when he'd strung together more than four or five hours of sleep, it was because he'd been soothed by the sound of the ocean.

"You still worried about us seein' Doubt's men again?" Jack's sudden switch of subjects guaranteed that four or five hours would be a long shot tonight.

"Every minute I'm here," Henry replied, somewhat embarrassed by the admission. He crossed his arms to hold off the shiver he knew would probably follow.

The SS *Persévérance* had a large and low belly—low enough that Henry felt he might be able to hide from Doubt's men in the hold if he saw them on board. Each passing day, though, had convinced him that the baleful apparitions probably weren't on board. They were likely on another ship somewhere ahead of them, maybe already in Paris. Mattie had told him she felt the same way, which explained why she'd gone up to the main deck four nights in a row.

Henry looked over to see if Jack had noticed the unsettled look on his face. Seemed as if he hadn't, his eyes still gazing upward.

"Aw, to hell with those ghouls," Jack muttered under his breath. "You and me? We'll knock 'em around good if we see 'em, ain't that right, Babbitt? We're gonna win this thing!"

"I hope so," Henry replied, sniffling his nose unconvincingly. *Got a ton ridin' on that, Great-Great-Grandfather. And only nine ledger boxes left to do it in.*

Jack finally turned his head to look at him. "I'm serious," he said. "And it ain't because of the money. That's the last reason I'm doing all this. I don't care how incalculable Skavenger's reward is."

Henry pushed himself up on his elbows, suddenly curious.

"Why are you doin' it then?" he asked, a set of thumping waves outside keeping the answer at bay for the moment. Jack waited until the eastern Atlantic decided to take a break.

"Know how many people in my life have told me what I can't do, Babbitt?" Jack's voice trailed off for a second. "Not what I *can* do. What I *can't*. Happens every day of my life."

He spun around in a single motion and put his feet on the floor, leaning forward to make certain Henry heard what he had to say next.

"I mean, sure, I know I've gotten myself into a little trouble a few times. And I know there's a chance I'm not goin' anywhere in life, but the fact is, it's a nuthin' chance, ya ask me! I'm gonna *make* my own chance!" Jack nodded and pursed his lips. "I'm smart, I can do stuff. You've seen it!"

"I have seen it." Henry sat up and put his feet on the floor as well, making sure Jack knew he was listening. "Might have felt it a couple times too, the way you grabbed my collar and all."

Jack looked as if he might grab it again, until his old familiar grin broke through. "Wiseass," he said.

Henry smiled, but didn't say a word.

"It's like you, Babbitt, right?" Jack continued. "You couldn't even walk through Vanderbilt's front door, and guess what? Ya did. Went to Jennings and you stood your ground with those two brothers. Till they had you thrown out, anyway. Point is, we're doin' pretty good, yeah?"

Henry nodded, more of a half nod, actually. The words caught him by surprise, especially considering the source.

Of all people, Jack really thinks I'm gettin' somewhere . . . Wow.

"I want the same thing you do, pal." Jack looked Henry straight in the eye. "Someone to say I did good, that I'm just as good as everybody else. I don't want anybody to *give* me nothing, to hell with that. That's for all those losers still back at the Dakota, right? Right?" With a devilish grin, he reached across and slapped his great-great-grandson's knee.

"Right," Henry answered. The two of them laughed quietly, but a laugh nonetheless.

Jack stood and snapped his suspenders. Then, as he had done more than a few times during their Atlantic crossing, he loudly announced to anyone who might care to hear, "I'm gonna go see if there's a line at the head. Back in a minute."

But before he could go too far—

"Hey, Jack?" Henry stopped him.

"Yeah?"

"Thanks for saying what you did. About me doing good. It's just that . . . ever since my father, y'know . . ."

Jack came back and sat down on Henry's bunk, right next to him. The twelve-year-old wondered if maybe he shouldn't have brought it up, until his great-great-grandfather spoke again a second later.

"Yeah. I do know," Jack assured him. "Okay? You don't have to say another word. Not about what happened, not about anything. Not unless ya want to."

Henry wanted to. At least a little.

"I mean, I wasn't there when it happened. I just heard how bad it was." He tapped his forehead. "Doesn't mean I haven't seen it up here, though. I . . . I don't think I can even remember what it feels like anymore. Me not bein' . . . well . . ."

He held back saying the last word. Not wanting to. Not needing to say anything from the look aimed his way.

"Here's the secret, pal," Jack said with an affable smirk. "And I'm talkin' to you here, all right?"

Henry nodded.

"Bad things happen sometimes, and there ain't nuthin' you can do about it." He raised his eyebrows to make his point. "And if ya come through it okay? What reason do ya still got to be afraid of anything?"

Huh. Never thought about it that way. Almost . . .

"Step by step? That's what you're sayin'?" Henry asked.

"Long as you're still takin' steps, that's my motto." Jack winked as he stood back up, snapping one suspender and then the other.

"So . . . Lah Toooooor Eiffel, huh?" he asked, apparently ready to switch subjects. "That's what the French call this towering vision thing of yours? Sure must be somethin' to see."

"That's what I hear." Henry nodded. "We're gonna see it firsthand soon enough."

Jack shook his head at the thought, then trundled off to take care of business with an appropriate, "*Oui, oui, oui!* Weee sure as heck will! And speaking of weeeeee."

Henry smiled and quietly laughed, deciding that with Jack now wandering off to relieve himself, and Ernie snoring through his seasickness, it was a good time to slip up to the main deck to find Mattie. He wiped his nose again, and headed on up—which was always kind of an obstacle course. The ceilings were barely six feet from the floor and the hallways were as narrow as a tiny closet, which made passing anyone an interesting dance. Not to mention the occasional overhead pipes threatening to rap anyone over five foot seven right in the head—which meant it was no problem for Mattie.

She'd become fast friends with a young family of four from Marseilles, who now served as the usual reason for her to wander away from the stale air of the *entrepont*.

She barely knew a word of French, but it hadn't mattered in the least. Mattie had a way with everyone, whether it was a nine-year-old girl from a far corner of France, a porter on a train to St. Louis . . . or Henry.

The steel stairs connecting the lower decks to the main level could be tricky when wet, he'd already learned from an unfortunate slip or two. They were dry tonight, though, and with a good chunk of the moon visible, going up the stairs was turning out to be problem free.

What was it Jack said? "Long as I'm still takin' steps"?

Once on the top deck, he walked along the starboard right-side railing toward the spot where he usually found Mattie. Typically, she liked to sit against the ship's very tallest smokestack, pointing out the stars to her new young friend Isabelle, who was all of seven years old.

The girls weren't there tonight, though. On a ship that was more than five hundred feet long and carrying thirteen hundred passengers, he knew they could be anywhere.

Henry moved to the railing to peer at the splashing waves below. The swells broke against the ship's hull, creating an enormous explosion of white foam and sea spray.

Just the sight of it was enough to bring a small smile to his face. Not only because it was spectacular, but because of where he was at that moment. What he was doing.

You're on a real steamship! Crossing the Atlantic Ocean, headed for France! Check this out, Mom . . . you hold on to the rail tight . . . you lean out . . . annnnnnd . . . all good! Noooooo worries.

"Be careful, young man," a menacing voice uttered from behind him, and Henry's knees buckled as he whipped around.

No.

No, no, no!

It was Grace.

The Dark Man.

Standing two feet away, close enough he could have thrown Henry over the rail without anyone ever knowing who'd done it. The man's sunken blue eyes glinted coldly.

"I told you I'd be ssseeing you again . . . soooooon." Grace raised a slender finger and pointed it threateningly as he moved closer still. "Tonight, though, is your lucky night, young man . . . for I actually have *nothing* to tell you. Nothing at all. Though ssssssomeone else does."

Tap . . .

Tap . . .

Tap . . .

Henry knew in a horrifying instant what was making the sound and who was behind it. He knew because he'd heard it before.

It was a cane. A cane coming up the same metal stairwell he'd scaled only a moment ago, prompting his heart to skip a beat.

The cold hand just above the wolf's head and its gold teeth was the first thing to come into view, with the worst most certainly yet to follow.

Tap . . .

Tap . . .

Tap . . .

Hiram Doubt's terrible gray eyes slowly came into view. The thin scar running the path of a teardrop down his cheek. The scraggly, almost silver eyebrows that Henry hadn't come close to forgetting.

Skavenger's bitter rival stopped for a moment after reaching the dry, but scuffed, surface of the main deck. He ran the tip of his black dress shoe over the still-rain-swollen wooden floor, as if wanting to make sure he wouldn't get a speck of dirt or water on it.

"Only one . . . more . . . day," Doubt finally said as he strolled toward Henry, moving slightly closer than Grace. "One more day until Paris. I'm guessing you'd forgotten about me, yes?"

Yes. No! But . . .

Henry looked ready to run, but the Dark Man's hand shot out fast as a snake, tightly grabbing hold of his collar.

"Ah-ah-ah." Doubt shook his head. "Not before you and I have an important conversation, one that wasn't necessary on the train to St. Louis . . . but is now."

Jack's words of encouragement now felt like a distant memory to Henry.

Somebody. Somebody, anybody, help!

But there was no one anywhere. Not just then, at least. Not in the isolated spot where Henry had mistakenly decided to watch the waves. It was just the three of them. And just as he'd done on the far side of the Vanderbilt Mansion, Doubt slowly raised his cane and let the teeth of the wolf's head softly land on Henry's nose.

"Now," Doubt said with both calm and yet terrifying eyes. "I have, shall we say, a problem. A problem I did not anticipate having, but one that *you* might be able to help me with."

Henry, now nearly choking with fear, looked from side to side for someone who might have just walked on deck. Hopefully. Anyone.

Doubt moved the wolf's head over to Henry's cheek and gently nudged it back so that he was looking at him, and him alone.

"Much better, thank you. As I was about to say," he said with a chilling smile, "I have a confession that is, well, difficult for me to make. Ever since I asked Mark Twain to give me the

clue that you now have as well, I've been . . . struggling somewhat with the answer. Aside from Paris, of course. So . . ."

No, no, no. Don't—

Grace tightened his grip on Henry's collar.

Doubt pulled back the head of his silver cane, then again
tapped it gently on the young boy's nose with each word
that followed.

"What. Do. You. Know?"

The gloomy-eyed man uttered the words with a low voice,
his cold gray eyes demanding an immediate reply.

Henry stammered, "I, what—"

"No *I*, no *what*," Doubt interrupted. "You must have *some*
thought, yes? A thought that convinced the four of you to
board a ship bound all this way for France?"

I'm gonna have to say something! He won't let me, I can't . . .

Henry's head was racing senselessly. "We don't," he tried to
get the words out, "I mean, we're not sure—"

"Stop," Doubt cut him off, his jaw now tightening with
simmering anger. "I asked you once, I will ask you only once
more. What is it you expect to find in Paris?"

A young Frenchman passed by, spotting the three of them
as he turned his head. *"Est-ce que tout est correct?"* The man
wore a worried look as he asked if everything was okay.

"Tout est très bien. Retournez vers le bas ci-dessous," replied
Doubt. The cold look he delivered to the young Frenchman
persuaded him to wheel around and run away.

Thump thump thump thump—gone.

Doubt turned his hard gaze back to Henry. "Well?" he
asked him.

"We don't . . . I . . . we . . . we don't know yet!"

Grace tightened his grip on Henry's collar and lifted him
into the air, dangerously close to the railing's highest bar, completely unconcerned with the young man's efforts to wriggle free.

SAY SOMETHING. HE KNOWS THE CLUE. SAY SOMETHING ABOUT THE CLUE!

"We need to find the visionary," Henry finally managed to gulp out. "We're pretty sure he's in Paris."

For the shortest of moments, Hiram Doubt looked . . . disappointed.

"No, no, nooooooo," he said, shaking his head. "I already know all of that. Tell me what else you know. Tell me everything you know. *Who* you believe the visionary is. *What* the vision is."

Barely able to take a breath, his feet still inches off the deck, Henry somehow mustered the nerve to simply say . . .

"We don't know yet, I promise! They got a lot of visionaries in France. The only thing we're sure of is that it doesn't make sense for Skavenger to bring the hunt back to New York yet."

Please believe it. Please, please.

Doubt waited to see if Henry might choose to say anything more. Waited until he looked convinced that he wouldn't.

"Brave boy," he said menacingly, motioning for Grace to lower him back down. "Brave, but foolish . . . and very, very impractical. I think you know very well who the visionary is, as do I. I suspect it is the vision that confuses you . . . as it does me."

Henry's feet finally touched the deck again. He could feel the heat coming off Grace's threatening breath.

Doubt softly rested his wolf-headed cane against his own shoulder. "We will be watching you and your friends every minute of every day," he warned in a deadly whisper. "As we have been ever since you boarded this ship. And should the vision somehow become clear to you? I strongly urge you to let me know."

He let the cane slide through his hand, strangling the wolf's head as he grasped it at the neck.

"Safe travels, young adventurer," the shadowy man said as he and Grace turned to disappear into the darkness. "Or as they say where we're going: *Voyage securise.*"

But the only thing Henry heard was . . .

Tap . . .

Tap . . .

Tap . . .

Tap . . .

Like nails being hammered into the lid of a coffin.

SEVENTEEN

Vision

"BONJOUR, JEUNE MONSIEUR Henri! Bienvenue vers la France!"

Juliet Bonnet extended her hand and Henry politely shook it—the young, smiling Parisian having already greeted the two other boys and Mattie. Apparently she'd also dismissed with the notion of calling Mattie anything but "Matilda," and her extreme accent placed a humorous emphasis on the middle syllable.

"So, Mateelda," she promptly asked after introductions were finished. "You are friends of Monsieur Tasse and his family, *oui?*"

"Oui," Mattie replied with a firm nod. Monsieur Tasse was the father of the young girl she'd befriended on SS *Persévérance*. Not only that, it had turned out that Isabelle and her family weren't exactly strangers to money. The Tasses, in fact, were loaded.

And so, before the family's tearful departure to the humble Tasse Estate, Isabelle's father had insisted upon purchasing four train tickets to Paris for the young hunters. He had also introduced them to the family acquaintance now standing right in front of them, who, as it turned out, had been on the same voyage they'd all just completed.

"Well," Juliet announced with a gracious tip of her head, "our train does not leave for Paris until tomorrow. So we, the five of us, will celebrate our arrival in Le Havre tonight, if that's acceptable with all of you, *oui*?"

"*Oui!*" Mattie clapped her hands, gleefully accepting the invitation no matter what any of the others might have said.

Henry had quickly noticed that Juliet had more than a passing command of the English language. Each word was spoken perfectly, aside from the occasional artistic flair with things like "Mateelda." She was certainly more bilingual than Jack and Ernie, whose noble efforts to speak French were interesting to say the least.

"Um, yes, *oui*. We would," Jack said haltingly. "I mean 'we' the way we'd spell it, not your '*oui*,' the one that means yes."

"I think Jack means it'd be great to celebrate," Ernie chimed in. "Especially with you, Mizz Bonnet."

Juliet was at least twenty-five, but Henry could see that Ernie was smitten. He had been from the minute the stunningly beautiful French woman—straight blond hair cascading from her Paris-gray beret—had reached for his hand. She had unknowingly completely sealed the deal with a wink that only managed to heighten Ernie's infatuation.

"And you, Henri?" Juliet asked, pronouncing his name "Awnray." "I'm quite certain you would welcome a good French meal and, perhaps, not that I'm being accusatory of course, a bath and fresh clothes? My friend Marguerite's apartment is not far from here."

Henry, however, had missed a good part of the question. He was too busy scanning the milling crowd for Doubt, Grace, or any of the other Dark Men.

The night before, Henry had tossed around in his cot without a second of sleep. He'd decided it wouldn't serve much purpose to tell the others of his encounter on the deck of the ship. They'd already been keeping an eye out for Doubt and his men—ever since the cavern-of-boxes affair on the train. Better to have them focused on the job at hand.

"Henri?" Juliet asked again. Ernie jabbed him in the ribs.

"Hey, Awnray," he chided. "Juliet wants to know if you want a bath before we celebrate."

"Hmm? Oh." Henry finally looked over. *"Merci, ce serait merveilleux,"* he replied with a smile.

"AH HAAAA! Really?!" Now it was Juliet's turn to clasp her hands in surprise. "Well, in that case, Henri Babbeet, *laissez la soirée de la célébration commencer!"*

"What did she say?" Ernie whispered to him.

"She said we should let the celebration begin," Henry whispered back. "Least I'm pretty sure that's what she said."

"You should be very sure, Henri." She motioned for them to follow her as she walked along the concrete landing of the massive port. "Your French is excellent for a young American; better than a good many Frenchmen, I might add."

"You're from Paris, Juliet?" Mattie cheerfully asked as they weaved their way through the just-arriving throng.

"Actually, Mateelda, I am from Montmartre." Juliet seemed to glide through the crowd, sidestepping suitcases and trunks. "It's where artists live. Music like you would not believe. And dancing?" She kissed her fingertips and sprung them open with a smacking *MmmmmmmWAH!*

She turned around as she walked, almost dancing. "What do you say, Ernie? Shall you and I dance tonight? No, I should call you Ernest, shouldn't I?"

"Ernest is good." He blushed. "I like Ernest."

Henry thought Ernie would have liked being called "Monsieur Stupide" at that point, long as the words were coming from Juliet.

"And what do you do, Juliet? In Montmar—*OW!*" Mattie bumped her hip into a stray trunk, thanks to Ernie paying no attention to anyone other than Miss Bonnet.

"In Montmartre?" Juliet threw her hands out. "I am one of the artists. Mainly sculpture. Baroque. Expressionism."

"Sounds great!" The words had come from Ernest . . . again, of course.

Jack rolled his eyes. "Is the train station right around here somewhere?" he finally got around to asking. "We don't want to miss it in the morning."

"Ah *merci*, Jack," Juliet assured him. "The only thing you are going to miss is France, after your return to America. It is a shame you cannot stay longer. There is so, so much to see!"

One thing in particular, Henry reminded himself.

A vision.

⌘

And so, once the four of them were cleaned up, Juliet and her friend Marguerite took them to the cobblestoned commons for their promised celebration. It was a bustling spot, closer to the train station than the luggage-littered docks. Accordion music and bistro tables surrounded dozens of couples slowly dancing. The entire area was illuminated by the soft light of French hall lanterns.

Juliet sat at the head of their table, holding a container of just-purchased wine. She cast a look toward Henry. "Awnray?" she asked. "Where did you learn to speak French the way you do?"

"My grandmother was French," he replied courteously and carefully. "She died a few years ago."

"Oh." Juliet's smile dropped to a frown. "And where in France was she from?" she asked.

"A town called Fontainebleau," he answered, hoping it had existed in 1885. "I think that's what it was called."

"Fontainebleau?" she declared with disbelief. "I have family in Fontainebleau! As we speak!"

Henry could see Jack shift uncomfortably. He was itching to get to the train station and would have absolutely taken an evening Paris-bound train had there been one. Juliet, to her credit, had promised more than once to get them to the station first thing in the morning.

"Jack, Jack, Jack, I want you to relax, *oui*?" she reassured him for the fourteenth time. "You are far too nervous about missing your train. And besides, I have another form of French art to show you."

She pushed the rustic wine container out into the middle of the table.

"My country's finest invention," Juliet announced with immense pride, "though you can only have a little. For many of you this may be your very first sip, I imagine?"

"Not me," Ernie piped up. "I've had vino plenty of times."

Jack snorted softly.

Mattie looked out of the corner of her eyes toward Henry, before informing Juliet with a somewhat sheepish voice, "You're right. I've . . . never really had any before."

Juliet clucked her tongue. "Oh, Mateelda, you are in for a treat." She pushed the wine closer to her. "Just one sip, the first sip—*that* is what wine is all about."

"And sometimes the second," Marguerite added with a wink, her wavy golden hair descending from her black beret to just below her shoulders.

"Wine is about history," Juliet told them all. "People. Stories. Maybe your own country will one day discover wine as our country has. Perhaps sometime soon."

A tingle ran up Henry's neck at the mere sound of the word: *Soooooooooooon* . . .

There were maybe a hundred people in the square at that moment, and he used every second to study as many of them as possible.

Mattie looked hesitant as she reached for the container, despite Marguerite clapping her hands in encouragement. "One of your presidents loved our wine, Mateelda," she urged her. "Thomas Jefferson! He would want you to at least try it!"

Mattie took the tiniest of sips, and for a second showed no reaction—right up until she did.

"It's . . ." She coughed once, then twice. "It's, um, very . . . it's very good," she was finally able to say after quickly clearing her throat.

Everyone at the table broke into laughter, even Jack, while Juliet's expression bordered on pure elation.

"Welcome, Mateelda, to a new world of adventure! Where every vintner has their own story to tell," Juliet fairly shouted as she nudged the wine toward Henry.

"Henri? Your turn," she insisted. "Then Jack and my little Ernest."

Henry reached for the container, spying to see if the term of affection could make Ernie even more infatuated with their hostess. Apparently it could.

Henry took a small sip from the jug, which really was his first sip ever. As the red hallmark of French history rolled down his throat, he noticed that it was . . .

Wow. Not too bad.

He could also tell that both Frenchwomen were waiting to see if there might be another coughing fit. *"Ouuuuuuuiiiiii?"* Juliet asked with a hopeful look.

"It's good," Henry offered after a few cough-free seconds. "Really. I mean, I think it's great."

"Ah, Henri, *très, très bon*! *Vous aimez?*" She asked if he really meant it.

"*Oui*, I sure did," he answered, sliding the wine over to Jack before leaning back with a somewhat victorious grin on his face. Until his great-great-grandfather took a huge sip.

Annnnnnd . . . of course . . .

Another one.

"*Très BONNNNN!*" Marguerite shouted at Jack's accomplishment. The big kid scooted the wine directly over to Ernie amid Juliet's sustained cheering.

Monsieur Stupide, though, already looked as if he might break into a sweat because of the pressure. Not wanting to buckle in front of the woman he'd just discovered was the woman of his dreams, Ernie confidently raised the crimson-colored jug and downed what turned out to be a bit more than probably would have been practical.

"*Uhmmph,*" Ernie immediately coughed. Half his mouthful of wine ended up on various locations around the table, followed by Juliet and Marguerite jumping to their feet, almost bursting as they laughed and cheered. Even the surrounding patrons and dancers turned to look as Ernie wiped his mouth with the back of his hand, covering his hangdog grin.

The two women sat back down and Juliet motioned for someone at the table to send the wine her way. Ernie practically fell over himself to make sure no one else got the honor. He placed it in front of her, and she poured herself a sizeable serving.

And it was in that moment that Henry first noticed a small but decided change in Juliet's demeanor. The joyful smile and laugh from only a second ago faded away, replaced with a much, much different look: a calculating countenance that he easily spotted in her eyes.

"Well . . . well." Juliet dipped her chin, perhaps to underscore what she was about to say. "Now that the four of you have had your share of our wine, I need to ask a few questions as to this most, most mysterious visit you've all made; a mysterious visit indeed. *Oui?*"

Juliet raised her glass to her lips, her tone of voice suddenly devious.

"So," she continued, "Which one of you is going to tell us exactly why you are here in France?" Her eyes grew even darker as she added, "Because if you don't, we know of people who can force you to tell us."

The words took the air right out of the festive moment. Mattie looked completely caught off guard, while Jack eyed the two young Frenchwomen evenly. Even Ernie looked worried about Juliet's unexpected change of tone.

And Henry—for very good reason, given his encounter from the night before—didn't know what to think.

Wait, wait, wait . . . these two? They know? They knew all along?

Of course. Juliet was on board the whole trip. With Doubt. With Grace. She's either with them or she's got one of Twain's envelopes herself.

The wine! That's why she gave us the—

"Ha! Ha! HAAA, OHHHH," Juliet suddenly exploded into laughter, apparently unable to keep her vibrant eyes dark any longer. "You thought I was serious, did you not? I am not just an artist, you know. I am a performer too. An actress. It is a joke. Funny? *Oui?*"

A joke! A JOKE! No! No oui! *No* oui!

Mattie let out a deep breath of relief and Juliet winked at her.

"Not to worry, little Mateelda, all is well," she said with her previously sunny voice. "I do, however, suspect there is a secret the four of you must be hiding from me. From Marguerite. I do. Coming all this way from home . . . so very, very young."

She took another sip of wine before continuing. "But secrets, Mateelda? Secrets can also be a beautiful and wonderful thing." She delicately wiped the edges of her mouth with her finger. "I don't wish you to worry, though. Monsieur Tasse entrusted me with your safety."

It was quiet for a long moment, aside from a pair of lingering accordions, and it was Jack who finally spoke up.

"We'll be fine, Juliet," he said to her. "We've been fine so far."

"*Merci*, Jack, I do hope so," she replied with a faint smile, until all of her concern seemed to drop away with a happy rush of joie de vivre.

"Ernest!" she announced, springing to her feet. "You and I are now going to dance! And should you refuse? I will be most disappointed."

"Okay," Ernie nodded faster than a racehorse past his mealtime. Marguerite stood and extended her hand to Jack, who looked more than happy to accept as well.

The music and the cobblestoned dance area of the square quickly swallowed up the four of them, leaving only Henry and Mattie at a suddenly lonely table.

Henry turned his head and smiled at her . . . awkwardly, or so he guessed. She returned it—a nice smile, he thought, without nearly as much clumsiness as his own effort.

Okay, so this is great. And by great, I mean really awful.

Dang it . . . look. Everyone's out there! We're here! The two of us. Me not even saying a word to her.

He sighed. They sat there for a long minute or two, just the two of them. The unmistakable, irresistible music of Le Havre was apparently not enough to lure either one to their feet.

Certainly not Henry.

Mattie finally dropped her eyes and quietly said, "We don't have to go out there. I mean, that's . . . that's another thing I've never really done before. Dance."

"Neither have I," Henry finally said something, also finally getting around to recalling Abigail Kentworth's invitation to the ice skating gala tomorrow.

Well, what would have been tomorrow.

Christmas morning at Central Park.

The accordion music continued under the moonlight. No real sign of Juliet, Marguerite, and their two swooning dance companions, who had both said *oui* to the invitation without anything even approaching a second thought.

Right at that moment, though, Henry was having second, third, fourth, and fifth thoughts—the kind he always had when it came to this kind of stuff.

Abigail. Now Mattie. Real smooth, pal.

Not so deep down, Henry knew that was the real reason he'd said no to Abigail's invitation on Christmas Eve. It wasn't that his mom was being too protective, or because he was getting a cold, or because of the downright nasty winter storm in New York.

It was the dancing part of it. What would have been his first-ever serious dance.

Chief was right. That one's on me.

Henry looked up as Juliet and Marguerite appeared—out there on the cobblestones, patiently teaching their young dance partners the proper steps. Ernie was far too busy swimming in Juliet's sky-blue eyes to be concerned with what his left or right foot needed to be doing. Jack, who was swaying only inches from Marguerite's brown eyes and black beret, looked pretty darn content himself.

Henry kept on watching from the safety of the table.

C'mon, could you just stop being so nervous for once? You've got accordion music, which . . . well . . . you've never really spent any time listening to, but sounds pretty amazing right now. You've got the moon, you've got Mattie sitting right there, obviously wanting you to dance with her. Okay? C'mon, get serious. Remember what Dad said, all right? Never let an extraordinary moment wait.

"I guess we could try it for a minute." Henry said the words before he knew it. "If you wanted to, that is. It's okay if you don't."

Mattie was standing before he even finished asking. "We should," she declared decisively. "I mean, *oui* . . . that's what I should say. Seems like we should while we're here."

Henry stood up and offered his hand. Mattie took it, not seeming to mind that it was a bit sweaty, and the two of them walked onto the dance area, unsure of where to even begin.

Almost all of the dancers were taller than they were. Mattie settled on a spot and turned to Henry as she smiled nervously. It felt as if they were surrounded by a moving curtain of people. Accordion music rose and fell all around them.

"HENRI!" Juliet called out, having finally noticed them. "You are a gentleman! Asking our Mateelda to dance!" His cheeks flushed red as the couples nearest them turned to look.

Juliet and Ernie moved closer.

"All right, now listen to me," Juliet directed him. "Put your left hand around her back." Henry promptly did so. "*Oui, parfait, Henri!* Now, Mateelda, hold your hand up to meet his, like so. And then . . . allow the music of my country to move you."

Now it was Mattie who was blushing.

"*Parfait?*" she asked Henry.

"It means 'perfect,'" he answered.

The moon had just risen over the top of an old warehouse, and while the light glowing from the collection of lanterns was more than enough, this was more romantic. The red in Mattie's hair, especially on the curls resting on her shoulders, shined brighter than it had all week.

"Maybe dancing's not so hard after all," Henry said to her.

"Maybe not, I guess," she agreed with a light laugh as they slowly moved a short distance from the others. "I like the name Awnray. How Juliet says it."

"Yeah, well, that's how my mom used to say it too when she was in a good mood. She was the one who made sure I learned to speak French."

"You haven't told me about her yet," Mattie said with nudging curiosity. "Mom . . . I haven't heard too many people use that word." She softly laughed again.

The music ended, but she squeezed his hand to tell him they should stay for the next song as well.

Henry knew he had to be careful when talking to Mattie about his past, which was her future, as he'd just found out by saying the word "mom." He wished he could talk about how he was feeling, but he also had to make sure he didn't say anything that would make his new friends think he was crazy.

"Yeah, my mom . . . it's kinda like a nickname," he said, which drew another smile out of her. "She used to live back in New York, before, and after my father . . ."

"Oh . . . right. I shouldn't have asked, I'm sorry," she said with a sad look.

"No, no, it's okay," Henry assured her, wanting very much to get that smile back. "She was really, really beautiful, especially when she was with him," he recalled, as much for himself as for Mattie.

"What happened to her?" she asked.

Now he really wasn't sure what to say.

Be smart here. Don't say "mom," make sure you say "mother," y'know that much. This question's the minefield. Take a minute, take a minute.

"She . . . left me," he said without taking the minute. "I think she didn't want to be around me anymore."

Seriously? Can you be any worse at lying? Yeah, you had to say something, otherwise she'll wanna know why you're here by yourself. But that was the best you could come up with? She's not gonna buy that!

The skeptical look in her eyes convinced him as much, their slow dance continuing despite the bump in the conversation.

"I don't believe you, Henry Babbitt," Mattie firmly replied. "I don't believe anyone, especially your own mother, would ever want to be away from you."

They were the most kindhearted words she could have ever said. He fumbled for something intelligent to say in response. Heck, at that point, he would have taken something even in the neighborhood of intelligent, but Mattie didn't appear to be done yet.

"I hope one day," she said to Henry, her soft smile returning, "when you're ready to tell the real story, not the one I just heard . . . I'll be the one you trust with it. Promise?"

"Promise," Henry answered with a smile of his own.

"Good."

The music coming from the accordion continued to play, maybe even slowing down a little, and Henry found himself as close to Mattie as ever, in more ways than one.

The music. The moon.

He looked into her eyes.

You can do this, Awnray.

You got it.

Come on.

Henry leaned closer. Mattie did the same. Their lips almost lightly touching—

"MATEELDA?" Juliet called out. Henry and Mattie sprang apart, both flushing red. The young Frenchwoman and Ernie eased their way through the curtain of dancing couples, neither seeming to notice Henry and Matilda's sudden embarrassment.

"We have come to watch you and Henri dance!" Juliet declared. "You cannot hide from us any longer."

Ernie still looked as if he might faint from sheer happiness.

Henry and Mattie shared one last look as Juliet and Ernie began to waltz around them. Jack and Marguerite were sure to follow.

Their private moment was gone.

But just as Henry had seen her do so many times, ever since she first tumbled out of Vanderbilt's tree, Matilda McGillin found the perfect way to seize the moment. She leaned close to whisper in his ear:

"We made it to France, Henry. Can you believe it?" She pulled back to look into his eyes. "And tomorrow? We're going to find the next clue in Hunter S. Skavenger's hunt!"

EIGHTEEN

Entrée au Monde

JACK HAD BEEN asleep during the entire train ride connecting Le Havre with the prize city of Paris, and for good reason. As Henry suspected might happen, the head suspender snapper had rustled everyone else awake that morning—much, much, much earlier than Juliet had said would be necessary.

The spark that lived in the Parisian woman's voice the night before was gone when she first awoke, but after several minutes and what looked to be two brutally strong cups of French coffee, it came back. She yawned and delivered an equally strong lecture on the value of those two commodities: time and coffee. Both were essential, in her eyes, to a life well lived.

Thanks to Jack's rousing, they'd arrived at the train station an hour and ten minutes earlier than needed. Even so, it was already packed with scores of Paris residents anxious to return home.

Le Gare Saint-Lazare was the name of their rail line, Henry had quickly discovered. The locomotive huffed steam into the air as it awaited its daily run.

Once on board, Juliet offered the two window seats to whoever wanted them most, which, not surprisingly, turned out to be Henry and Mattie—last night's dance still bright in their otherwise sleepy minds.

The seats would be ideal, Juliet informed the two of them, for seeing the amazing sights of the city once they drew near: the Left Bank and its dazzling architecture, the bridges offering access to the breathtaking collection of elaborate palaces.

Jack hadn't argued with the seat assignments in the least. He fell into the first open seat and was dead asleep before the train's first churn of working steam. Ernie, meanwhile, wanted to sit in one place and one place only: right next to Juliet.

With Paris now only minutes away, Henry couldn't resist leaning closely against the window, wanting to be the very first to see "la vision."

La Tour Eiffel. La Dame de Fer.

"The Iron Lady"—that's what his French lessons had taught him it was called here in France.

In America, it's just the good ol' Eiffel Tower.

Henry remembered also being taught that it could be seen from pretty much any point in the city. The Empire State Building? The Chrysler? Both were staggering visions, sure, but they were packed in tight with the rest of New York. Even if you were walking the long blocks of Manhattan, you needed to be really close to even see those buildings.

The Eiffel Tower, though? She stood alone and majestic. A true vision.

"You look anxious," Mattie quietly observed from her seat.

"Uhhh, *yeah*," Henry replied. "Aren't you?"

"Nope, I'm fine. Because you were the one who figured it out." She smiled and then nudged Ernie. "How about you, Ernest? Are you nervous?"

Juliet's eyes were closed, so it was difficult to tell if she was asleep or listening. Ernie, whom Henry knew was still enchanted, but also practical, leaned closer to the two of them.

"I'm scared," he whispered under his breath. "Scared of not finding it, yeah, but I might be even more scared of finding it. That's when really bad people start lookin' for you."

"Aw, we'll be fine" Mattie said to Ernie with a dismissive, yet reassuring, wave of her hand. "We haven't seen anyone since the train. We're either way out in front of them or way behind." She winked at Henry. "I vote for ahead."

Henry struggled for a smile, not saying a word.

"Or maybe the hunt's already over," Ernie whispered. "Maybe we came all this way for nothing."

"Ah . . . Monsieur Skavenger and his amazing hunt," Juliet said as she cracked open one eye and then the other. "I should have guessed."

She'd been awake through the entire conversation—or at least the important part of it. The three of them looked at her, the sparkle in her eyes now sparkling even brighter.

"*S'il vous plaît*, my trio of adventurers." She held up her hands to calm them. "This is *your* hunt, not mine. I would never, ever do anything to interfere."

Her eyebrows, however, sprung up high with budding excitement.

"Having said that," Juliet continued, "I read about his grand hunts of last year and the year before." Her voice seemed to climb an octave. "I was sure he would hold another. You, *mes jeuenes amis*? You have actually found some of his clues?"

"We have," Mattie told her, eliciting a squeal out of Juliet. "Shh, shh, shh, shh, shh, shhhhhh, quiet," she had to remind her.

It was all enough to awaken Jack, Henry had just noticed, right as the slowing train passed through the outskirts of Paris. The River Seine and the Left Bank were now coming into view.

"Jack, Jack, Jack!" Juliet thumped him on the knee, her voice climbing another octave still. "One of my little determined Skavenger Hunters!"

Jack sat up in an instant. "You told her?" he threw out the accusation in three different directions.

"Jaaaack," Juliet cut him off with a kind, yet scornful look that told him not to worry. "It was an accident. It was no one's fault. I'm your friend, remember? *Ton meilleur ami.*"

She then curled a finger for all four of them to huddle closer. "But how exciting!" she whispered. "Juliet Bonnet of Montmartre shall guide you to your victory!"

She then sat up prim and proper and clasped her hands in her lap. "So . . . where is it I will be taking you today?"

The steady puffing of the train was slowing even more, easing Le Gare Saint-Lazare to its imminent stop. Henry took his eyes off Juliet long enough to glance at the others. He picked up a pair of nods from Mattie and Ernie, and a cautious look from Jack.

"We're going to the Tower," he quietly answered Juliet.

She quietly gasped and clutched her hands close to her chin with delight.

"The TOWER! Oh my goodness, Henri! Oh, this is incredible! This is remarkable! This is incredibly remarkable!" Then she leaned very, very close to ask him . . .

"And what tower is that?"

WOOOSHchuggachugga WOOOSHchuggachugga WOOO-OOOOOOOOOOSH . . .

The sound of the gradually slowing train was the only thing Henry could hear for a long moment.

What tower? How could she not know what tower?

It was as if he'd asked someone in Nepal to show him "the mountain" and they'd replied: "And what mountain is that?"

Henry repeated his question, only this time he did so out loud.

"What tower?"

"*Oui*, what tower?" Juliet nodded, brimming with excitement. "What tower in Paris holds Monsieur Skavenger's next clue?" She lowered her voice, suddenly aware. "Sorry, am I being too loud?"

No, you're not too loud. But, Juliet, there's only one tower in Paris that means anything. Why are you even . . . ?

Henry was now beginning to feel the weight of Jack's and Ernie's worried looks, Mattie having lowered her eyes with the first twinge of growing concern as well.

"Well . . . the Eiffel Tower of course," Henry answered, already fearing what he might hear next.

Don't say it. Don't say it.

"Eiffel Tower?" Juliet responded with a confused smile. "But Henry . . . there is no Eiffel Tower."

No, no, no. There is, there is, there has to be!

Mattie worriedly glanced toward Henry before informing Juliet, "Henry told us about the great tower in the middle of Paris."

The one you can see from everywhere!

"But . . . no." Juliet looked toward Henry, still baffled. "You mean Monsieur Eiffel? Is that who you're talking about?"

Henry, though, was back looking out the window. His breath coming in short bursts. The low skyline of Paris was there, but it was blue and barren, La Dame de Fer nowhere to be seen.

The first hint of sadness moved into Juliet's eyes.

"Henri, I'm sorry," she softly said, putting a hand on his shoulder. "Monsieur Eiffel has never built a tower. He has built many wonderful things, *oui*, but not that."

Something's wrong. Something has gotta be wrong. I need to . . .

The train lurched to a stop and Henry bolted from his seat, wanting to get outside to see for himself. The French porter, a young man wearing a round blue-brimmed hat, grasped for him and yelled . . .

"SÉJOUR POSÉ, JEUNE HOMME!"

But Henry was already through the door and had jumped down to the boarding platform, his head spinning.

You can't have been that stupid! The Eiffel Tower's been here forever. FOREVER! This is France! Everything's been here forever!

"HÉ!" the porter yelled again from the lowest step on the train. *"ÊTES-VOUS FOU! SAUTER COMME ÇA?!"*

They're wrong, it's here. They must call it something else.

Henry surveyed the short, mostly equal-in-height buildings adorning the view of the already legendary city.

The vision. The visionary. Where are you?!

Except there was no vision. Nothing towering to the eye. He looked wildly in every direction, seeing nothing more than . . .

Thwamp!

The ground under his nose.

Henry struck his forehead hard, rolling over to see a furious Jack hovering over him.

"No tower! NO TOWER!!" he howled. His fist cracked wickedly against Henry's jaw. Ernie and Juliet lunged at Jack, trying to hold him back; but Mattie was already there, trying to also hold back a quick surge of her own tears at the same time.

"WE TRUSTED YOU!!!" Jack screamed at Henry. "HOW COULD YOU DO THIS!! WE WERE THIS CLOSE!!"

Ernie somehow found a way to pry Jack away, enough that Mattie and Juliet were able to help Henry to his feet, his cheek already growing red. The Frenchwoman yanked a kerchief out of her pocket, licked it, and dabbed it at his face.

"It's okay." Henry brushed her hand aside, still shaken.

"Okay?" Jack lunged at him again, but Mattie stepped in between the two of them with a fierce look on her face.

"STOP IT, JACK!" she yelled. "Stop it right now!"

"No." Henry held up his hand. "He's right. I was wrong. I was wrong about everything."

"Oh, you were wrong, all right! 'Bout as wrong as anyone could ever get!" Jack shouted over Mattie's head.

"Would you please PIPE DOWN, JACK?!" Ernie joined in, seemingly having reached the end of his own rope. "We just got here. We'll find it."

"We're not finding anything," Jack seethed. "Because of him, right there." The train station security agents were headed their way now, while a good many of the disembarking travelers were watching and murmuring among themselves.

Mattie turned again on Jack, pointing an angry finger into his face. "All right, give up then! Just quit, Jack! But I'M NOT! We can still finish this!"

Henry could see that her words were having no effect. The only thing Jack wanted to do was take another couple good swings at him. Mattie wiped away a tear, took in a deep breath, and tried one more time.

"Let's find the visionary, Jack," she calmly urged him. "We find the visionary, maybe we find the vision."

ಌ

A summer rain shower soaked Paris that afternoon, and it didn't really stop until an hour after nightfall. The lingering mist had left Mattie a little chilled, but Henry, who was walking alongside her, was numb for a much different reason.

They'd broken into two teams shortly after the Le Gare Saint-Lazare incident: Jack, Ernie, and Juliet in one group, Henry and Mattie in the other. The decision was made for two very practical reasons: number one being the risk that Jack might still coldcock Henry at any given moment; number two being that both teams needed someone who could speak French.

With that settled—or as settled as things could be—they'd taken off in search of one Gustave Eiffel, agreeing to meet back at the train station every three hours to report on their progress.

Progress, though, had been in short supply. Juliet had warned them all that Monsieur Eiffel had a reputation for valuing his privacy, to the point that it often proved difficult to even find him. If they were fortunate enough to track him down, chances were good he might not be in a mood to talk.

So far, her words had proved prophetic.

Henry had politely asked dozens of Parisians if they knew where they might find the noted designer, but he and Mattie were met with either indifferent shrugs, or even worse, arrogant comments along the lines of *"Personne ne sait où Monsieur Eiffel dessine ses conceptions."*

"What's that mean, Henry?" Mattie had asked him.

"It means we should mind our own business," Henry had answered.

She hadn't bothered asking for more translations after that.

They walked along the Trocadéro, site of the Palais de Chaillot, with barely a word between them for the longest of stretches. Henry could tell she was worried. Worried and disappointed that their remarkable run of skill may have officially dried up.

She'd yet to say anything even close to hurtful, and Henry was hopeful the night before had something to do with that. But the one thing he couldn't overlook was the simple fact he'd promised Mattie a tower in Paris—and it was a tower that didn't exist.

Mattie's stride slowed a bit as she nodded toward the Palais du Trocadéro. It was an immense and elaborate palace graced by high, elegant arches and protected by brilliantly sculpted horses. Even now, after everything that had happened that day, it was impossible to resist gawking at it.

The gardens were sprawling and fragrant. The center structure looked similar to the Colosseum in Rome yet was flanked by two skyscraping towers, and all of this drew the gaze of a gigantic elephant statue in front. An African elephant, Henry could tell, same as the one in the Natural History Museum back home.

"It's beautiful, isn't it?" Mattie quietly noted.

"Yep . . . it sure is," Henry agreed.

The most recent Parisian they'd talked with had been nice enough to give them a short history of the Palais. It was surprisingly new, the man had told them, built only a few years ago and designed by the well-regarded French architect Gabriel Davioud—best known for the spectacular Fontaine Saint-Michel.

"It's a big fountain," Henry had whisper-translated for Mattie.

The Parisian man complimented Henry on his fine command of the language, and was off to finish his nightly stroll.

The two of them once again walked in silence for a bit.

"Can I ask you something, Henry?" Mattie finally turned to look at him.

"Sure you can."

She scrunched the collar of her wrinkled coat up higher around her neck. It was Marguerite's coat, actually. The cape had been gone for a while now—Mattie having ditched it a few days before arriving in France.

"Never mind." She apparently decided not to ask. Instead, she tipped her head toward the bridge straight ahead of them, the one that spanned the Seine toward the Left Bank.

"What did that man say the name of this was again?" she asked. "Pont duh-what?"

"Pont d'Lena." Henry smiled. "It crosses over the water to where I thought the tower was going to be."

It'll be there one day, Mattie. I promise. A tower so amazing that people all over the world will come to see it. Bright lights at nighttime . . . sparkling.

Tonight, though, the only thing the Pont d'Lena led to was a dark and empty night sky. They walked across the bridge, Henry deep in his own thoughts, until Mattie walked to the middle overlook and looked as if she wanted to ask her question after all.

"How did you make that mistake, Henry?" she gently asked as she stared at the river below. "All this time, the whole entire hunt, ever since I met you . . . you've known so much. Where to look, where we should go . . ."

He didn't answer at first, waiting for one last couple walking across the bridge to move past them. Mattie patiently waited too, until they disappeared into the darkness.

Henry sighed and told her the only thing he could think to tell her:

"I just thought I knew."

He waited a bit longer before continuing. "I don't know . . . maybe it was something I read about Eiffel wanting to build a tower, and he hadn't started it yet."

"Henry, there's a big difference between wanting to build something and actually building it." It was as close as she'd ever come to giving him a tongue-lashing.

"I know there is," he quietly admitted, knowing he deserved it. "I'm sorry, Mattie. Really."

She turned to look at him, the twinkle in her eye already thinking about returning. "Well, Henry Babbitt," she announced, "whatever newspaper you read that in, I give you full permission not to use anything from that paper ever again. Agreed?"

"Agr—"

Scrrrrr-whump.

A silent hand grabbed the scruff of Mattie's collar from behind, the other hand quickly covering her mouth. Any scream she might have considered was smothered before she even had a chance to breathe.

The same went for Henry, courtesy of another set of hands.

The Dark Men!

"No, no, no, no. Don't even think about yelling," a deep, familiar voice whispered into his ear.

Henry glanced over at Mattie. She was struggling to break free, her muffled protests silent and useless on the now empty bridge.

Even before he and Mattie had started to cross the bridge, Henry noticed that the Pont d'Lena was just like the streets surrounding the Vanderbilt Mansion: thin, infrequent triangles of dim light surrounded by massive areas of pitch-black darkness. The couple that had passed by them only a few moments earlier hadn't traveled far before disappearing into the gloom.

Henry felt himself being pushed toward the side of the bridge. Mattie's legs furiously churned to keep her own Dark Man from forcing her to the same destination—and for good reason.

Oh no. She doesn't know how to swim.

The concrete side of the bridge, even for someone as small as Mattie, barely rose higher than her waist. The River Seine swept past twenty feet below.

"Where's the clue?" the man behind Henry snarled to him.

"I told you! We didn't find it!" Henry managed to yell, digging and pushing his heels into the lower bricks of the bridge. Out of the corner of his eye, he saw the man holding Mattie; he was dressed black as midnight.

"Lemme GO!!!" she managed to scream, wrenching her head free from her attacker's grasp for a second. The Dark Man, who was easily twice her size, quickly covered her mouth again with his hand. She wriggled and kicked, but it was hopeless.

The voice behind Henry, which had sounded so eerily familiar, leaned close to his ear once more. "Should have told us what you knew back in New York. We gave you the chance, remember?"

What?! The Colton Brothers?!

"This one here could have told us too." Clifford Colton twisted Mattie around to face him. She kneed him hard in the stomach, knocking some of the wind out of him, but it only made him angrier.

"You tell us NOW!" he roared. And with a surge of fury, he pushed Mattie up against the concrete siding.

"She doesn't know! We haven't found it!" Henry yelled a second time, only to have Clyde whip him around as well.

"You're lying to us, Henry! Just like before!"

Mattie had clearly decided she was done with all of this. She ripped one of her arms free from Clifford's lock-fingered grip and hammered at him in the hope of breaking free.

But Clifford squeezed tighter. And with a single unimaginable motion he lifted Mattie with both of his hands and . . .

. . . held her out over the flowing Seine River. She hung from his hands, hovering there on the wrong side of the Pont d'Lena's concrete wall, her feet dangling and kicking in midair.

"NOOOO!" Henry screamed as loudly as he could. Loud enough that the twin brothers could tell they'd be out of time any second.

"CLIFFORD!" Clyde looked at his brother with slack-jawed disbelief. "What . . . what are you doing?! Pull her back!"

"Not until she tells us," Clifford hissed through clenched teeth, not even bothering to shake his head.

The unsettling calm on his face was the opposite of the panic taking root in Mattie's expression. Her legs flailed even faster than before; the cloth of her already old and weakened shirt had ripped slightly; and the threatening water, only a scant distance below, moved along at an ominous pace.

"Last chance, little girl." Clifford gave her one more furious shake, somehow finding a way to hold her out a few inches farther.

"I don't . . ." Mattie gasped. "I don't . . . know!"

Henry could hear a rush of running footsteps finally thundering their way, but he could tell they were coming from the far edge of the bridge.

They're not gonna get here in time!

"Pull her back!" Clyde shouted again.

"Don't worry, brother," Clifford replied. "We'll get it out of 'em somehow."

Slowly he began to ease her back, but then he stopped, taunting her one last time. So close and absolutely so far. Silently terrorizing her for one last moment . . .

Riiiiippppp . . .

Suddenly he found himself holding nothing more than a handful of fabric as her frayed and battered shirt tore and gave way—

And Mattie McGillin fell toward the Seine River.

"HEEEENNNNNNRRRRRYYYYY!!!"

"NOOOOOOO!!!" Henry yelled, hearing her splash into the water a half second later.

Clyde let go of him, stunned, rushing to the bridge's concrete barrier to look down.

"I didn't want . . . I didn't mean to . . ." Clifford was now in his own private panic, staring at the fluttering piece of cloth in his hand, then glancing down toward the river. "I'm sorry, I'm sorry, I'm sorry . . ."

Without a twinge of hesitation, Henry pressed his hands against the top of the barrier and vaulted over, spiraling down and smacking into the cold water.

The next few seconds turned dark and hazy.

Gray water surrounded him as he scrambled to kick his way back up to the surface. He'd landed in the water on his side, and the ringing in his ears was nothing but a steady hum until he burst through the surface of the river and into the night air.

"MATTIE!!"

He shouted blindly, frantically rubbing his eyes, looking all around. "MATTIE, WHERE ARE YOU!!" he tried again, but heard and saw nothing.

Whereareyouwhereareyouwhereareyou!

"MATTTTTIE!!" Henry started swimming in the direction the water was taking him, which had to be the same direction it was taking Mattie. He could hear shouting coming from the bridge above, but none of it made sense—every word, every shout coming from a stranger.

But there was nothing from Mattie.

Until . . .

"HENR—"

Finally. Mattie's cry—cut short by the river—didn't seem far away, but it was hard to tell from which direction it came.

"HENRY!!!" Another cry, this one farther away and to the south of him.

Henry paddled in that direction, but his wool coat was beginning to soak up the water of the Seine and weigh him down. He'd jumped in without even thinking about it.

"MATTIE!"

This time, there was no reply. Only the steady lapping sound of the River Seine's current.

His arms were getting heavier with each desperate stroke. Heavier and heavier. He was still whipping his head around, looking in every direction.

Henry yelled as loudly as he could.

"WHERE ARE Y—"

The first rush of water spilled into his mouth as his drenched coat decided it was time to start pulling him down. He threw his head back to take in as much air as he could . . .

. . . but each breath was coming faster and faster. Too fast. The sky above him . . .

Gray.

Darker than gray.

All except for the sliver of bright moon directly overhead. The same moon he and Mattie had danced underneath last night. The night she told him, with the smile and the words that somehow now filled his mind in the middle of this un-imaginable horror:

"We made it to France, Henry! Can you believe it?"

He heard more shouting coming from up on the bridge. Distant now, but it sounded like a lot of people.

Fading, though.

Fading, fading, fading.

Another cold funnel of water found its way into Henry's mouth. His coat pulled him down even more, until the last thing left for him to see was . . .

Gray. Nothing.

NINETEEN

Au Revoir

"JEUNE HOMME, AVEZ-VOUS toute autre chose que vous vous inquiétez pour ajouter?"

Henry blinked as he looked up at the old, steady-voiced police detective, who'd introduced himself as Francois DeLacorte only two hours earlier.

"I'm sorry. What?"

DeLacorte sighed. The sixty-year-old veteran of the Police de Paris—a short, amply built, gray-bearded man with a more-than-patient countenance—sat in a simple chair in front of an uncluttered desk.

"Is there anything else we should know, Henry?" he asked. His questions had gone back and forth between seamless French and heavily accented but more-than-passable English, having already learned that Henry could speak both languages well.

The old policeman had made a point of speaking to him in the most welcoming room of the medical clinic, where Henry had been taken after being rescued from the river. In addition to the simple chair and tidy desk, the physician's office where they were speaking also had a sofa and a set of high-backed chairs, rather than the steel chairs and benches in the exam rooms.

"No," Henry finally answered him with a tired and wrecked voice. "I, uh . . . I think that's everything I can remember."

Juliet's hand rested on his shoulder. She'd been crying ever since she arrived, Henry having told DeLacorte that she and Jack and Ernie would be at the train station waiting.

The detective solemnly nodded and reviewed his investigative notepad, flipping through page after page, while Henry stared straight ahead with the blankest of expressions.

Mattie.

He choked back a sudden heaving sob, just one of many so far. There'd be many more to come, of course. He'd learned that from his father's death. Ernie gave him a pat on the back, inconsolable himself.

"There was nothing you coulda done, Henry," he told him. "You did your best."

Jack had been in his own silent daze since showing up, saying little to anyone. All of his fury from that morning was gone, and right now he looked like nothing more than what Henry knew all three of them were: young boys who just wanted to get out of France.

"So . . . Henry, to summarize," DeLacorte said, still busy reviewing his notes. "You and Miss McGillin were walking the Pont d'Lena in search of clues to Monsieur Skavenger's Hunt, *oui?*"

"Yes, I mean . . . *oui*, sorry," Henry haltingly replied through eyes brimming with tears.

"*Oui*, of course," DeLacorte said as he patiently turned to the next page. "You were at the center span, overlooking the river, when the two of you were attacked by two young men.

American twin brothers you'd encountered before, back in New York City. Clyde and Cleeford Colton, yes?"

Henry nodded. DeLacorte's strong accent had mangled the name every time he said it. "The latter of whom," the portly detective continued reading from his notes, "dropped Miss McGillin into the River Seine."

Henry lowered his head and said nothing, his shoulders shaking.

The detective compassionately closed his notebook, having now reached the most difficult part.

"We, of course, regret very, very much that we've not been able to locate your friend, young Matilda," the detective said with as much empathy as he could muster. "Fortunately, these two brothers have been found and taken into custody. I assure you all that proper justice will be served."

Juliet wiped her nose with her now-damp kerchief. *"Mis leur en prison pour toujours,"* she angrily told DeLacorte, before offering an equally angry translation for the boys. "Put them in prison forever. For what they did to our poor Mateelda."

The detective offered his own handkerchief to Juliet. She took it and nodded her thanks.

"I am . . . quite certain," DeLacorte grimly added, "that Monsieur Skavenger would be appalled by what happened here tonight. Such a joyful enterprise, these hunts of his. Only to come to this."

The detective turned to Juliet and asked her in perfect French, "You'll make certain these three are on the first available vessel back to the United States?"

Juliet nodded. "Yes, I, uh, I know a family that's emigrating. They're leaving tomorrow morning. I'm confident they'll agree to accompany them back home."

Home. What home?

Henry shook his head.

"Very good." DeLacorte sighed again and stood, putting a hand on Henry's shoulder. "Young man, you have my deepest sympathy." He looked toward the others in the room. "All of you do."

The detective smiled sadly and made a quiet, respectful exit from the room.

Juliet quickly gathered up their things. "All right, boys," she said, wiping the current round of tears from her cheeks, "Marguerite will have something for you to eat, I'm sure. You'll all need your strength for tomorrow."

She headed through the door to the main exit, not wanting them to see her next round of sobs. Jack and Ernie stayed behind for the moment, silently waiting for Henry.

The twelve-year-old sat motionless in the same high-backed chair he'd been in for the past two hours, his forehead resting heavily on one hand.

"Hey, Jack? Ern?" he asked with a weary voice.

"What is it, pal?" Ernie answered him.

"I'm sorry."

Neither of them answered right away, until Jack quietly replied:

"C'mon. Let's go home, Henry."

The two of them headed through the same door Juliet had cried her way through a moment earlier, which meant that Henry Babbitt once again was, as he had been at so many important times in his young life . . .

Alone.

He shook his head, not ready to stand quite yet. He'd already come to terms with the knowledge that today was one of the two worst days of his life—no matter what century he was in.

One day for Dad. Now one day for Mattie.

He'd revealed to Jack, back there in the cold lower quarters of *entrepont* days ago, back before the now meaningless encounter with Doubt and Grace, that he hadn't been there the day he lost his dad. That he hadn't seen what had happened, but that he'd imagined the moment in his head more times than he could count.

This moment he had seen.

The sound of her voice in the river, the look on her face as Clifford dropped her—those awful, awful details that he'd now remember forever.

He was sure of that, just as he was sure of one other detail. A detail that felt so incredibly trivial after Mattie's death:

Skavenger's Hunt was over.

ॐ

The churning Atlantic, which had been temperamental enough between New York and Le Havre, was in an even nastier mood for their returning voyage. Appropriate, it seemed.

It had been seven days since the SS *Le Chasseur* obeyed its captain's orders and pointed her bow into the stronger-than-usual prevailing current. And while the weather had gotten better over the last two days, the first five had been rough enough to cause problems for a lot of the passengers.

None of which mattered in the least to Henry.

Even had the ocean been as calm as a summer lake, he would have wallowed in the same grief and despair he'd lived with the past week.

The haunting image of Mattie falling. Her calling his name. His failure to find her. Those were things his brain simply refused to put away into storage. It simply would not do it, nor should it, as Henry had already convinced himself countless times.

It was his fault she was even in Paris at all. He was the one who'd mistakenly said a tower was waiting for them there. If he hadn't said it, they wouldn't have gone. And if they hadn't gone . . .

Mattie wouldn't be gone either.

Henry squeezed his eyes closed a little tighter, lying on his side on the sagging green cot that had been designated for him—the one Juliet's friend Phillippe made a point of checking in on every couple of hours to make sure Henry was okay.

The twelve-year-old reached into his coat pocket, a habit he'd retained even after his jump into the Seine.

There was nothing there anymore, of course.

Absolutely nothing.

That was the other staggering loss from what happened the night on the Pont d'Lena—something Henry hadn't realized right away.

The ledger page was gone too.

The sheet that included Skavenger's instructions for Henry and the destinations he'd visited: lost in the Seine.

There had been only six boxes left on the ledger page—a half dozen precious date and destination slots that had told Henry how many chances he had left to meet Skavenger. As long as there was an empty box on the sheet, Henry could at least hope for a path to get back home.

No way back now.

Even if he somehow won the hunt and found himself face-to-face with Skavenger, he'd still need the ledger sheet to go back. It was written right up there, clear as could be, at the top.

Or had been.

Henry opened his eyes and glumly stared at the ship's rivet-filled wall, having decided days ago there would be no winning anything. How could there be? They were stuck in the middle of the Atlantic while Hiram Doubt and his men were still back in Paris, drawing closer to Skavenger's prize.

Henry blinked back the morning's first set of tears, staring hard at the ship's miserable coloring. When they'd left Le Havre for New York, which seemed like months ago now, Juliet had managed a sad smile for Henry as she pointed to the name of their sea-crossing vessel.

"*Le Chasseur*, Henri," she'd said to him. "You know what that means, *oui*?"

"'The hunter,'" he'd answered her.

She had then hugged him, tightly through her own tears. "May your next hunt bring you peace, young friend," she said, before sending him on his way.

That had been a week ago. And the chill of *Le Chasseur*—the hunter—had yet to warm.

Most hours of the day he'd spent on his cot, doing nothing aside from staring numbly at the wall while Jack and Ernie played cards on the main deck with two young men from Bulgaria. It was their way of dealing with what had happened.

Henry didn't get up there too much. The last place he wanted to venture on the ship was the railing overlooking the pounding ocean, black and forbidding, even on the one day the sun had come out.

He'd glanced at the waves once, but his recollections of water had gotten the best of him. Remembering the sight of Mattie slipping from Clifford Colton's hands into the Seine. Trying to rescue her himself; unable to even find her.

And in the few moments when he wasn't thinking about the loss of Mattie, he'd catch himself thinking about the family he'd also lost.

A father who was definitely gone. A mother and grandparents he suspected he'd never see again.

"Henry?"

He let out a deep breath. His head had decided to tease him with his father's voice again.

"Look at your mother . . ."

And Henry was back under his father's arm, watching an old movie that hadn't kept Eloise from drifting off to sleep, her head peacefully resting on Nathan's lap.

"She's beautiful, isn't she?" Henry could hear the smile in his father's voice. *"Not a care in the world."*

That was the other thing Henry thought about. His mother. All those times he'd gotten so frustrated with her for protecting him from everything.

No on recess, yes on French class. No to the rides at the school carnival, yes to the library.

It was all because she loved him. Simple as that. She just needed a little more time with everything that had happened—same as he did.

Henry restlessly pushed himself out of his cot and headed for the nearest set of stairs, his legs ached from doing pretty much zip for hours on end. Yesterday he'd gone down to wander the ship's lower hallways, just to stretch out a bit. It had taken him all of maybe a half hour to discover that *Le Chasseur* was, when you got right down to it, a pretty boring ship—built to transport passengers and not much else.

Clank clank clank clank . . .

Henry's footsteps echoed on the narrow metal stairs that led down to the storage areas, louder than he'd hoped. Even though he hadn't seen anyone during his first venture down there, he still didn't want to attract attention.

Same as yesterday, someone had left the main door to the area slightly open.

The forward side of the storage hold was where all the wooden trunks were kept. He had little desire to see those again.

Way too easy to picture Mattie sittin' on the box of clothes on the train to St. Louis. Thumping her heels against the side.

Seemed like the littlest of things could trigger a memory of her.

A rolling empty bottle did the trick a week ago, whipping him straight back to Mattie peering at the empty beer glass outside of the Jennings Establishment. The moment when she'd handed it to Henry and he'd spotted the same clue she had, prompting her to roll onto her back and shout up to the sky in celebration:

YEEEEESSSSSSS!!!

Henry shivered as he turned and set out toward the other side of the lower level. There was more light than he expected, but just as many trunks and stacks of luggage, almost forming a long corridor of sorts.

Even if it had been darker, Henry's fear of bumping into Doubt was gone.

Nuthin' to be afraid of. He's there, I'm here.

A few beams of light streamed through the slats above, joined by the raindrops also finding their way in. It was starting to get just a little darker back in the far stern, made darker still by the hallway of baggage that reached to the ceiling.

Thanks to the stray beams of light, though, he could see where he was going. See the boxes, see the floor, see the . . .

Door.

Big door.

Henry noticed it as he reached the end of the luggage corridor; it was tightly padlocked and enormous, and it was at least fifteen feet high from top to bottom, perhaps more, constructed of what looked to be extremely thick and unyielding steel.

Whaaaaat is behind that? The ship's engines sound pretty close. That could be it, right?

Henry moved closer. The sound of the engines remained muffled and distant.

All right. Can't be the engines. They're close, but not behind-this-door close.

Henry reached out a cautious finger to give the five-inch-wide padlock an easy tug.

It clanked, but held tight. He tried again, this time using his whole hand, pulling hard enough for it to make a dull clunking sound as it fell back against the door.

He softly exhaled, perplexed.

Well, it's somethin', that's for sure. Nobody puts that kind of lock on an empty ro—

Which was precisely the same moment a hand fell on his shoulder. Henry whipped around mid-gasp.

"Y a il quelque chose que je peux vous aider avec, jeune homme?"

An unfamiliar man stood directly in front of Henry. He had strangely sleepy eyes and wore a perfectly tailored black suit with a crisp vest and a green ascot. A gold watch chain led to the pocket where his timepiece no doubt was ticking with precision right now.

The man wasn't Hiram Doubt, wasn't the shadowy Grace, wasn't anyone Henry had ever seen before—though he certainly would have guessed he was French had he not even said a word.

"Whew, man . . . dude, you scared me." Henry took in a breath to calm himself.

"Man? Dude? *Moi?*" the unfamiliar man inquired with a bemused, somewhat puzzled expression on his face. "I confess I am not too familiar with your country's . . . how should I say it? The manner in which you young Americans speak?"

"Sorry . . . sir," Henry apologized. "I was just looking around. *Je regardais juste autour.*"

The man—who looked to be in his early fifties, with a fine beard and mustache and carrying a thick satchel—smiled and seemed to be mildly impressed.

"Ah . . . I see," he replied in decent English. "What is it going to be then? Français . . . or Anglais?"

The gentleman's words, and more importantly, the tone in which he said them, quickly put Henry at ease.

"English would be great, thanks." Henry nodded. "I guess I probably shouldn't be here, should I?"

"I don't see why not. You do have a ticket for travel, *oui*?"

"Oh, *oui*, I do," Henry assured him, patting at his pockets, forgetting for a moment which one held it. The man was rummaging through his own pockets as well.

"No need to offer proof," he said with a smile. "I was an explorer when I was your age too. I remain an explorer. So yes . . . you should absolutely be here."

The man pulled a key out from one of his other coat pockets. *"Excusez-moi?"* he politely asked as he gave a nod to the massive door.

"Oui, sure."

Henry stepped aside as the gentleman slipped the key into the lock and asked him, "And what is your name, young explorer?"

"Oh, it's, uh . . . Henry Babbitt."

"Monsieur Henry Babbitt," the man repeated as he removed the lock and gave a mighty pull on the door. "I am Monsieur . . . *ummpph.*"

The gentleman gave a short groan as the door opened a bit. He gave another mighty pull.

". . . Gustave . . ."

Followed by one more.

". . . Eiffel."

TWENTY

Mother of Exiles

THE VISIONARY CLAPPED his hands free of dust and motioned for Henry to lead the way inside the mysterious room.

But the twelve-year-old was unable to take a step.

Ei . . . Ei . . . Ei . . . Ei . . . Ei? As in Eiffel *Eiffel? One of Riggin's* Three E's Eiffel? *Here? Me? Him?*

"I'm sorry, you're . . . you . . ." Henry was having a little trouble standing. "You're Gustave Eiffel?"

"Indeed," the man confirmed, gesturing a second time for Henry to go in. "Well, you wanted a look inside? Let's look inside."

Henry stepped in, never once taking his eyes off his unexpected host. Monsieur Eiffel closed the door behind him, latching it on the inside while tucking his thick satchel under one arm.

"Where are you from, Henry?" Gustave wiped the last bit of dust from his hands before walking to the center of the cavernous area.

"Well, sir . . ." Henry followed, until his eyes rose and his voice dropped away.

Scattered on the floor of the mostly empty room were seven very substantial . . . well . . . Henry wasn't quite sure what they were. The closest thing they resembled was a long, thin pyramid—ten feet long and spiked at one end. The base of each was about three feet wide.

"Henry?" Eiffel asked again. "Your hometown? Where is it?"

"Oh, New York," his still-stunned young guest answered.

"Ah. So your family is here with you then. On *Le Chasseur*."

The long spikes rested on heavy sections of canvas, which Eiffel was busily inspecting. Impressive as they were, and as impressive as the legendary designer himself was, Henry had fallen silent again because of a trio of tarp-covered items taking up most of the large storage room.

"Henry?" Monsieur Eiffel's sleepy eyes still twinkled as he moved from one spike to the next. "Your family?"

"Oh, no. I'm, uh . . . I'm here with two friends," Henry finally answered.

Eiffel looked genuinely surprised, shocked even. "Just you and two friends? Crossing the Atlantic?" he asked as he leaned against the base of one of the pyramids, gesturing that it was fine for Henry to do the same.

Henry hesitated to say much more. "We're traveling with this family from Paris. The father's name is Philippe. It's kind of a long story."

"The best ones always are, *jeune ami*." Eiffel pushed himself away from the long pyramid he'd been leaning against, smiling at the wonder in the young man's eyes.

"What is this?" Henry finally asked. "Something you've designed, something you're building?"

"This?" Gustave held his arms out. "Oh no, this is something a friend asked me to help him finish. His design, not mine. Though I did make the framework, which . . . was a distinct challenge to be sure."

He cocked his head and fixed Henry with a curious look. "How is it a young American knows I am a designer?" he asked. "I haven't found many your age that know of my work, especially across the Atlantic."

"Pffft. Who hasn't heard of Gustave Eiffel?" Henry asked. "I mean, you're the reason my friends and I went to . . ."

Oh c'mon, can you think before you talk just once?

"The reason your friends and you did what, Henry?" Eiffel put two fingers on his perfectly bearded chin. His was the curious expression now.

For the first time since he'd walked in the room, Henry looked at Eiffel instead of everything else. He should have done it sooner, because no matter what was in that room, Eiffel was the reason they'd all ventured to Paris in the first place.

Gustave Eiffel. Looking at him right now. Standing in front of . . . something. Something big.

Wait . . . I may have been right about the clue after all! "Find me on a nine-day journey. Paris. New York." We're going from Paris to New York now! THIS was the journey all along. We just had to turn around and come back. Le Chasseur. The HUNTER!

Henry took in a nervous breath.

"Monsieur Eiffel? My friends and I came to Paris because we thought you might be part of Mr. Skavenger's Hunt."

The churning of the steam engines was the only sound for a moment.

Eiffel now scratched the corner of his mouth, just below his also-perfect mustache. "Monsieur *Hunter* Skavenger?" he asked. "The man behind the greatest of adventures?"

Henry nodded.

"And why would you think that I might be part of his hunt?" Gustave asked in all seriousness.

Well . . . because . . .

Henry was hoping this part of the conversation might end the same as the other encounters. Vanderbilt had been part of Skavenger's Hunt. The same went for Mark Twain. Maybe Eiffel was no different.

Henry decided to roll the dice. "Well, sir," he began, "we found a clue that pointed us to one of your designs. I mean . . . at least I thought it did. Turned out I was wrong."

Monsieur Eiffel's interest went up a notch. "A design of what?" he inquired, moving closer.

Henry knew he had to be careful. Very careful. He looked up at the great designer and very subtly revised his earlier words. "What I meant to say was . . . we found a clue that pointed us to you."

"No, no, no." Gustave shook his head. "I am a student of detail. You said the clue pointed to one of my designs."

The young man now really did need one of the metal pyramids for support.

"Go on, you can tell me," Eiffel encouraged him.

"Well," Henry tried again. "I thought I'd read somewhere that you wanted to design a tower. In Paris." He sighed and then added, "But . . . like I said, I was wrong."

Gustave Eiffel didn't say a word. Long enough to convince Henry that he'd blundered once again.

Super. Terrific. Not only hasn't he designed a tower, he hasn't even thought of a tower yet! How'd you ever get that A in histo—

Henry's private kicking of his own rear end screeched to a stop as the great designer gently rolled up his shirt cuffs, reached into his leather satchel, and removed a large drafting paper which had been carefully and meticulously folded several times.

He crouched down, placed it on the floor, and slowly, fold by fold by fold, revealed the plans for . . .

The Tower. It's right there. HIS Tower!

Henry's eyes grew wide.

Without even realizing it, he was down on his hands and knees getting a closer look, resting his palms on the design's edge—then moving them back as if he'd touched a vase in an expensive store.

"No, no, it's all right," Gustave assured him. "It's a rough draft, I know." He paused before adding, "I call her *La Dame de Fer*, which means . . ."

"The Iron Lady," Henry jumped in to make the translation. The design was the Eiffel Tower, and it wasn't a rough draft at all.

Eiffel was still puzzled, though. "I hadn't heard of anything being written about it yet," Eiffel said to Henry. "Guess it's my turn to be wrong, *oui*?" He looked at him with a smile.

Prob'ly not, E. But I think I'll save that part of the story for some other time.

"So, Henry Babbitt . . ." Eiffel looked down at his design again. "What do you think?"

Henry could only shake his head, awestruck. "I think it's incredible, sir," he quietly answered.

The visionary looked pleased. "I first thought of it just last year," he said. "But I fear it will be too dramatic for a good many of my countrymen."

He pointed to the first level, near the base. "I added an arch here, just below the landing." His voice held the enthusiasm of an eager schoolboy. "That way it matches the narrowing angle at the very top. *Oui*? You see?" he asked.

"I do see," Henry marveled.

"I still worry it will not be well received." Eiffel sighed.

"No, no, no, it will be," Henry promised with foresight even the great designer didn't have. "Where do you want to build it?"

Yeah, yeah, you know the answer, but playing dumb for once might help.

"The Champs de Mars," was Eiffel's confident reply. "It will be a thousand feet tall, can you believe that, Henry? It will be the tallest structure in the entire world."

"The whole world will love it," Henry said, mesmerized by the piece of history just inches below him. A piece of art—born in a distant corner of a great man's imagination.

"So, young man." Gustave seemingly couldn't resist. "What was the clue that drew you to me? In Paris?"

Henry looked up, just as Eiffel quickly held up his hand to reassure him. "No, no. Please understand, Henry, I am not a part in any way of Monsieur Skavenger's hunt, nor do I wish to interfere with your own search. I am, however, a great admirer of adventure, and I'd be honored to help if I can."

There wasn't a shred of doubt in Henry's mind as to whether he could trust Gustave Eiffel. He spoke each word of the riddle as precisely as he could.

"The clue read: a towering vision to the eye. Full and . . ." Henry couldn't resist stopping. "Eye? Full? Get it?"

Eiffel nodded.

The young man continued, "Impressive as any continent or sea. Find me on a nine-day journey. Paris. New York. The visionary and the vision."

He leaned back for a moment, sitting on his heels.

"That's what it was." Henry put his hands on his hips. "That's why we tried to find you."

Eiffel looked stunned, slowly repeating Henry's own mannerisms, sitting back, hands on hips, before slowly standing.

"Monsieur Hunter Skavenger." Gustave shook his head, turning to walk toward something in the room. "He is a brilliant, brilliant man, is he not? These great quests of his, more enticing and creative than even I could ever imagine."

He heard something. Just now. In the riddle!

"It IS the tower, isn't it?" Henry quickly asked as he pushed himself up. "Skavenger knew something about the tower. Your tower!"

"No, Henry." Eiffel slowly stepped toward the very largest of the tarp-covered items, reaching for a handful of the heavy cloth. "Monsieur Skavenger knew about this."

He tugged the tarp free and it slowly parachuted to the floor. A half second later, Henry Babbitt found himself staring into the face of . . .

The Statue of Liberty?

"Allow me to introduce you to another Iron Lady," Gustave said with great pride. "My friend Frédéric Bartholdi's grand vision. She is a gift to your country, Henry. *Liberté éclairant le monde.*"

Lady Liberty's gaze was fixed high over Henry's head, her serious yet somehow welcoming eyes a dozen feet above his own.

As overwhelmed as he'd been holding one of the first copies of *Huck Finn* in his hands, this moment was simply overpowering. Henry knew he was viewing the face of freedom from a vantage point that would be impossible to future visitors.

Yep, pretty sure nobody *gets to look at Lady Liberty one foot right in front of her nose.*

He glanced over at Eiffel, asking for permission without a single word. The designer smiled and nodded.

Henry reached out and placed his hand, with great respect, on the edge of her frowning lips, then gently touched the tip of her nose. Lady Liberty wasn't the greenish gray Henry was used to; that, as Dr. Riggins had explained once, would come later with the weather of the New York Harbor. Right now she was brand new—nothing more than a simple slate gray.

He pushed himself up onto the very tips of his toes, looking at the top with a quizzical expression.

No crown on her forehead. What's the deal with that?

Whoosh.

Eiffel pulled the tarp from the second item and revealed half of the statue's crown. The openings below the crest were smaller than Henry would have guessed. Gustave then yanked the final tarp away, revealing the crown's other half.

"You've heard of her, *oui?*"

"Oui," was all Henry could manage to utter.

"The rest of her is being shipped a few months from now, but this part? This part I did not want making the trip alone."

Henry stammered, "Mr. Eiffel, I . . . I . . ."

"Breathtaking, is she not? I have a friend in the newspaper business—your country, not mine—who has been raising money for the pedestal that will be her new home. It is incredible, Henry. Young children have been reaching into their own pockets to give ten cents, twenty-five cents, whatever they can afford . . . all because of one man's vision."

Henry felt Eiffel's hand on his shoulder. "Full and impressive as any continent or sea." The visionary smiled proudly as he gazed up at her. "She is that, isn't she?"

The young, once former, hunter standing next to Eiffel felt a tingle at the base of his own neck. A flutter of sudden revelation. Two words that made him realize he was hunting once again.

Continent. Sea.

Sea. Continent.

Henry whipped his head around and looked at the long metal pyramids scattered around on the floor.

"Mr. Eiffel, what are these exactly? The big ten-foot-long spiky things?"

"Those?" The great designer nodded toward the nearest one. "Well those are the rays to—"

"Her crown," Henry finished the sentence without even realizing he had, already knowing the answer—already suspecting he might have just figured out the answer to everything.

The young current hunter dashed straight over to the closest of the pyramids, pointing a counting finger at it and then doing the same with all the others.

"One, two, three, four, five, six, and . . . seven."

The visionary, still puzzled, moved next to Henry's side. "*Oui*, seven," he confirmed. "*Sept rayons de sa couronne.*"

"No." Henry shook his head with a growing smile. "Not just seven rays of her crown. Seven . . ."

"Continents!" Eiffel suddenly realized what Henry had just pieced together. "Seven seas! *Oui, bien sûr!* That's why Frédéric chose the number, I know this! He even did so because he has seven children!"

Henry took in a deep breath.

"Mr. Eiffel . . . sir. Would it be all right if I took a minute to look at the seven rays of Lady Liberty's crown?"

With a gleam of childlike excitement in his eyes, the visionary replied, "Young man, I want to find out if you're correct as much as you do. So please, be my guest."

The closest was right in front of Henry, who rushed over to its tip, slowly peering at every inch along its dull gray metal, running his hand over the sandpaper-textured surface as he searched for hidden words.

Until he reached the opening to the three-foot-wide base at the opposite end.

The ray was hollow.

All seven of them were.

Henry looked at Eiffel with a knowing grin. The great designer's lips pursed into an adventurous smile.

"As I said . . . be my guest," Gustave said to the young hunter.

Henry couldn't get to his hands and knees quickly enough. The hollow base of the ray was actually wide enough that he was able to crawl inside about four feet before it became too narrow. He took a look around—the dim light from behind now barely bright enough for him to see beyond another foot or two. Henry reached as far as he could . . . his fingers finding . . .

Nothing.

He pushed himself back out.

Okay, it's just one. I've still got—

"Six more, Henry! Go!" Eiffel encouraged him as the young man emerged. "It could be any one of them!"

But Henry was already scrambling into the second ray. The ray that represented a great sea, a great continent, a visionary's child. Looking, reaching, finding . . . nothing.

"Five more, Henry! Keep looking!"

Monsieur Eiffel could barely contain his own delight, straining to look over Henry's shoulder at each stop. And at each of these stops, Lady Liberty's crowning rays proved empty. A hollow third; a fourth spike that merely echoed; a fifth and sixth that teased him with a stray set of bolts, but turned out to be as vacant as the rest.

Dang. Only one left. Dang, dang, dang.

Henry approached the seventh ray, and then stopped. Unable to hide a growing look of disappointment, he turned his head toward Eiffel.

"Listen to me, Henry," the great designer said, moving closer. "There is a measure of providence in every discovery. It led me to my vision for the tower. It led you to me. To Madame Liberty. Why should you be surprised that it will be the *seventh* sea? The *seventh* continent?"

Henry nodded.

Gustave, his sleepy eyes vibrantly awake now, squeezed the young adventurer's shoulder and wished him luck, *"Bonne chance, jeune homme!"*

The words, and the manner in which he'd said them, put Henry back at Mark Twain's desk for a quick moment. He remembered Mattie standing next to him, feeling her excitement as he sensed he was on the brink of getting the best of Skavenger.

"Go ahead, Henry! Go on!"

Henry Babbitt crawled in and reached deep inside the seventh sea, the seventh continent, as far as he possibly could. Slowly his hand circled the cold interior of the final ray. Looking. Reaching. Finding . . .

SOMETHING!

SOMETHING'S IN THERE!

The tip of his finger brushed over the edge of whatever-it-was-he-couldn't-tell-yet and a rush of air burst through his tightened lips.

"I found something!" he yelled, his voice echoing in the final ray of *La Liberté éclairant le monde*'s crown.

"What is it?!" Eiffel excitedly called back.

"I'm not sure yet!"

A year or two more of growth and Henry would have been able to reach it with ease, but not yet. Instead, he had to wriggle his way in a bit more so that his outstretched hand could finally grasp:

AN ENVELOPE.

He grabbed it and twisted his way back out, where Eiffel was waiting with keen anticipation. Feeling better than he had in a week, Henry held up the envelope for the visionary to see. It was the same brilliant yellow as the one given to him by Mark Twain, though this one featured an even deeper hue of sparkling gold.

"Open it!" Eiffel urged him.

Henry's finger was already under the envelope's flap, neatly ripping it open on the first try.

I found it, Chief! I found it, Dad! Skavenger's next clue. Right inside the Statue of Liberty's crown!

Henry's hands shook as he pulled out a small, elegant card within. He held it up to his astonished eyes.

There it is. The next riddle. The next clue.

"'Congratulations, worthy adventurer,'" Henry read the words out loud, until Gustave interrupted him.

"No, Henry," he said kindly. "This is your clue, not mine." Henry nodded and gulped, and then silently read the entire clue to himself.

Okay, here we go . . .

Your prize awaits you in Old New Amsterdam.

His eyes took in the words.

Mulberry, Little Water, Anthony, Cross, Orange. Enter the door that bears my name, but know that it will take ALL your courage, ALL your bravery, for ONLY YOU will have the chance to declare yourself winner of my incalculable treasure.

He looked up at Eiffel, having decided to read the next four words, the *last four words*, out loud for him to hear . . .

"'Good luck, lone adventurer.'"

The visionary shook his head in wonder and breathlessly asked, "Do you know where it is?!"

Henry looked at the words again. "I'm not sure yet," he replied, turning the card over and finding it blank. "I think it's in New York somewhere."

Just then, the first trickle of fear crept into the pit of his stomach. Fear at the meaning of the words he'd just read.

He had the *only* clue.

The one clue that others had already shown they were willing to kill for. Doubt. Grace. Who might not be in Paris for too much longer.

What do I do now? I can't just . . .

Suddenly overwhelmed by his discovery, he slowly looked up at one of Riggin's Three E's. His eyes begged the great designer for any words that might help him.

"I have faith in you, young man." Eiffel smiled reassuringly. "You are the lone adventurer. You stand on the threshold of doing what no one has done. You, and you alone."

Monsieur Gustave Eiffel patted Henry on the shoulder as he reaffirmed what they both now realized.

"Henry. You are the only one who can find Skavenger's treasure!"

TWENTY-ONE

Three of a Kind

HENRY TRIED HIS best not to run toward the front of the boat, even though not running after this little discovery was like asking the wind not to blow.

Countless thoughts and questions hammered through his mind as he walked . . . quickly: *The hunt's back on! If there's only one clue, no one else can find it. Okay, what do you do, what do you do? Figure it out, there's a start.*

Doubt. Dark Men. They were on the train. They could be here. No, no, no, don't go there. Keep your eye on the ball. Figure out the clue.

Mulberry. Little Water. Anthony. Cross. Orange.

Mulberry. Little Water . . .

What the heck does any of that mean? All right, just think it through. One at a time.

Anthony's a name, that feels like a safe bet. Cross? Could be a code maybe. Maybe, maybe not. Could be . . . well . . . okay, you can come back to Cross. What about Orange? Orange could be anything.

He walked faster, looking over his shoulder—double-checking his pocket to make sure the envelope was still in there.

It was.

What if you're able to solve it? This, the last clue? I mean, yeah, you don't have the ledger sheet anymore, but if you figure this one out and show up where you're s'posed to show up? You'll finally get to see Skavenger! He's gotta be able to help you get back somehow!

The port side of *Le Chasseur*—the hunter—was where he was headed. There was a little area wedged between the lifeboats where Jack and Ernie usually played cards with the Bulgarians. Henry had found them there days earlier while taking a rare walk, after hearing Jack crow that he'd drawn a spades flush.

This time it was Ernie he could hear as he drew closer.

"Full house, Nikolai! Nines and fours!"

The proud declaration was followed by the sound of the loser's cards being slapped to the wooden deck in disgust. Henry glanced in every direction before crouching low to find himself a foot away from Jack.

"Hey," he said to him with his widest smile of the last week.

"Whoa, Babbitt," Jack said as he gathered up the cards. "Decided to get out for a walk, huh? Good for you."

"You got room for another player?" Henry grinned as he pulled the envelope from his coat pocket. "I might be able to throw this into the pot."

Ernie's eyes grew wider than the pair of life rings hanging above his head.

"That's a different one, that's a different color, that one's new, isn't it?" He rattled off the words in half a second as he dropped the worn, yet winning, playing cards in front of him.

"It's not just a different one, and it's not just a new one," Henry answered. "It's the only one."

Jack threw down his cards and hopped into the air like a rocket. "We're out, boys, sorry," he informed the suddenly confused Bulgarians.

"What do you mean, to be out?" Nikolai protested. His fellow Bulgarian, Toma, merely held up his hands in dismay.

Jack and Ernie, though, were already smack-dab in front of Henry, their sudden, sharp attention focused on the envelope he held like treasure in his two hands.

"You found it?!" Ern asked him in amazement. "Where? When?"

"Here! Just now! All right, here's the deal," Henry started to babble. "Eiffel's on the ship. This ship. I found him. Down below. Storage. Eiffel!"

"Wait, wait, wait . . . slow down, Babbitt," Jack said, his hands urging Henry to keep his voice low. "What do you mean Eiffel's here? *The* Eiffel? The one you messed up on?"

Henry's head nodded like a steam piston hard at work. "That Eiffel. The Eiffel I messed up on. It wasn't the Tower we should have been looking for! The Tower's not there yet."

"Yeah, yeah, we kinda know that already," Ernie replied. "So what should we have been lookin' for?"

"The Statue!"

"Statue? What statue?" Jack whispered.

"The Statue of Lib—" Henry stopped, realizing it might not have been given that name quite yet. "It's the statue the French built; the one they're sending as a gift."

"I'VE HEARD OF THIS STATUE!" Ernie shouted. Jack's glare advised him to pipe down too.

"It's on this boat, Ern!" Henry had picked up on the whispering. "That's where I found it. Eiffel's making sure it gets to New York okay."

"And you think the clue you're holdin' right now, in your two hands, you think that's the only one?" Jack already looked convinced enough to start watching for anyone trying to overhear.

Henry looked around as well before opening the envelope. After his runaway breathing settled down, he gently pulled the card up just enough to reveal Skavenger's puzzle.

In a quiet and discreet voice, he read every word of it to them, then handed the envelope to Jack so he could take a look for himself. The twelve-year-old hunter swallowed as Jack repeated the last few words that Henry already knew by heart . . .

"'Good luck, lone adventurer.'"

Jack studied the handwritten words a second time before handing the clue back to Henry, shaking his head and saying, "You did it, Babbitt. You really did it! We're back in this thing!"

He gave Henry a proud pop in the shoulder—much different from the pop he'd given him on the Paris train platform a week earlier.

"We all did it," Henry said with a smile. "All of us. Mattie especially."

As he said those last few words, he noticed a look of dread beginning to overtake Ernie.

"Ern? Ernie?!" Henry asked with a quickly worried look. "What's wrong?"

Jack turned to look as well. Ernie's eyes had an almost-glazed look to them.

"I . . . I don't know if I can do this," he said to the two of them, a wavering tone in his voice.

"What do you mean, you can't do it?" Henry asked, growing more and more worried by the second. "We've got the very last—"

"I mean, I don't think I can walk through that door, that's what," Ernie interrupted. "I don't even wanna get close to that door."

Henry had seen Ernie afraid more than once, but this was beyond that. This time he wasn't just afraid. He was frozen with terror.

Even Jack looked more concerned than Henry'd ever seen him. "Ern, hey, what's the matter here, pal?" he asked.

Out of the blue, Ernie erupted. "What's the matter?!" he shouted loudly. "You really have no idea what's the matter here, Jack?!"

A thinly built ship purser with a hastily trimmed graying beard approached, drawn by Ernie's bubbling meltdown. "*Est-ce que messieurs, là m'excusent sont un problème?*" he inquired.

"No. No, sir," Henry quickly reassured him as he tucked the envelope back into his pocket. "*Aucun problème.*"

Appearing to be unconvinced, the purser turned his attention back to Ernie, apparently wanting to hear it straight out of him. "*Problème?*" he asked again.

C'mon, Ern, calm down now. Calm down. Envelope's in the pocket. Just get him to walk away. Lower your voice. We're all good.

Ernie shook his head. "No," he answered the purser, less than convincingly in Henry's mind at least. "No problem. No problem at all."

The purser said nothing for a long moment or two before giving Ernie and the boys nothing more than a curt nod and a simple "*bon*" as he turned and walked away.

The very second he was out of sight, Jack whipped around to confront Ernie. "No *problème*? No problem?" He somehow managed to keep his voice under control. "I'd say we've got a big problem, Ernie pal! Now tell me what's got you so spooked."

"THINK ABOUT THE—" Ernie started to reply, before realizing he was still too loud. "Think about the clue, Jack," he whispered. "You're so excited Henry found it, you didn't even listen to it!"

Henry took in a quick breath.

Ernie's already solved it. That's why he's scared. He's got it!

"Lemme see it again." Jack curled his finger toward Henry, who pulled out the envelope again and handed it over.

"You figured it out, didn't you?" Henry asked Ernie as he took a step closer to him.

Ernie nodded, but said nothing. The fear that had overtaken him a few minutes earlier seemed to be getting a second wind.

"It's gotta be in New York, right?" Henry asked. "Right?"

"Oh, it's in New York all right." Ernie sat against the edge of a nearby lifeboat and put his head in his hands. "It's in New York. At Mulberry . . . and Little Water . . . and Anthony . . . and Cross . . . and Orange."

Jack's chin dropped with what looked to be a rush of sickening understanding. Slowly, he placed the card containing the clue back into the envelope.

Henry was confused. "Okay . . ." he calmly said to both of them. "So the way you just said that makes it sound like you're talking about streets."

"He is talking about streets." Jack handed the envelope back to him. "Skavenger's right. This is gonna take all the courage and all the bravery we've got, if we can even find this door that's got his name on it."

Henry was now completely lost.

All right, so we're talking New York streets. Got it. Mulberry and Orange annnnnd three others. So?

"They aren't just five streets, Babbitt," Jack uttered, as if he'd heard Henry's silent question. "You're from New York, you should know what they are. They're five points."

TWENTY-TWO

Five Points

THE TWO DAYS following the discovery of Skavenger's final clue were incredibly tense. Nearly every moment, Henry and the boys thought about what awaited them in New York.

Mulberry.

Little Water.

Anthony.

Cross.

Orange.

Five Points. The notorious spot in lower Manhattan where Ernie's parents had confidently gone to spread the word of God and failed to return.

Where they'd been murdered.

Even though it was still difficult for Ernie to talk about, he managed to tell Henry that the intersection of the five streets remained home to the most vicious gangs New York had ever seen.

Crime could be found on almost every corner, which made it clear in Henry's mind that the final step in Skavenger's Hunt was simple, yet so, so difficult.

It was a test of courage.

Now, finally, the two days were behind them and they had arrived in New York. It was raining as their horse-drawn carriage—provided by Eiffel himself—pulled away from Castle Garden in the Battery, home to New York's port of entry.

More than once, Chief had told Henry about the history of this spot. The rugged port had felt the first footsteps taken in America by thousands of arriving men and women, all seeking the hope of a new land.

When Henry saw it, though, it had been a strange sight.

Jack and Ernie, along with almost all of the hopeful immigrants, crowded shoulder to shoulder on the ship's railing as the southern edge of Manhattan prowled into view.

Henry and Eiffel, however, had chosen to gaze out at a tiny, empty island.

That's where you're headin', Lady Liberty. The young hunter smiled. *You'll be the first thing everyone sees in America. Torch high in the air. Sayin' hello to all your tired, your poor, your huddled masses yearnin' to breathe free.*

Despite the hope provided by that sight, Henry couldn't help but think about what was ahead of them. Monsieur Eiffel had promised that his New York host would take exceptional care of all of them upon their arrival. And so the awaiting gentleman had, welcoming them outside immigration with the finest of carriages and then accompanying them for the ride into the city.

Now, Eiffel glanced at the three boys sitting across from him in the bouncing coach.

"If you boys wish for someone to go with you," the great designer suggested, "it's certainly not too late."

Henry didn't reply, waiting to see if Jack or Ernie might. He kept a steady gaze through the rain-specked carriage window.

"Henry?" Eiffel asked again, this time with a growing hint of concern. "Would you like someone to go with you?"

Jack turned to look at him, while Ernie kept his vacant stare on the floor of the carriage.

"No, *merci*," Henry answered Eiffel. "We're supposed to do this alone."

"So you've told me several times." The visionary nodded. "I just wish to make sure before we bid farewell."

Henry smiled at Eiffel, then turned to look through the window again. The sight of New York, especially with a bit of unseasonal weather, reminded him of . . .

Christmas Eve.

Snow comin' down. Mom driving you next to the park. Thinking you were about to start two days of nothing-but-being-inside.

Heck, Jeremy's prob'ly still watching "The Tick Loves Santa!" I can hear him right now. Hey "H," what'd you do over break?

Ohhhh, not much. Crossed the Atlantic twice, hitched a train ride to Missouri, snuck inside the Vanderbilt Mansion. Oh yeah, I also met Mark Twain, Gustave Eiffel, and this legendary newspaper publisher who's kinda sittin' across from me right now. The guy whose name is still on the biggest writing prizes in the whole entire world. The guy who raised a hundred thousand dollars for the pedestal the Statue of Liberty's gonna stand on? Y'know . . . that guy.

The publisher with the bushy black mustache and equally thick beard glanced at Henry over the top of his reading glasses. "Don't forget, we have a deal, yes?" he reminded him. "Should you solve Skavenger's riddle, I'll want an exclusive for all of my papers."

"Well, Mr. Pulitzer," Henry answered him. "I think maybe we should do the solving part first."

"Fair enough," Joseph Pulitzer replied, smiling as he turned the page of the newspaper he was reading. The newspaper he owned. Not just this one, but each and every copy printed in the city.

The patter of late-night rain had started to ease on the carriage roof. Jack straightened his cap and pulled his jacket collar tight. "This is close enough, thanks," he said.

Pulitzer removed his glasses and immediately struck a worried tone. "You boys want to be dropped in this neighborhood?" he asked.

Henry nodded.

Pulitzer knew nothing of Skavenger's clue, but the youngest of the three hunters could see he hadn't expected the edge of the most dangerous neighborhood in New York City to be their destination.

The great publisher tapped the window nearest him and nodded to the streets on that side. "That is the direction you need to take. Or I'm afraid I cannot let you out."

He then pointed toward the opposite window. "Because if you go that way?" Pulitzer simply shook his head, not needing to say a single word.

Henry could see that the direction in which he'd pointed was nothing more than a gateway into despair. Rickety old buildings—some made of brick, some made of damp and sagging wood—loomed over a host of dark alleyways.

"Which way does the clue take you, Henry?" Eiffel solemnly asked.

Henry had trouble looking him in the eye. "We'll take the good way, don't worry," he quietly lied.

The visionary waited several seconds before nodding. "I want all three of you to remember the words of Aristotle," he said with a serious tone of voice. "'Courage is the first of human qualities because it is the quality which guarantees the others.'"

Pulitzer lifted his cane and tapped the roof. The driver above whistled for his two horses to stop, and the lumbering carriage came to a halt. All was silent aside from an impatient snort from one of the two rain-soaked steeds.

"Be careful and safe," Pulitzer cautioned one last time. "And remember our deal."

Henry gave one last look toward Eiffel, hoping the Frenchman's reassuring smile would put him at ease, but finding that it didn't.

"*Bonne chance*, Henry," Gustave told him, his voice thick with concern. "My worthy adventurer."

They shook hands all around, and Eiffel opened the carriage door. Jack almost had to drag Ernie out, but Henry followed readily. A handful of thumping heartbeats later, the three boys watched as the sanctuary of Joseph Pulitzer's carriage rolled away.

CLIP CLOP CLIP CLOP clip clop clip clop . . .

Leaving them alone on the outskirts of Five Points.

❧

Jack, of course, was the first to disregard Pulitzer's warning, heading for the risky edge of Anthony Street the minute the sound of the carriage was gone.

"All right, follow me," he said to both of them over his shoulder.

Henry took a deep settling breath. "Okay, Ern, you ready to do this?" He stepped forward, right into a puddle he'd missed in the dim twilight.

He stopped. And not because of the puddle or the darkness.

Ernie hadn't moved.

Ernie wouldn't move, Henry could tell.

"I can't, I'm sorry," Ernie said to him with a ragged tone. His own wet shoes looked firmly anchored to the street.

"Jack! Hey, Jack!" Henry called out, hoping he wasn't too loud. Jack turned and was back to the two of them in an instant. Ernie looked stricken when he got there.

"Sorry. I'm sorry. Sorry," he said to both of them.

"Hey . . . we'll make it, pal, all right? We'll be okay." Jack put a hand on his shoulder, but Ernie shook his head.

"I can't go in there." He gulped hard to keep the tears from rolling. "I thought I could. But . . ."

Jack tried one more time. "Nuthin's gonna happen, Ern. I prom—"

"You can't promise, Jack," Ernie cut him off short with a weary smile. "You can't. People promised my mother, people promised my father. Look what happened to them. They got killed in there!"

The first tear found its way onto his cheek.

"Ernie, we can't just leave you here," Henry said. "I mean, what are you gonna do?"

"I'm goin' to Aunt Hazel's and Uncle Phil's, that's what I'm gonna do." He answered the question as if he'd decided days ago. "I've still got a family, you heard what she said. She said I was welcome anytime."

"Ernie, wait." Jack lowered his head so he could look his friend straight in the eye. "You need to finish this first. You'll regret it if you don't."

Ernie smiled and shook his head. "Nah, I'll regret it if I do, Jack. Think about it. Everything my folks did was just them tryin' to show I could do somethin' myself. Make things better. That was a big part of why they walked in there."

He nodded to the Points and then looked at Henry. "Wouldn't have figured that out if you hadn't solved that first clue and dragged me halfway around the world."

Henry felt a hard pull of emotion.

Can't argue with that. At least you got somewhere to go.

"You sure about this?" Henry asked, even though he already knew the answer.

"Yeah. Yeah, I'm sure. Thanks."

Ernie had one more thing to say, though.

"Don't go in there," he said to both of them. "Aunt Hazel, she'll take care of all of us. I know she will. It's like Mark Twain said. All we gotta do is ask."

The rain had just now broken into a fading shower. The nearest alleyway leading into Five Points beckoned.

"Sorry, I gotta see this through to the end," Jack told his friend. "Same reason you shouldn't."

"I know you do." Ernie exhaled with a worried look. He cast a hopeful look toward Henry. "You?"

"Yeah," Henry answered. "I gotta see it through too."

Ernie sadly nodded, holding out his hand to wish them both luck. "You'll know where to find me," he said, making sure to add, "Promise you'll turn back if it goes bad in there."

"We will," Jack promised, though Henry knew better.

Ernie backed away, not wanting to turn quite yet. After a few more steps, he finally gave a wave and turned to head toward the somewhat brighter lights of safety a block away.

Good luck, Ernie. Thanks for everything.

Ernie spun around one last time.

"Hey, Henry!" he shouted and held up his raggedy old journal. "All those days on the train? The ship?" He thumped the cover and tucked it away again. "I was finishin' writin' my mother's book! Turns out it's not a piece of crap after all!"

A few seconds and another wave later, Ernie Samuels was gone around the corner. Gone for good. Same as Pulitzer's carriage had been for minutes now. Same as anyone with a sane mind would be if they accidentally found themselves in this neighborhood.

"Well?" Jack said as he turned to Henry. "We've got ourselves two Babbitts." He puffed his cheeks wide. "Better than just one, yeah?"

"I hope so," Henry answered.

Together, they stepped into the alleyway that led to the Points.

❧

The first match flared three blocks later at the opening of another darkened alley. A thickly browed man, twenty or so very rough years old, sparked half a cigarette before handing the match to someone next to him.

The man took a long pull before grunting to Jack and Henry, "Doubt you'll wanna be goin' any farther than right here, lads."

You got that right. Henry shuddered. *Just keep walkin'. Don't say a thing. Get to Mulberry, get to Orange. Find the door with Skavenger's name on it.*

Both Henry and Jack peered back to see the two men step out from the alley. They were motionless as they watched them, aside from the jumping light coming off their cigarettes. The two men stared for a few seconds more and then cackled, apparently deciding the boys weren't worth pursuing.

That was the one thing Jack had told Henry could be in their favor—that the two of them would appear worthless to anyone who saw them. Their frayed and drenched coats, cracked shoes, even their expressions seemed to shout that they had nothing of value.

Henry, though, worried that their shabby appearance might not make any difference in Five Points. Too many people had been hurt there. Or in the case of Ernie's parents, much worse.

The stench of rotten things came and went as they walked deeper in. Even when the smell occasionally eased, it never fully went away. Worse yet, Henry could sometimes see where the reeking smell came from—dead rats bloated and infested with white maggots, rusty metal buckets half-filled with things he didn't want to get any closer to.

There were no more broken and twisted fire escapes on the sides of the buildings, as there had been the first few blocks. Only high-reaching scorch marks from fires that looked to have been barely fought.

The bleak surroundings seemed to press in on them, and Henry tried swallowing what little moisture he had left in his mouth.

Door with Skavenger's name on it. Keep looking, keep looking, keep moving.

They kept walking, their shoes squishing into the muddy gravel that served as somewhat of a makeshift sidewalk. Faster, but not too fast, passing another alley opening without so much as a glance.

They heard footsteps. The sound of the footsteps was steady; not growing louder, not growing softer.

"Don't say anything," Jack whispered.

"Don't worry," Henry answered, unable to resist taking a quick look back. Two men were walking toward them. One wore a tattered dark vest and a cap that shadowed his eyes completely; the other was shrouded in dreary and dirty ill-fitting clothes from head to toe.

The larger of the two men—the one in the tattered vest—spit onto the gravel, then reached down to scoop up a handful of the small stones without breaking his steady, unsettling pace.

"AYY," the man called out.

The boys ignored him. Still walking, still looking for Skavenger's door.

"Ayy, you!" the man demanded in a louder voice, punctuating his sentence with a gurgling cough.

"What?" Jack tried growling over his shoulder.

"What? You're asking me what?" The man lazily tossed a single stone in their direction, and then another.

Plink . . . plink . . . plunk.

The third of the small rocks ricocheted off Henry's head.

"I'll tell ya what," the man said as he reached to the ground for more. With almost every word that followed, he threw another stone. "Why don't you . . . tell me . . . what the two of ya are doin' in my neighborhood? Middle of the night."

A mucky gray rat, very much alive and close to a foot in length, scurried out of a gutter and right between Henry's feet.

"Aaaaagggh!" *Rat! RAAAAT!*

"Welcome to the neighborhood," Jack uttered under his breath. "Just keep walkin'."

The clockwork-steady footsteps behind them continued. A scream broke the quiet from somewhere up ahead. It was hard to tell whether it had come from a man or a woman, but the one thing that *was* certain? The scream was not followed by a second.

"HEY." It was the man from behind again. "I asked the two of ya a question." He sounded as if he was losing patience.

Jack stayed quiet for a few more strides before yelling over his shoulder, "We're meetin' our uncle at Little Water. Johnny Flynn? You know him?"

Johnny Flynn? C'mon, Jack, least you can do is come up with a scarier name.

The man scoffed. "Never heard of no Johnny Flynn at Little Water. You?" he asked his smaller, equally sketchy accomplice.

"Nah." The smaller man blew snot from his nose. The large man sent another small stone sailing through the air, this one bouncing off Jack's shoulder. He was smart enough to ignore it.

Henry closed his eyes for a second, hoping that last word might actually be the last word. The steady crunch of gravel behind them, though, gave him his answer.

Crunnnnch crunnnnch crunnnnch crunnnnch . . .

"All right . . . whatta ya say the two of you stop right now," the larger man finally threatened. "So we can have ourselves a talk."

Henry's breathing started to race—loud enough that he knew Jack could hear it.

His great-great-grandfather quietly, yet firmly, said under his own quickening breath, "All right, Babbitt. I got an idea. Here's what I need you to do. All your bravery, all your courage, I need you to reach down deep for it. It's there, I know it is. These two guys are a wreck; they can't hurt us."

"What do you mean, they can't hurt us?" Henry asked, still moving ahead. "What are you gonna do?"

But Jack had already wheeled around and was now waiting for the two men to draw closer. Henry zipped back with just enough time to ask him, "What are you doing?"

"Haven't decided yet," Jack whispered back. "Remember, though, whatever I do? You do."

Haven't decided yet?! C'mon, Jack, look at these guys!

Both were covered in scars and welts of varying age—some new, some not. The smaller man had a ragged pink scar on his upper neck that dried up the last remaining spit in Henry's mouth. The scroungy, intimidating pair slowed as they drew close to the boys.

"Well, well. See?" The larger man came to a stop. "That wasn't so hard, was it?"

"Can't believe you ain't never heard of Johnny Flynn," Jack said, trying to lower his voice. He rammed his hands into his coat pockets, as if he were carrying something they should be worried about.

The large man smirked at his partner, jabbing a thumb in Jack's direction. He tossed the remaining stones in his hand onto the ground, then slowly reached into his own pocket.

"I ain't never heard of no Johnny Flynn, no Jimmy Flynn, no nobody Flynn," he said as he pulled out a rusted knife. "This, however," he warned, "you can call whatever you want."

"Jack?" Henry quietly, yet urgently, asked.

But Johnny Flynn's so-called nephew was already tough-talking the knife-wielding man again. "Well, that's too bad," he said with his low voice. "Because we have heard of him, and I think we're already late. Babbitt! Time to go!"

Jack whipped around and gave Henry a shove in the back. Both boys bolted in the opposite direction, the walkway gravel flying from beneath their shoes. The scarred men came right after them.

In a dead sprint the hunters ran. Not out of Five Points, but deeper into it. Down one street, then down another. A block this way, a block that way.

Still . . . the ragged, scarred men gave chase. Faster than Henry thought they might.

The next few blocks felt like the twisty and winding path Jack had led Henry through back in Hell's Kitchen, only they were covering this route a whole lot faster.

Up and over a broken and leaning fence; dashing through two dark, but fortunately empty, wet alleyways; then down a pair of garbage-strewn streets. Thankfully, the boys didn't encounter any people. Not so thankfully, their path seemed to be leading them deeper and deeper into danger.

"Keep going, Babbitt!" Jack yelled as he glanced over his shoulder. "Faster! We got 'em!"

"You boys are DEAD! DEAD!" the knife-packing man shouted from behind, but his voice was already beginning to fade in the distance.

Neither Jack nor Henry, though, looked as if they were about to risk slowing down. Not here. Not now.

Keep goin', keep goin'! I don't care where we end up, let's just get away from these guys!

Jack skidded around the corner of a seedy broken building, his shoulder brushing the bricks while Henry stayed right behind him. Still running. Running, running, running.

One more block . . . one more street . . . just to make sure . . .

. . . until Jack allowed himself one final look and a quiet laugh as he slowed to a stop. He leaned over, hands on his knees. His breathing was deep and loud.

Henry slowed and stopped right in front of him. He cocked his head in each direction, not wanting to say a single word until his breathing settled and he was sure the two scarred men were gone.

Once he felt it was safe, he finally turned his head and looked Jack right in the eye.

"*That* . . . was your . . . idea? *That*?!" he asked in between heaving breaths. "Johnny Flynn . . . and then RUN?!"

Jack grinned at him.

"Game . . . ON . . . Babbitt!" he answered, his laughter making it even harder to catch his own breath.

Henry couldn't help but laugh too. And then they were both laughing. Right there in the worst part of New York . . . laughing harder at their near-death experience than at any time since they'd met.

"Okay, 'nuff of that," Jack said, finally pushing himself up. "Let's find out where we are, all right?"

∽

Ten minutes and four blocks later, they both knew. Through the darkness of that last stretch, there had been a shimmer of dull light, illuminating what appeared to be an opening to a common area of some sort.

A handful of people walked back and forth. Their faces were filled with despair and their eyes were vacant. Not so with the seedy panhandlers. Their eyes were alert and darting, seeking unfamiliar faces who might be able to spare something. Anything.

The boys turned down a few of them as they walked into the open square between the pale and narrowing buildings. They then stopped and took a long, depressing look all around them.

The area resembled a rotting center hub of a disgusting wheel.

They had just walked past Little Water, the street name simply carved into a crumbling brick wall. Cross looked to be up ahead at eleven o'clock. Mulberry and Orange had to be the two streets on their left. And Anthony was where they now stood.

They were standing in the heart of Five Points.

Old leaking barrels of unknown ooze spilled into the muddy ruts that ran through the filthy epicenter of the neighborhood. The open windows on some of the taller buildings looked like glaring eyes, silently asking the two boys why they had even bothered to come.

Henry and Jack looked around the sorrowful gloom, looking for a door with Skavenger's name and making sure to avoid meeting the gaze of anyone. The few looks they did receive were largely indifferent. Even the painted ladies of the aptly named Orange Street looked bored and disinterested in them.

"All right, this is where he said it'd be," Jack muttered as he looked at the decaying neighborhood. "See any doors look promising? Anything with 'Skavenger' carved right into the wood? Maybe it might even be burned in. Who knows?"

Henry was trying to figure that part out himself.

Even if Skavenger managed to put his name on a door, it had to be dangerous for him too. What'd he do? Bring his fancy carriage right down the middle of Anthony Street into Five Points?

Henry glanced to his left, checking Orange Street again. Most of the buildings over there were completely dark except for a few flickering candles. Best he could tell, there wasn't a single door with a name on it. Not that he could see.

He turned to Mulberry Street, which looked just as desolate.

Maybe we already walked by it. He glanced back in the direction from which they'd come. *Maybe it was back there on Little Water . . . or here on—*

He took in a sudden and sharp breath.

No.

No, no, no.

Henry couldn't move. He couldn't even breathe.

There . . . beyond one of the dripping wedge-shaped buildings, under a broken streetlamp, a figure stood in the shadows. Its blackened outline was darker than the surrounding night.

The Dark Man.

And not just *any* Dark Man.

Grace.

He was there. Somehow, he'd found them. It was past midnight in Five Points, and yet there he stood, Henry was absolutely sure of it. A silhouette, yes, but it was Grace all the same. Just like Henry had known it was him on the train heading to St. Louis.

"All right, sooo where ya wanna start, Babbitt?" Jack sighed, unaware of what—of *whom*—Henry was looking at.

He can't be here. There was no clue for him to find, no way he could have known we left Paris. How? Wha . . ? They must have been on Le Chasseur *all along!*

"Ja . . ." he tried whispering. "Jac . . ."

SOOOOOOOOOOON . . .

The cold word chillingly rolled through Henry's head as Jack finally turned.

"All right, what do you say we go over—" His voice caught as he saw the look on Henry's face. "Holy smokes, Babbitt! What's wrong?!"

Henry could only dip his forehead toward the dark image under the streetlamp.

"It's him." He gulped, seeing the icy-blue glint of the man's devious eyes, even from a distance. "It's Grace."

Jack fell silent as he looked, his eyes quickly finding him as well. "No, no. It can't be," he said, shaking his head. "That's impossible."

For a short moment, all they could do was stare. Stare and stare some more, in growing disbelief.

Until, with one intimidating stride, Grace began to walk toward them. Slowly, steadily, moving closer.

And then the nightmare grew worse.

With Grace now heading for Henry and Jack, two more of the Dark Men appeared at the ends of Anthony and Cross. They began to walk toward the boys. Then the fourth emerged from the gloom of Little Water behind them.

"All of them," Henry's voice quivered. "We gotta do something, we gotta do something, Jack. What do we do?"

Jack let out a deep breath. But Henry could tell there was something strangely different about it, even here . . . even now.

It was an angry breath.

"We do what we came here to do," Jack growled as he shoved Henry toward Cross Street. "Nobody's takin' my chance or your chance away from us. This is our hunt, not theirs!"

They walked as fast as they could, not wanting to run unless it was absolutely necessary. Even so, the gaunt neighborhood stragglers despondently leaning against the crumbling brick buildings seemed to know something out of the ordinary was taking place.

Jack shook his head as he quickened his stride. "Maybe they'll walk away like they did on the train."

"They were on the ship going to Paris too," Henry chose to admit.

"You saw 'em? All four of 'em?!"

Henry looked back again. "Just the one out front." He nodded at Grace. "Doubt was there too."

"*Doubt* was on the ship?!" Jack sped up a little more. "How come you never told us?!"

"Would it have helped?"

"I dunno. Prob'ly not, I guess."

Jack skirted an approaching panhandler, and Henry now had to work to keep up. It wasn't that hard to do, though, thanks to the sound growing louder behind him.

Kuhthump kuhthump kuhthump kuhthump . . .

The boots of the four Dark Men seemed to thunder against the wet grit of the street. Striding side by side. Insistent.

Henry looked back just as a rat scurried in front of Grace. His boot landed on the grimy rodent's tail. The rat squealed with pain, but Grace didn't blink.

We gotta get outta here! We gotta get outta here NOW!

"No, no, we stay. We finish this," Jack firmly ordered as if sensing what Henry was feeling.

Stay? We can't stay! They're gonna herd us right into some dead end. Look at 'em, Jack! They're right back there!

Henry's rattling thoughts stopped for a short second when he heard Jack laugh under his breath. An actual laugh.

"Heck of an adventure, huh, Babbitt?" Jack looked over his shoulder again. "When you and I get outta here, we're gonna do somethin' like this again. Maybe not with these four jokers, but somethin', that's for sure. And then we'll go on another one and another one after that. You with me?"

The words, so similar to his own father's, made Henry stand up straighter. "Yeah. Yeah, I'm with you," Henry replied as he turned to smile at his great-great-grandfather . . .

And then he stopped.

Stopped right in the very middle of Cross Street. Stopped, even though he could still hear the Dark Men approaching.

Kuhthump kuhthump kuhthump kuhthump . . .

"Come on, Babbitt! C'mon!" Jack spun around and reached for Henry's jacket. "We can't stop. Gotta keep walkin', gotta keep . . . NOOOO! BABBITT!"

Henry had already started running.

Not running away from the foursome of pursuing men, but running toward something. Something else. His beaten shoes slipped on the scattered gravel, but he kept on moving.

"Hey! HEY!" Jack shouted as he ran after him. "Babbitt! Stop!"

Henry took the steps leading up to a broken building two at a time. He stopped on the landing, facing a single front door that featured two solitary letters:

H S

The letters had been carved right into the wood, and they were fresh. Henry reached out to touch them as Jack came running up the steps. Seeing the Dark Men still on approach, he took them three by three, jumping over a broken whiskey bottle with his long final leap.

Henry reached for the doorknob . . . and then hesitated. Not out of fear, but with the panic-laced knowledge that . . .

It's the last door. The last one. This is it.

"Open it!" Jack yelled as the four men drew near.

Henry gave it a turn.

Click.

The doorknob turned the width of only a fingernail before firmly catching.

C'mon, c'mon, not here! Not now!

It was locked. Seemingly locked tight. But it had turned just enough to convince him to give it one more try—heck, ten more tries.

Henry closed his eyes.

Under his breath, he said the words that had worked once before at a mansion in this same city.

"Your journey . . ."

The Dark Men were nearly at the bottom of the stairs. Henry had to catch his breath before trying again.

"Your journey shall be . . . unlocked."

The twelve-year-old hunter twisted the knob and heard the tumbler give way. Jack reached over his shoulder and thumped the door open with the heel of his hand.

In.

And.

Thump.

SHUT!

They slammed the door closed behind them. The corridor in which they now found themselves was dark, but there were hints of light coming from within. Henry and Jack looked down a long, barren hallway, and it was the lure of that feeble light that almost made Henry forget to—

"Lock the door!" He whirled around, but Jack was already clicking the bolts, of which there were two. Hopefully they were strong ones.

The two boys looked at each other. They were trapped, Henry knew that much, but there was something else he knew.

"Jack!" he whispered, still short on breath. "We made it! We're here!"

"Yeah, I know. We're *all* here, if ya know what I mean. Whatta we do now?"

Henry turned his head and looked down the paint-peeled hallway, a crackling sound coming from deep inside the room—the part that was hidden around a corner twenty feet ahead of them.

Orange and yellow light danced on the weary ceiling at the far end of the hall; it was enough to convince Henry of at least one thing about the section of the room neither of them could see.

A fireplace? With a fire in it? Here in Five Points?

There was a *click* as the knob on the front door began to turn, one way and then the other, followed by the unsettling tapping of a long fingernail against the knob itself.

They're trying to get in.

Right now.

The four Dark Men.

Henry tried to ignore it, while Jack nodded his head toward the wavering light coming from inside. Slowly, quietly, the two of them stepped their way along the splintered wood floor to the tempting opening.

Jack bumped into Henry as he stopped at the threshold. "Sorry," he said, but it wasn't necessary . . .

Because of what they saw.

The room stood nearly empty except for an oak table situated to one side of a roaring fireplace. An even older leather case, a satchel, was positioned precisely in the center of the table, six burning candles surrounding it.

There was an old gray chair facing the fire, its high-arching back blocking any view of who might be sitting in it.

But Henry knew there was someone there.

He could see a hand on top of a walking stick. Its owner, face still unseen, basked in the warmth of the curling flames.

"Congratulations," Henry heard a familiar voice coldly utter. He felt his throat go dry.

Can't be . . . no . . .

Hiram Doubt slowly stood and prodded the fire with the tip of his cane, not looking at either of the young men. He flicked a stray burning ember back into the hot pit, then turned to his two guests. The wicked grin Henry first saw outside the Vanderbilt Mansion was on the sinister man's face once more; a shadow crept over the teardrop scar as he turned his back on the fire. In this very moment, though, the smile wasn't just wicked—it was much worse than that.

It was victorious.

Henry's shoulders sagged.

We lost. It's over. I don't know how, but it is. Everything the four of us did. Every clue, every step to get here. Mattie. All of it for nothing.

The malevolent winner of the hunt stepped closer to Henry. His cold features began to take shape as the young man's eyes adjusted to the dim light.

"Seems we meet once more, my friend," Doubt said with his icy tone. "Though I'm quite sure I've neglected, up until now at least, to give you my proper name."

He held out his hand, the deadly chill of his bleak eyes filling with sudden and unexpected warmth.

"Hunter S. Skavenger," he smiled as he introduced himself. "The honor is mine."

TWENTY-THREE

Find Me

SKAVENGER? SKAVENGER!

The shock of the introduction was so great, Henry's hands shook worse than if he actually had been greeted by Hiram Doubt. In that very moment, he realized there was no Doubt. There never had been. All along, the legendary villain had been nothing more than a brilliant idea inside the head of the man before him—the man who had designed and constructed the hunt.

The hunt the boys had just won.

"You're Hunter Skavenger?" Jack asked, his mouth hanging half-open.

"Indeed," the gentleman replied as they shook hands. "And you," he added with a now-steady smile, "you are Jackson Babbitt, yes?"

"Uhhh, yes, I . . ." Jack started to reply, then stopped. "How'd you know that?"

Skavenger winked and left the question unanswered as he extended his hand to Henry. The twelve-year-old victorious hunter held out his own trembling hand, and the mythical creator of the Great Hunt took it with a reassuring grip.

"Hi." Henry finally found a word he could form. "I'm . . ."

"Henry Babbitt, I know," Skavenger kindly acknowledged, his voice no longer holding its sinister edge. "Such bravery, such courage. The both of you."

Neither of them had heard the front door open, and Henry felt a familiar hand fall onto his shoulder from behind. A hand that was no longer cold.

It was Grace, backed by his three shadowy friends—not a one of them frightening any longer, just as Doubt was no longer Doubt.

"My closest associate," Skavenger informed them. "Mr. Jonathan Grace."

"A pleasure to make your acquaintance," Grace said as he squeezed Henry's shoulder, though very gently this time. "And not a moment too *soon*, it seems."

This time there was no chill in the word. No hissing that had taken up residence in Henry's nightmares. Simply a good supply of genuine warmth in both his voice and his eyes.

Grace offered the same gesture and words to Jack.

There was a protective look to all four of the men, which, now, in this moment of stunning revelation, made perfect sense to Henry.

"I tasked Mr. Grace and his men with watching over all of you," Skavenger explained with a now tender voice. "Testing you as well, of course, since you began solving my riddles faster than the other hunters. Even faster than that pesky Hiram Doubt."

He gave the two of them a sly and subtle look as he added, "You shouldn't have worried, you know. All you had to do was consider the name I'd given him to decide if he was a real threat."

Ohhhh, of course . . . of course that's what you did. Doubt!

Skavenger stood in front of them, softly placing a hand on each boy's shoulder. "They were guarding you, Henry. You too, Jackson. And your good friend, Ernest." Then he smiled sadly as he said, "Unfortunately, though . . . we very much failed one of you."

Grace moved closer to face both of them. One in particular.

"Henry," he said with an almost broken voice. "We tried our best to save her that night in Paris. But the river had already taken her away." His voice began to struggle, now nothing more than a pained whisper. "I'm glad I was at least able to pull you out."

Henry looked up at the man who'd been the source of so much of his own fear. The man who'd glided past him on the distant side of Cornelius Vanderbilt's mansion, who had silently stood outside the cavern of boxes on the train, who had held him high against the railing of the SS *Persévérance*.

The man who had saved his life.

"That . . . that was you?" Henry managed, even though he was close to speechless. "I . . . I didn't know who . . . I wasn't sure . . ."

His voice trailed off as he looked up to offer Grace a nod of extreme gratitude. "Thank you . . . and . . . thanks for trying to save Mattie."

The once-but-no-longer Dark Man gave Henry a sorrowful nod as Skavenger moved behind the brown oak table and placed his hands on each side of the leather case.

"Gentlemen . . . I think it's time we discuss the reason that you and many others risked so much during my hunt." His voice softened as his fingers tapped the small leather satchel. "A fortune both enormous and incalculable."

It's NOT money. Not in that tiny thing. It's gotta be something else. Something better.

Henry saw Jack giving him a puzzled glance—one that Skavenger caught as well. *"Problème?"* he asked with a wry smile.

"Oh . . . no, sir," Jack answered. "No problem. I just . . . I guess I wasn't expecting . . . whatever it is, to be in that."

Henry thought it best to wait for the right moment to ask his own question. The question that involved Skavenger's name on the ledger sheet that had been lost in France.

Not only his name, but also a promise.

To whoever has found this page from my ledger: find me. There is a way back.

Henry's eyes rose up to the architect of the Great Hunt.

"Henry, I have something to ask you," Skavenger said in his most serious voice yet. "What do you believe is the enormous and incalculable reward for winning this hunt that I constructed? Something no one aside from you and Jackson has ever been able to do."

Henry didn't have to ponder long. "I think it's something we don't expect it to be," he answered.

Skavenger said nothing, content to let the small smile now growing on his face speak for itself. He looked toward Jack.

"And you, Jackson?"

Same as Henry, Jack barely wasted a second.

"I think, Mr. Skavenger," he said almost sheepishly, "I think I've already won enough, just by doin' what nobody thought I could. That's the real reason I did this in the first place. To show I wasn't nuthin'." He then stopped for a moment before finishing. "Whatever your reward is . . . I want Henry to have it."

Henry was overwhelmed. Not only by what Jack had just said, but because he could have sworn he heard more than one of the Dark Men sniffling back tears.

Skavenger placed his palms on top of the small satchel. His smile had now grown into one of immense pride.

"And now I know," he said, his hands moving toward the small latch. "Now I know that my reward will go to someone truly worthy. Because it must only go to someone who proves themselves worthy or truly needful in the moment. Someone clever. Someone brave and adventurous. Someone who will make certain my greatest treasure will be used well for their entire lifetime."

The fire crackled and spit as Skavenger opened the satchel and pulled out a perfectly bound leather journal. Its cover was hard and weathered. He laid it down on the table in front of them.

Henry took in a swift breath.

There it is. That has to be it.

"My father was given this by his father," Skavenger began, the tips of his fingers now softly pressing down on the cover. "I lost my own father far too soon . . . and . . . I have no child to give it to. And being as I am no longer the young man I once was . . ."

With a single grand move, he folded the leather cover open . . . revealing a hundred, perhaps more, crisp and bright white . . .

LEDGER PAGES!

All of them precisely the same as the single sheet that had brought Henry to 1885.

Each box on the first page was full. Each date and destination complete. The very first line declared that Skavenger saw the Declaration of Independence being signed!

The creator of the Great Hunt looked at the two awestruck young men in front of him. "The origins of this journal are uncertain," he said with reverence. "But its powers? Its magic? Those are undeniable."

Jack looked understandably confused. "I'm sorry," he said. "But . . . whaaaat exactly is that?"

"The key to anytime and anywhere, Jackson," Skavenger answered as if it made all the sense in the world. "A book that can take you to another place, another time. Just tell the ledger when and where you wish to go, out loud"—he snapped his fingers—"and you're there! Great moments, great rewards! A book that will give you—"

"Another life," Henry whispered, not quite realizing he'd even said it.

Skavenger tilted his head and fixed him with a long and curious look. "No, Henry," he said. "We will always have just this one life. But the ledger? The ledger lets us experience the great adventure that our lives are meant to be."

Jack still looked lost, which, had Henry not used one of the book's pages himself on Christmas Eve, would have been his look as well.

"Mr. Skavenger?" Henry asked. "If this journal . . . these ledger pages . . . can take us anytime, anywhere. Can we go back and stop things from . . ."

He held back from saying the rest. The old gentleman's teardrop scar now seemed especially appropriate, because his eyes were quickly welling with tears.

"I'm sorry, Henry," Skavenger sadly answered. "The things we do, the decisions we make when the ledger takes us somewhere, they can affect the small, inconsequential fragments of one's history, but they cannot change our destiny." He swallowed back the emotion overtaking him. "If you hadn't traveled to Paris, Matilda would have met her fate in a different manner, but she would have met it all the same. At that same age, that same time, that same moment."

Henry nodded, his eyes falling back on the journal.

"Young man, you have more than proven yourself these past few weeks," Skavenger assured him, then pushed the ancient ledger forward. "Go on, pick it up! There are hundreds of pages filled with the adventures of my lifetime. If you are truly meant to be its new owner, Henry"—he pointed a long finger at the ghostly-written entries—"My adventures will disappear . . . to make way for yours."

Henry looked at every face in the room, and the kindness he saw made his own eyes well up with tears.

I've only got one adventure I want to take.

Just one.

Even though he'd lost his own ledger page, he now realized he'd found a way back after all. It was resting right there on the table in front of him. A way back . . .

Home.

Carefully, Henry gathered up each side of the journal's heavy cover and slowly lifted it. There, on the inside, etched into the aged and experienced leather, were the words:

The Adventures of Hunter S. Skavenger

An orange ember snapped in the fireplace as Henry turned to the first page, and then the second; countless adventures and destinations jumped out at him in deep, bold black . . .

Wait . . . wait, hold on . . . aren't the words supposed to be . . . ?

He looked up to see a grave expression on Skavenger's face, as well as those of all four Dark Men.

Henry realized in a heartbeat what they were thinking. What he was thinking too. His eyes quickly fell back onto the book in his hands . . . the words on the first page still as dark and black as they were a second earlier.

He sighed the deepest of sighs. All of the places he'd worked to find, all of the places he'd been . . .

The telephone exchange in Hell's Kitchen. The Vanderbilt Mansion at 5th and 57th. The Jennings Establishment, where he'd first encountered the Colton brothers. The *Natchez* riverboat on which he'd met Mark Twain. Paris. *Le Chasseur*. Gustave Eiffel. All of those names, all of those places—they were still only in Henry's mind and not on the pages of the ledger below.

Henry's shoulders sagged as he looked up. "It's not meant for me, is it?"

Because of Mattie, that's why. If I hadn't promised her a tower . . .

The creator of the Great Hunt sighed as well. "I'm so sorry, Henry," was all Skavenger could bring himself to say.

I'm not going home after all. Not ever. I'm stuck in 1885.

Overwhelmed with that knowledge, Henry gently lowered the journal back onto the table. A tear rolled down his cheek.

"No!" Jack angrily shouted and reached for the old ledger. "Don't give up, Henry! Just hold it longer! Maybe that's . . ."

A twinkle of soft blue light sparkled and burst from the cover, brightly snaking its way around Jack's fingers the second they touched the book. He yanked his hand back as if it had just touched a blazing-hot cast-iron skillet.

The eyes of the graceful old gentleman locked on what they'd just seen, and he shook his head in wonder.

Henry understood as well. Even in the middle of his own crushing disappointment, he felt a strong sense of satisfaction that if the ledger wasn't meant for him, at least it might be meant for . . .

"Jack." Henry smiled. He reached over and once again lifted the book, but now offered it to the young man who'd taught him so much about fear and how to conquer it.

The hardscrabble street kid who'd always been the toughest and most cynical of the bunch, from when he first grabbed

Henry by the collar in Central Park, all the way to their race through Five Points . . . gulped.

Jack's hands hovered over the book as if he felt he might not really deserve to touch it. For the first time since he'd met him, Henry could see that his great-great-grandfather . . . was frightened.

Jack looked at him and shook his head—not much, but enough to let Henry know he wasn't sure what to do.

"Hey, it's okay," Henry assured him. "What was it you told me on the ship to France? 'If you come through it, what reason you got to still be afraid of anything?'"

He then picked up the old leather journal and placed it into Jack's reluctant hands.

The same burst of twinkling blue light they'd all seen a moment ago flowed outward from the cover and wrapped around the book itself this time; brightly enough that Jack could see the words on the first page. But only for a second or two.

JULY 4ᵗʰ, 1776, PHILADELPH . . .

July 4th, 1776, Phil . . .

July . . .

One by one, the words began to fade and disappear from the ledger. Henry held his breath as he watched each entry become nothing more than a vacant white box. Jack turned the page with a trembling hand, witnessing the same thing happening on the second page.

It is *for him. It's always been for him.*

Jack fanned the entire ledger and the hundred or more pages blurred from a graying charcoal into a nearly eye-blinding white as they quickly whipped by in his hand.

Skavenger's list of adventures . . . now completely gone.

"Turn back to the cover, on the inside," Skavenger instructed with a knowing smile.

Jack did just that. And there . . . elegantly etched in the interior of the front leather cover were the words:

The Adventures of Jackson Babbitt

He lifted his head to look at Skavenger, who then said the words the young man had waited a lifetime to hear.

"Well done, Jackson."

"Thank you," Jack managed to somehow reply through a sudden and obvious swirl of emotion. Even the Dark Men, all four, gave him a thump on the back to congratulate him.

"We have much, much to talk about, you and I, which shall begin in just a moment." Skavenger gestured with his hand for Jack to give the journal back to him. "Not to worry, the ledger's yours and yours alone. However . . . I do wish to have a private word with Henry, if you don't mind."

"Oh, sure, of course," Jack replied, handing it back to him before exchanging a dazed, bewildered smile with Henry and then following the Dark Men out of the room.

All was quiet aside from the snapping, bright fire.

Skavenger held the ledger with one hand and his cane with the other. "Quite a night, wouldn't you say?" he asked.

"Yes," Henry replied, looking down for a second. "It sure has been."

Skavenger's curious look returned, now that it was just the two of them. "Henry Babbitt," he said, cocking his head, "there are things I suspect about you, things I'm quite certain would be difficult for you to explain. Would I be correct in that assumption?"

"I think you might be, sir," Henry answered.

"I thought so." Skavenger sighed and Henry could tell he was pondering what to do. "Young man, I have two options for you," the creator of the Great Hunt went on to say. "I have a carriage outside that can take you to your home, wherever it is here in the city, safe and sound. Or . . ."

Skavenger opened the journal to the very back and ripped out . . . a single, precious ledger sheet. He held it up between two fingers as he closed the cover with his other hand.

"Perhaps this would be of more help," he suggested with a prying twinkle in his eye.

The young man's eyebrows furrowed in puzzlement. "But it won't work for me. Will it?"

The graceful gentleman stood and moved closer to him. "You're forgetting what I said about the journal and its powers, Henry. It works for those who are worthy or truly needful in the moment. Why this will work for you now, while the journal as a whole won't, you should be able to figure out." Skavenger offered the young boy a kind smile.

Henry did the same in return. It wasn't the largest of smiles quite yet, but rather a faint and hopeful one.

"Unless you choose the carriage ride, that is." Skavenger held the ledger sheet a short, tantalizing distance away from the young hunter. "I was thinking of keeping a single sheet anyway, had no one solved this year's hunt. Maybe leave it somewhere. You know, one last clue to be found . . . whenever."

"Maybe in the Astor Library," Henry suggested. "Two hundred and fourteen pages inside some book."

Skavenger no longer "suspected" a thing. He knew.

"You should definitely take this." He twisted his fingers to let the ledger sheet dip in Henry's direction, followed a second later by the ancient journal. The hopeful young boy took both.

"Give the journal back to Jackson." Skavenger smiled. "Then the two of you meet me in the carriage. I'm sure you can offer directions as to where I should probably take you."

Henry somehow found a way to nod. It wasn't easy, given the flutter of anticipation he now felt with the blank ledger sheet right there in his quivering hand.

Skavenger gave him a proud pat on the shoulder and then walked toward the door, but not before stopping to look back one more time.

"Henry," he quietly said as he leaned the wolf-headed cane against the wall, never to retrieve it. "You should know that you and Jackson were both more than worthy of the journal." He then turned and looked straight at him.

"It's just not your time yet. Is it?"

And with that, Hunter S. Skavenger smiled and walked out.

A moment later, Henry found Jack waiting by himself just inside the front door. He handed him the age-old ledger.

"Thanks," Jack quietly said, and then broke into still-stunned laughter. "He wants me to go with him so he can show me how this thing even works. Can you believe it?"

"It's pretty incredible." Henry grinned.

"No kiddin', it is."

Jack poked his thumb toward the door. "Well . . . you ready to go? Should be a little easier going out of here than coming in. Carriage and Dark Men and all. I'm gonna need you to be there for me when—"

Jack's voice stopped cold. He'd just noticed the single ledger sheet in Henry's hands.

"Oh, yeah." Henry held it up, knowing it all probably looked confusing. "Mr. Skavenger gave me this one so that I can, well, it's uhhhh . . . kind of a really, really long story, Jack. I'll tell you everything on the way to where you're gonna drop me off."

"Wait . . . you . . . drop you off?" Jack stammered.

Henry held up a hand to calm him. "Don't worry," he said. "I'll be okay. I hope." He could tell things were now starting to tumble into place for his fourteen-year-old, maybe fifteen-year-old, ancestor.

"But," Jack sputtered some more, "the only reason you'd need one of those is so you could . . . wait, you mean . . . all this time . . . *Babbitt?*"

Yeah.

All this time.

More than a hundred years' worth.

If he'd been back in his own time, Henry would have wrapped his great-great-grandfather in the tightest of embraces. But this was 1885, and as he'd learned on his adventure, things were a lot different here. Then.

So Henry extended his hand and simply said, "Thanks, Jack, for showing me a few things. Now what do you say we finally get out of this neighborhood, huh?"

ల

A short time later and a few miles removed from Five Points, the carriage pulled to a stop in front of the building Henry knew would be 142 Central Park West more than a hundred years later.

Skavenger had offered both young men a unique piece of advice on the ride over, actually stopping Henry as he was about to reveal the truth of his tale to Jack.

"One thing I learned on my travels," he'd calmly interrupted. "Never say a word about what might be to come. And, Jackson? Never ask. If the two of you truly do have the connection that it appears you do? Don't tell each other a thing more."

"Why?" the two of them had asked in unison.

"Why?" Skavenger repeated their question, but with a tone that suggested they should know better. "Let Jackson live his life without the pressure of making decisions based on when and where you, Henry, live yours. You could be one generation removed, you could be a half dozen, who knows? Small things will change because of you being here, but too much information will make larger things change. That, neither one of you want. Be content to let time go where it will."

Now that they were standing in the lights below what would one day be Chief's and Gigi's home, everything—Skavenger's speech, the ledger, the revelations of their victorious hunt—all seemed, in Henry's mind, very much like a dream.

"Safe travels," Skavenger said to him with a tip of his hat, heading back to the carriage to give Jack and Henry a last moment alone.

As soon as the man behind the greatest scavenger hunt ever held was inside, Jack wheeled around to Henry and said with a wicked grin, "Okay, tell me everything!"

"Jack, we can't! You heard what . . ."

"Yeah, yeah. I know. I was just kiddin' ya."

They grinned awkwardly at each other. The only thing left to say was the one thing Henry figured would be okay for him to ask.

He nodded to the leather-bound ledger clamped tightly in Jack's right hand, a whole lifetime thicker than the single sheet in his own hand.

"Keep it in the family. Okay?" Henry asked with a smile.

"Will do, lunky-boy." Jack winked, already starting to back away, but not before adding a final comment of his own.

"To the next adventure," he said with a salute as he stepped on the carriage stair. The four horses started to move, carrying him and Skavenger down the street. "For the both of us!" he shouted over the clipping and clopping. A moment later, he was gone.

Henry smiled and turned to look at the door that had locked behind him seemingly so long ago.

The place really does look a lot like Chief's and Gigi's, he thought. The same perfect steps, the outcroppings with the royal shields, everything was close to the same—except for that half foot of snow on Christmas Eve.

Y'know, if this ledger thing works right now, I don't even want to think about if I could have done this that very first day. The sheet said to find Skavenger. So I found Skavenger!

The answer, though, popped into his head right away, as Skavenger had told him it would at some point.

It wouldn't have worked. The ledger only works if someone is truly worthy.

You had to prove yourself, Henry Babbitt.

Besides, it wasn't your time yet. Your time's right through that door up there. With the family you still have.

Henry walked up to the very top step and sat down, looking out toward the dark, small trees of Central Park. They were only a hint of what they'd grow up to be—same as his twelve-year-old self.

The young, victorious hunter knew how much he'd changed over these last few days and weeks. Years and decades, to be more accurate.

Learned a lot. Lost a lot, Henry thought to himself, feeling a bittersweet smile tug at the corners of his mouth.

Maybe it really would be better if it was all just a dream.

With that, and with a hopeful smile, Henry Babbitt lifted the bright white sheet of ledger paper and closed his eyes. Quietly, he said one last time, for luck, really . . . for more luck than he'd ever asked for . . .

"Go ahead, Henry. Go on."

Then he spoke the date and destination he had given up hope of ever seeing again.

TWENTY-FOUR

Golden Days of Yore

CHRIIIISTMAS EVE WILL find me . . . wherrrrrre the lovelight gleams . . . Oh, I'll be home for Christmas . . . if only in my . . .

Henry's eyes were still closed. *Squeezed* closed, actually—with the side of his face resting flat against the surface of an old desk.

It was precisely this kind of moment that the squeeze-the-eyes-tight-as-you-can trick was designed to remedy. Whenever a dream, or a nightmare—as was more often the case—got out of hand. It was a guarantee to wake Henry up.

Therrrrre ya go, he thought to himself. *Back in bed.*

Nope. Not in bed.

Where am I again? What day is it?

All right, squeeze the eyes a little more, little more, waking up, waking up, here we go. Can still hear the Christmas music downstairs . . .

Henry's head popped up in a flash.

CHRISTMAS MUSIC! I HEAR CHRISTMAS MUSIC!

His eyes were now open wide and his hair matted so tight on his forehead that he had to give it a swipe or two before he could even see straight.

Christmas music. Downstairs. Chief's and Gigi's place!

Which should have been obvious, he now realized, being as he was sitting right there in . . .

Chief's chair! I'm at his desk!

Henry pounded his hands on top of the old desk to make sure it was real and wouldn't fade away to nothing. *Smack! Smack! Thump!* His palms sharply slapped against the deep, old, very, very, very familiar red mahogany surface.

"HA!" Henry laughed, unable to help himself. "Ha ha HAAAAA!" he shouted at the ceiling and then gave the room a quick once-over to make doubly sure of everything.

Okay. Let's run through everything. Chief's desk? Check.

Chair that disappeared and made me fall on my, well . . . Check.

Stack of old New York Times? *Yankee Stadium first base? Yup.*

His head was still fuzzy, but not so fuzzy that he would have questioned where he was . . . or *when* it was.

I'm home! I'm back!

He spun the chair around for a quick look out the window. A light snowfall was still coming down outside, easing a little, but falling all the same.

He whirled the chair around two or three times.

It's Christmas in New York! It's not July!

Thump, thump, thump, thump, thump.

A pair of slippers scaled the stairs as a familiar voice called out to him:

"Well, it's about time, sleepyhead. You have been OUT, OUT, OUT!"

MOM!!!!!

Henry's mother whipped into the study with the brightest smile in the world on her face. "I don't think I've ever seen you sleep in this much on Christmas morn . . . OH!"

She ran smack-dab into Henry's embrace, the tightest he'd ever given her.

"Whoa, hey!" Eloise said. "I guess you did get some good sleep." She hugged him back, kissing him on the top of his head. "Merry Christmas, sweetheart."

"Merry Christmas, Mom," he said to her, hanging on longer than he could ever remember. "I love ya. Love ya a lot."

"Well, I love you too, Awnray. Or should I say, *Je t'aime?*" she finally pulled away, with a hint of pleasant puzzlement in her eyes. "You feeling okay?" she had to ask.

Henry looked up at her, seeing what his father had seen the night she'd fallen asleep watching that old movie. She was beautiful then, and with her traditional green slippers and red Christmas robe, she was even more beautiful now.

"Yep, all good," he assured her.

"All right, your grandfather's a whirlwind this morning, I gotta warn ya." She popped him another quick kiss. "I don't know what he's got up his sleeve, but I do know you're not supposed to open *that* until later on."

Eloise nodded toward a wrapped gift on the corner of Chief's desk, before turning to go back downstairs. "I'll tell him you're up!" she shouted on her way down. "Breakfast in, like, five minutes, 'kay?!"

"'Kay," Henry quietly replied and smiled, listening to her as she headed to the kitchen.

Gigi's joyful voice pierced through a few seconds later. "HE'S UP?!" he heard her almost burst. "Finally! Henry Babbitt! Christmas breakfast will be served in FOUR MINUTES!"

Henry smiled. He turned and walked back, once again taking his seat—more accurately *Chief's* seat—at the old desk.

Whew, okay. It's like I read Dickens last night. That was the craziest thing ever! Skavenger, Jack, Five Points, the ledger . . .

Henry glanced toward the corner of his grandfather's desk. Sure enough, there was a gift in a strangely familiar-sized box, wrapped in brilliant yellow paper.

Not just any yellow paper. That's the Skavenger clue yellow paper. And check out that box. Same size, same shape, same . . .

Nahhhhhhhhhhhhh. It can't be.

Henry looked at the gift for a good long moment, listening to the bustle and excitement percolating downstairs.

Gigi was still in the kitchen, he knew that. His mother was down there too. And there was no sign of Chief yet.

Ya still got three minutes till Gigi makes her big breakfast announcement. C'mon, it's sittin' right there. RIGHT THERE!

Henry smiled. His waking brain was still busy churning away, trying to convince him that his journey had been nothing more than only a vibrant, spectacular dream. And there was a good part of Henry that wanted to believe that.

Not because of Jack and Ernie. Or Mark Twain and Gustave Eiffel. Or meeting Skavenger. Or solving the puzzles and riddles that came with the greatest adventure ever.

Nope. Those things were all great.

It was because of Mattie. It was better that his adventure in 1885 was a dream because of what had happened to her.

Yup. A dream. Got it? Got it.

Except he didn't get it.

Something felt different.

The hum of the holiday music took a break downstairs. The gift sat in front of him.

Beckoning him.

The yellow wrapping . . . it's on the box and the lid! If you open it right now, you can whip the lid back on and Chief'll never know. Not in a million years. C'mon, it's like Dad said . . . never let an extraordinary moment wait.

Tick. Tick. Tick. Tick. His grandfather's grandfather clock seemed to be telling him that time was, as always, a-wastin'.

Henry quickly pulled the gift close to him and popped it open with an easy motion, waiting a second in case there was a new round of thumping coming up the stairs. He used the time, now having learned that every second of it is precious, to look at the gift's tag.

To Henry—Love, Chief

Still, even then, Henry hesitated. A rush of certainty told him that whatever was underneath the bright yellow tissue paper would convince him of everything. One way or the other.

C'mon, get a grip. It's prob'ly just a Giants jersey to go with the hoody you got last . . . wait . . . hold on here . . .

For the first time since waking up, he noticed he was once again wearing the New York Giants hoody that Gigi had given him the night before.

See? Stop. You can fold up a Giants jersey and fit it in a box that size just fine.

He couldn't resist any longer. Henry pushed away the light tissue paper and discovered . . .

A large book stared up at him. Not *the* book, but a very old one nonetheless. A book that settled everything in a single Christmas Day second. Henry picked it up and read the title on the cover.

HUNTER OF SOULS
REVEREND ERNEST SAMUELS

Ernie wrote the book! The one his mom started!

Henry smiled at the mere sight of his good friend's name. But there was another item now looking up at him from the box, resting just beneath where the good Reverend Ernie's novel had been only a handful of seconds ago.

"Henry . . . when you get a little older, we're gonna sail somewhere. We'll climb the highest mountain we can find. And when we're done with that adventure? We'll find the next one. Okay?"

"Okay," Henry Babbitt quietly said to himself as he looked down on the leather-bound book he'd seen only minutes ago in his great-great-grandfather Jackson's hand.

The ledger.

The age-old book looked no different than it had in Five Points, either in the moment when Skavenger had pulled it out of his old satchel with such reverence, or the moment when Jack had held it tight under his arm during their good-byes.

"Two minutes!" Gigi called out from downstairs.

Henry moved his hand toward it ever so slowly, hesitating once more, the same as his great-great-grandfather had . . . then let his finger lightly brush against the cover.

A thin sparkle of soft blue light wrapped around the tip of his finger like the tendril of a vine. This time it was Henry's quick breath that had to push its way through a tightening smile of pure wonder.

It's meant for me! It is my time now!

He opened the old leather cover, seeing the words his heart hoped would be there . . .

The Adventures of Nathan Babbitt

And as Henry looked at his late father's name, the letters began to fade. The twelve-year-old quickly turned to the first ledger page where all of his father's early adventures were listed.

Dates. Destinations. Dreams. All fading to bright white, but for the reason Nathan Babbitt would have wanted most: a lifetime of adventure for his only son.

Henry turned back to where his father's name had disappeared, and discovered that it now read . . .

The Adventures of Henry Babbitt

This time, there was no welling of tears as he took in the old ledger's new title.

There were just tears.

Tears he needed to quickly wipe away, and a gift he had to just as quickly put back, as he heard Chief's lumbering stride pounding up the stairs.

"Tell him Christmas breakfast is now SERVED!" Henry heard Gigi proudly proclaim as he scurried to get everything back into place.

"Oh, I will!" the old man called back to her.

"Henry Nathan Babbitt!" Chief's voice brimmed with excitement as he bounced through the doorway, a pair of ice skates over his shoulder and another pair held tightly in his hand.

"Finally, there you are!" the old man said as he walked in and saw his grandson's face. "You okay?" he asked, even though Henry thought he had wiped away the last tear.

"Yeah, fine," Henry answered, faking a quick sniffle. "Just the last of that cold, I guess." A cold that Henry realized he didn't have this morning.

"Cold shmold, pffft," Chief scoffed. "You and me, ice skating in the park after breakfast. You might be able to say no to Abigail Kentworth, but you can't say no to ol' Chiefy boy."

The old man shot a suspicious glance at the reconstructed gift and asked, "You didn't open that, did you?" Henry shook his head faster than a hummingbird's wings.

"Good! Oh, and Merry Christmas," his grandfather continued. "You and I have much, much, much to talk about later.
Did I say 'much'?"

"You did," Henry answered with a nod and a smile. "Merry
Christmas to you too, Chief."

His grandfather had already thumped the frame of the
door and was on his way downstairs. "Wait'll you see this
breakfast your grandmother constructed!" he called back. "It
looks amazing!"

Henry stood up out of Chief's chair and quickly dashed
into the bedroom where he hadn't been able to sleep the night
before, grabbing his coat.

He whipped back into the hallway, cradled the box new-
el post as he leaned into the first stair, then finished the next
few steps—

And came to a stop halfway down.

An old photograph, once again on the wall, had caught his
eye: the one of Henry, Nathan, and Chief—taken under the
elephant's watchful eye at the museum. Henry's favorite photo
ever. The three of them all caught in that perfect moment of
laughter, the kind that only comes once in a great while.

But just above it now was an even older photograph. One
that Henry knew wasn't there *before*.

In sharp, yet elegant black-and-white, three Babbitts
laughed and smiled—long, long ago—in a photo that had
been taken at the base of . . . the Eiffel Tower.

The youngest in this photo, though, wasn't Henry. It was
Chief. When he was maybe seven or eight years old. His father, Sam, stood next to him, an arm around his laughing
son's shoulder, while on the other side, proudly smiling with
his thumbs inside a sharp new set of suspenders, stood Chief's
grandfather.

Jack. Looking proud, smart, and successful. Looking very much as if he'd made quite a life for himself, without the help of anyone else. Checkered past no more.

Eloise poked her head out from the kitchen and looked up the stairs. "Remember your coat and gloves, okay?" she reminded Henry with a smile. "And have fun, that's the most important thing."

Whoa. Where'd that come from?

"Let's get goin', Grandson!" he heard Chief call out from the dining room. "We gotta eat. This snow is officially beginning to STOP."

There was a knock on the front door.

The same kind of knock Henry had heard the night before.

Daaaaaaaaang, I forgot. Abigail. Abigail Kentworth.

Only this time, the familiar rush of blood didn't rush to his cheeks as much. "I got it!" he called out as he made his way down the last few stairs and reached for the doorknob . . .

. . . before stopping just short of it.

That same sliver of hesitation he'd felt the night before had suddenly decided to return. Again, not as much as he'd felt twelve hours and more than a century ago, but it was there all the same.

Oh, c'mon! You're better than this! You can do this! You did it!

Yeah, but what do you tell her?

I'll tell you what you tell her. You tell her your cold's gone. You tell her you're feelin' better, and yes, you'd like to go skating in the park. Soon as you finish with Gigi's legendary Christmas morning breakfast, which, if Abigail hasn't eaten yet and wouldn't mind joining them . . .

Henry smiled.

Small things. Inconsequential. Just like Skavenger had said.

Time isn't about time. Time's about the moment. The moment that was right there on the other side of this door probably wondering why he hadn't opened it yet.

"Go ahead, Henry," he whispered to himself as his hand wrapped around the doorknob. "Don't wait."

He opened the heavy walnut door.

Woooosh.

And she was there on his grandparents' doorstep, as stunning as ever.

New coat, brand-new winter hat, curly hair tumbling down over her shoulders. Standing there at the very moment that two straight days of New York snowfall had finally decided to stop for good.

Henry couldn't say a word. And there was a very good reason for that.

It was because it wasn't Abigail Kentworth standing right there on his grandparents' doorstep.

It was Mattie McGillin.

She looked at Henry with a smile he'd pictured every night since France. A smile he thought he'd never see again.

She held a single sheet of water-streaked paper. And he could tell, without really even looking, that every word was still right there. Central Park, the telephone exchange in Hell's Kitchen, the Vanderbilt Mansion.

And yes, even the address and the date he'd written to remind himself of the very place and time where he'd wanted to get back to . . . and where she now stood.

"Merry Christmas, Henry."

Mattie's smile was brighter than the glowing sun behind her. She held out the ledger sheet.

"I think you might have lost something in Paris."

ACKNOWLEDGMENTS

Hey! You're reading the acknowledgments—thanks!

To L. Frank Baum, C. S. Lewis, and Roald Dahl, thank you for the inspiration I first felt for this kind of story back at Rich and Judy Wandschneider's "Book Loft" in my hometown of Enterprise, Oregon. Population two thousand then, population two thousand now.

To my high school English teacher, Sharon Forster, for teaching me where to put a period in a sentence. Better yet, what to put before that period.

To the many, many, many individuals at United Talent Agency who helped make not only this story a reality but also the screenplays I've had the good fortune of writing over the years. Special thanks to Charlie Ferraro, Aaron Kaplan, and Stewart Brookman. An extra tip of the hat to Charlie for the brainstorming strategy sessions at 301 North Canon Drive.

To Adam Gomolin, the greatest champion of *Skavenger's Hunt* from start to finish, as well as the Inkshares team of Avalon Radys, Angela Melamud, Elena Stofle, and Thad Woodman, for their incredible support.

To Staton Rabin, Matt Harry, Pamela McElroy, Jessica Gardner, and Ryan Quinn, for letting me know which chapters, paragraphs, sentences, and words made sense, and which ones might need a second look.

To Will Staehle for his amazing cover design, and to Kevin Summers for his beautiful design work on everything inside.

To all of you for dropping a few hard-earned dollars and taking a leap of faith on a screenwriter who had never written a novel before.

To my children and grandchildren, who I often thought of while searching for the next elusive string of words during the snowy, icy, rainy, and flat-out cold Oregon winter of 2016–17. I couldn't have done it without you.

And finally, to my wife.

Grace.

I gave your name to a key character in this story only because I, and everyone who is blessed to know you, realize that you are the very opposite. I figured it would get a smile and a laugh from family and friends alike.

Having you next to me is what I live for.

GRAND PATRONS

Aaron Kaplan

Adam Gomolin

Al and Marla Hanna

Amber Sagnotti

Angie Machado

Becki Saltzman

Ben and Simon Policy

Bess Adams

Beth Oliphant Hoover

Bob and Kathryn Rich

Bob and Katy Barman

Brad and Heidi Pihas

Brian Fee

Bryan and Kathryn Semke

Bryce and Angela Schroeder

Carly Moran

Charlie Ferraro

Cherian Lautermilch

Christy Shaver

College of Liberal Arts,
Oregon State University

Craig and Janet Correll

Dan and Karen Peterson

Dan and Sharon Blickenstaff

Dan and Susan Kehler

Darrell and
Denise Hovander

Dave and Sally Sullivan

David and Jennifer Arbanas

David and Kris McHone

David Digilio

Dean and Patty Cocchiarella

Dennis and Nancy Marley

Diane Hoffine

Dick and Karen Oldfield

Dirk Davis

Ed and Beth Irish

Ed Medak

Elmo L. Robinson Jr

Erica Smiley

Frank and Shelley Buhler

Fred and Lori Charley

Frosty and Vicki Comer

Gail Hjorth

Grace "Gigi" Rich

Grant Jones

Greg Robeson

Gretchen Sherwood

Guy and Tina Cowart

Harold Reynolds

Harry and Colleen Craig

Helen Sollinger

Jamie and Angela Kingery

Jamie and Mindy Franklin

Jeff Meader

Jeff and Tracy Powelson

Jim and Cathy Rudd

Jim Mendenhall

Jo Waidely

Joe Gaber

Joel, Jessica, Jack, and Hunter Steitzer

John and Jill Turville

John Springer

Jon and Jeanne Paul

Judy Strickler

Julie England

Justin and Andrea Rich

Karen Mason

Kim Bronson

Kristina McMorris

Kstorey Green

Linda Weston

Lisa Kellogg

Mark Auxier

Mary Coucher

Matt and Kris Spathas

Michael and Hilary LaTondre

Michael and Marietta Harrison

Michael Gallagher

Michael J. Rich

Michael Orth

Michelle Smithpeter

Mike and Amy Baltzell

Mike and Anne Goetze

Mike and Diana Newdall

Mike and Jan Bubalo

Nathan Hungate

Parker, Caitlin, and
Harper Craig

Patricia Kellar

Patty Chapman

Peggy LaPoint

Peter Garrow

Peter Klemens

Phil and Angie Fogg

Ray Benson

Renée Price

Rick and Erika Miller

Roderick Cruickshank

Ruth Beyer

Ruth Johnson

Ryen Toft

Scott and Becky Robertson

Scott and Kathy Kiever

Scott and Mary Lee Alder

Scott Lynn

Shawn and Bevin Heilbron

Shawn Engelberg

Stein and Martha Nielsen

Stephen and Esther Abouaf

Stephen Feltz

Steve and Karen Preece

Steve and Mary Frantz

Susan L. Kelpe

Taylor and Mandy
Close Kavanaugh

Ted and Andrea Davis

Tim and Tracy Krevanko

Tod Perkins

Todd Stein

Tom Brian

Tom Soma and
Susanne Olin

Tony and Kim Click

Willamette Valley Vineyards

Wyatt and Stefanie Webb

Zack Lassiter

INKSHARES

INKSHARES is a reader-driven publisher and producer based in Oakland, California. Our books are selected not by a group of editors, but by readers worldwide.

While we've published books by established writers like *Big Fish* author Daniel Wallace and *Star Wars: Rogue One* scribe Gary Whitta, our aim remains surfacing and developing the new author voices of tomorrow.

Previously unknown Inkshares authors have received starred reviews and been featured in the *New York Times*. Their books are on the front tables of Barnes & Noble and hundreds of independents nationwide, and many have been licensed by publishers in other major markets. They are also being adapted by Oscar-winning screenwriters at the biggest studios and networks.

Interested in making your own story a reality? Visit Inkshares.com to start your own project or find other great books.